Noelle Holten is an award-winning blogger at www.crimebookjunkie.co.uk. She is the PR & Social Media Manager for Bookouture, a leading digital publisher in the UK, and worked as a Senior Probation Officer for eighteen years, covering a variety of risk cases as well as working in a multi-agency setting. She has three Hons BA's – Philosophy, Sociology (Crime & Deviance) and Community Justice – and a Master's in Criminology. Noelle's hobbies include reading, attending as many book festivals as she can afford and sharing the book love via her blog.

Dead Inside – her debut novel with One More Chapter / HarperCollins UK is an international Kindle bestseller and the start of a new series featuring DC Maggie Jamieson. All books in the series can be found on her Amazon author page. *6 Ripley Avenue* is her first, but hopefully not her last, standalone novel.

www.crimebookjunkie.co.uk

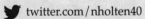

twitter.com/nholten40
facebook.com/noelleholtenauthor
instagram.com/author_noelleholten
bookbub.com/authors/noelle-holten

D1153837

Also by Noelle Holten

6 RIPLEY AVENUE

NOELLE HOLTEN

One More Chapter
a division of HarperCollins*Publishers*
1 London Bridge Street
London SE1 9GF
www.harpercollins.co.uk

HarperCollins*Publishers*
1st Floor, Watermarque Building, Ringsend Road
Dublin 4, Ireland

This paperback edition 2022
1
First published in Great Britain in ebook format
by HarperCollins*Publishers* 2022

A catalogue record of this book is available from the British Library

ISBN: 978-0-00-852533-0

Printed and bound in the UK using 100% Renewable Electricity
by CPI Group (UK) Ltd

For Julie. Your tenacity, strength and courage amaze me every day. Your laugh brightens my darkest days. Let's keep slaying those dragons! Love you, sis!

Prologue

I always thought my mother abandoned me.

That is until I read the letter and discovered that any chance of meeting her – of hearing her story, maybe even forgiving her – was taken away from me.

When you're given the opportunity to confront your mother's killer, do you take it?

I did.

No words were spoken though.

I just killed him.

Was it worth it?

Absolutely.

Do I have any regrets?

Only that I didn't make him suffer longer.

Maybe that will change over time, but I doubt it. They say I have the rest of my life to think about my actions and, as I stare through the cold metal bars that line the windows of my new home, I know instinctively that I did the right thing.

ONE

Sloane

S loane Armstrong was a freelance investigative journalist, and her focus was on crime. When asked to describe herself, she'd tell people she was confident while others called her aggressive, especially when it came to getting a story. An ex-boyfriend, Noah, who also happened to be a police officer, once told her he believed she had multiple personalities because she changed her mood and approach so often that he didn't know who she was most of the time. Manipulation was no stranger to her – but in her line of work she needed to think on her feet, respond to others to get the story, and she did whatever was necessary.

When Sloane was sixteen, her world had been turned upside down when her older sister had been murdered. A lump formed in her throat as she remembered how her life had spiralled into self-destruction – she tried every drug she could get her hands on, drank until she blacked out, and hung around people who did *anything* to get what they wanted. At the age of nineteen, she broke into a house, drugged-up and barely able to focus. As she rummaged through some drawers looking for anything she could pawn, she was confronted by the owners and this was when her life changed. It was her parents' house. They shouted that she was no better than the scum who had killed her sister and something inside her snapped. There were times at night, when she struggled to sleep, that she could still hear her father crying. The detox and therapy her parents had arranged helped her to realise she'd been using substances to push down her feelings when she should have been directing all that anger, confusion, and grief to make sure that people like her sister's killer never saw the light of day again. She had found her calling as an investigative journalist – and when Ripley House opened up around the corner from her two years before, she knew that one day she would inevitably get her breakthrough story.

Sloane was ready for bed but she couldn't help thinking about #6 Ripley Avenue. As she leafed through the photographs she'd used for a previous article on the probation hostel, her eyes were drawn to the sign on the big metal door that read *Ripley House Approved Premises*. From the outside, the building could easily be mistaken for a family home. In fact, it looked like every other house on the street – the redbrick fascia, the large windows – with its three floors of what one would imagine were cosy but character-filled rooms. But there was nothing cosy about the inside of that house because, unlike every other house on the street, inside lived some of the UK's most heinous violent offenders – released on licence to serve the remainder of their time in the community.

The local residents and the neighbourhood watch scheme, run by her friend Helen Burgess, had complained when they were first informed of the probation hostel location. Helen had protested almost daily in the run-up to its opening two years previously. It was the perfect opportunity for Sloane to weave in her own opinions on the ridiculous idea that convicted killers could be upstanding members of the community. The public had lapped up her articles about the high staff turnover rate, the increase of crime in the area since the hostel opened, and the seeming lack of security evidenced by the broken CCTV camera positioned over the front door. Just like her, the public were seekers of truth, only sometimes they needed a nudge in the right direction.

When Sloane came across the photo of Jeanette Macey, the Senior Probation Officer (more commonly referred to as SPO) responsible for managing the hostel, she bit her lip. The woman was not her biggest fan after Sloane portrayed her in one article in the local paper as insincere in her assurances of public safety at town council meetings. No matter what Jeanette said, if Sloane was around, she'd never be able to convince the locals that the hostel was a safe place to manage the high-risk individuals regardless of whether the hostel was to open or not. Jeanette's motto appeared to be 'better the devil you know'. Sloane disagreed and would do whatever it took to prove the probation manager wrong.

When the community had heard that Danny Wells was going to be released to the hostel, the level of anger rose tenfold. Details of his previous convictions had been leaked and Sloane made sure the public were made aware of his continued aggressive behaviour behind bars. Unfortunately, prison overcrowding, a convincing parole report, an expert solicitor who argued the appeal when he was first turned down, and a parole board panel hugely in favour of the idea that everyone deserved a second chance, meant that he would be released but under tight and controlled supervision – and that's where Ripley House Approved Premises came into the picture.

To reassure the community, further public meetings were held at the main council building in the run-up to Mr Wells's release a few months previously. Probation shared the rules of the hostel and confirmed that Danny's history of substance misuse and violence meant he'd be drug tested daily in the hostel and a 7pm to 7am curfew imposed. Other measures in place included the expectation that he attend daily keyworker sessions within the hostel, with the addition that his allocated home probation officer would attend the hostel and meet with him at least once a week. Danny was automatically placed under Multi Agency Public Protection Arrangements, also known as MAPPA – Level 1 restrictions due to the nature of his offence. To restore confidence in the release decision, those who attended the meeting were informed it would be reviewed regularly and raised to Level 2 if there were any signs that his risk of serious harm had escalated.

All of this should have eased the minds of the local community, but it didn't, and a sly smile crept over Sloane's face. Neighbours observed the police at Ripley House at least once or twice a week. They saw who they classed as the *undesirables* hanging around outside the hostel and even when staff came out and threatened to call the police, it wouldn't be long before another group of drunk or drugged-up loudmouths reappeared... and from everything that Sloane had learned, Danny Wells seemed to be the one encouraging them.

Through her contacts, Sloane had discovered that neighbours had witnessed Danny passing money in exchange for packages and even though the hostel staff were made aware, whenever Danny was drug tested he came up clean.

Random room searches also found no drugs or alcohol – so even though it seemed the staff had their own concerns, their hands were tied.

Sloane ascertained that Danny had received verbal warnings for his abusive and aggressive language not only towards staff and other residents but also towards members of the community. The claim that he could be rehabilitated had no merit in the eyes of those who lived on the street where the hostel was located.

No one liked Danny.

Something had to be done.

TWO

Killer
_____

D anny Wells was a cocky bastard from the moment he stepped through the hostel door, and I had been looking forward to finally wiping that smirk off his face. I knew the moment I slipped the note under his door that he'd be down those stairs so fast. Prison hadn't changed him – it had made him worse. In group, he tried to blame his behaviour on his childhood, but he wasn't born evil, he just loved violence. So why not give him a taste of his own medicine?

When I tiptoed into the living room, he'd already taken the bait. The amphetamine bag was gone and the three spliffs I had rolled and set alongside the bag of weed were being scooped up into his hands when he turned and looked at me.

'What the fuck are you doing here?'

'I see you got my note…'

'You? Well fuck me sideways. I thought you played by the rules with your _yes sir, no sir, three bags full sir_ babble.' His shoulders shook as he laughed and turned away from me.

Big mistake.

'I'm not paying you for this – you know that, right?' He

turned once again, and the slimy smirk appeared on his pocked face. 'You wouldn't want me to tell anyone, would ya?' He lay back into the sofa and put his hands behind his head. He really didn't think I was a threat.

It was now or never. I made my move. I pulled the needle from my pocket and jabbed it in his neck, hoping it was a vein I'd hit but I wasn't too worried if not. Next, I slid the knife down my sleeve and placed a gloved hand over his mouth as I sliced his throat from ear to ear.

Now that's one smile from this bastard that I could handle. I pushed him forwards and crept out the way I came in. I needed to get rid of everything before he was discovered.

I stepped outside and felt the cold air on my face. No time to stop and think. I knew where the camera was pointed and avoided being caught in its sights. I pulled out the plastic bag from my pocket and shoved the hoodie, knife, and gloves inside and stuffed them in the hole I had dug earlier. I threw dirt over the evidence and would collect them all to dispose of properly the moment I could. There would be no need for the police to look here.

Would the world miss Danny Wells? Not a chance.

I thought I would feel relieved, vindicated... happy. Perhaps I will once my transfer comes through. Leaving Ripley House would be the icing on the cake – I could move on.

At least, that's the plan.

THREE

Jeanette

The shrill tone of the mobile phone on her nightstand woke Jeanette Macey with a start. It was 3.30am and the only people who called her at that time were the police or her staff from the Approved Premises. The caller ID confirmed the latter.

'Hello?' She rubbed an eye as she waited for the caller to identify themselves.

'Jeanette! We've got a problem. A serious problem. The police are here. Oh man. You... we need... uh...' Frank Brown, a probation service officer, wasn't making any sense. His high-pitched voice alerted Jeanette to the fact that something was wrong, but having just woken up from a deep sleep, she wasn't processing the situation.

'Hang on. Take a deep breath and slow down. Is it an emergency recall?' Jeanette sat up and looked around for her glasses, her eyes darting around the room. She spotted them on the dressing table, got up and went to put them on. She hurried around her bed and grabbed the notebook she kept on the nightstand.

'It's Danny Wells. Bloody hell! I don't know how it happened. I mean we were... I was...'

'Is someone else there I can talk to, Frank? Go and grab a cigarette. If one of the police officers is available, put them on perhaps? I still don't understand what's happened.'

'Yeah, OK. Irene is here.' Jeanette put the phone on speaker and went over to her closet, pulling out a clean blouse, some black trousers, and a light cardigan. There wasn't time to worry whether they matched; she began to get dressed while she waited for Frank to pass the phone over.

'Hi Jeanette.' Irene's voice was low. 'It's Danny Wells. He's dead. Police are questioning everyone as we speak. You really need to get here, and I'll explain more then.'

Jeanette's heart palpitated as the seriousness of the situation took hold. 'OK, I'm on my way. I'll notify the area manager.'

This can't be happening.

All the residents for the most part were doing well – or as well as could be expected. At least that's what she'd thought. She ran her fingers through her hair.

Jeanette dashed around her flat, grabbing her keys and security pass from the porcelain bowl on the coffee table and picking up her leather satchel as she ran out the door. She threw them onto the passenger seat as she got into her car. The hostel was less than forty minutes away and at this time of the morning the traffic would be light; she was sure she could make it in under half an hour whilst keeping to the speed limit. Jeanette used the hands-free system to contact the area head of probation to advise them of the situation at the hostel and confirm that she'd be in touch after she had spoken to the police. Her head ached after ending the call. The blunt instructions and periods of silence spoke volumes in terms of her manager's feelings.

Once she had reached the hostel, she turned into the gravel driveway, heading towards the back where staff parking spaces were allocated. It was still dark, except for the light of the moon that shone through the trees like a spotlight on the hostel. Using her pass, she swiped the security pad and waited for the click before pulling the door open. There were a lot of people in the house – police, CSI, hostel staff and residents – and she had to squeeze her way past to get to the main office. Jeanette made a beeline for Frank and Irene who were both wide-eyed as they listened to the police officer standing in front of them. Whether they were absorbing anything the officer was saying was questionable.

Jeanette interrupted as much to let her team members know she was there as to give them a breather. 'Can I get either of you anything? I'm going to make some coffee – I think we all could use one.' They both nodded.

As she waited for the coffee to brew, Jeanette used the time to try and formulate a plan of action from the limited information she knew.

The newspapers would be all over this. The hostel had been getting grief ever since it opened. As hard as she tried, she knew there would be no positive way to spin the situation. A man had been murdered. It didn't get any worse than that – even if he was a criminal.

Once the coffee was made, she returned to her colleagues, placing the tray on the table. She waited as the officer finished up and gave him a side smile as he walked away before she grabbed her mug and sat across from Frank and Irene. 'OK. Speak. I need to know exactly what we're facing here. Who found the body?' She looked between Frank and Irene, waiting for a response. When one wasn't forthcoming, she snapped her fingers. 'Hey. The police will be asking you more difficult questions. I know this wasn't something you expected to happen on your watch, but I need to know how one of the residents was murdered right under our noses.' She said the last part a little sharper than she had intended, and Irene began to cry.

'I don't know what happened. I was... on a break. Frank was supposed to be watching the CCTV.' Irene shifted her body away from Frank and Jeanette turned her glare on to him.

'Well? Is that true? What were *you* doing, Frank?'

'Irene wasn't on a break. She obviously fell asleep.' He looked directly at his colleague and her eyes dropped to the floor. '*I* was the one on a break. I hadn't realised she was napping until I came back in to the office to do the final room checks. That's when I found him in the living room. There was a lot of blood; I've never seen so much blood. I didn't go near him though – I shouted for Irene to call an ambulance. But with that much blood, I assumed he was dead...'

'What time was this?' Jeanette glared at Frank wondering why he needed to think about something he just told the police.

'About – ' Frank looked up at the ceiling.

'Hang on...' She didn't let him finish. Something dawned on Jeanette. Room checks usually happened before midnight but Frank had called her much later. 'How come you only called me at 3.30?' Jeanette's hands clenched. She felt the heat rise on her neck as she thought about all the forms she'd need to complete, questions she had no answers for, and her staff, as much as they tried, weren't helping. She took a deep breath – playing the blame game at this stage wouldn't help anyone. They'd just found a dead body. 'Sorry. I don't mean to sound accusatory. I'm sure you have a very good reason to have waited.'

'Of course we… uh… did. The police wouldn't let us make any calls until we spoke to them first.' Frank looked over Jeanette's shoulder. 'How long do you think they're going to be?'

Jeanette turned and looked through the open door where people in white suits were moving about. 'A while.' Another thought crept into her head. 'Where are all the residents?' They'd need to secure them into a single part of the house. The hostel would be a crime scene, and no one would be allowed to wander about. Normally they'd try to find some temporary accommodation but with these being high-risk offenders, that just wasn't possible – murder or no murder.

'They're in the dining hall. Two detectives wanted to speak with them.' Irene wiped her eyes.

'Is Harvi with them? I haven't seen him yet.' Jeanette's eyes scanned the open-plan office. Harvi Gates was one of the more experienced PSOs in the hostel. He preferred to work the night shifts because of his insomnia.

'He called in sick. Flu or something…' Frank shrugged.

The other thing about Harvi was that he had a lot of time off sick. Jeanette hid her anger at the fact that she was just hearing about his absence now. She'd deal with that another time.

'So, there's no staff with them now? One of us should be in there. Will you both be OK if I just check what's happening? Irene, can you make a list of places we can reach out to for some temporary day placements? We'll have to find out roughly how long the communal areas will be unavailable. Frank, can you text Anwar and tell him I need him to get in as soon as possible?'

Anwar was Jeanette's deputy manager and she'd need him in to have oversight whilst she dealt with everything else. She stood and headed to the dining hall.

The door was closed, so she tapped first before entering. All eyes turned to her when she walked in.

'And you are?' A gruff voice projected from across the room. The man had his arms crossed, and a notebook held in one hand peeked out the side.

'Jeanette Macey. I'm the Senior Probation Officer. Who are you?'

The man introduced himself as DS Kurt Brady and mumbled the name of his colleague standing opposite, but something else had caught Jeanette's attention. One of the residents kept shifting in his seat and the chair leg screeched on the wood floor with each movement.

He refused to look her in the eye.

She suspected the blood on his shirt was the reason why.

FOUR

Jeanette

A s the detective approached, Jeanette focused on the article written by Sloane Armstrong when Ripley House first opened two years previously. She wasn't ready to hear what he had to say, and couldn't think about what she'd just seen. The feature was hung on the wall by her Area Manager, despite Jeanette's protestations at the time, as a reminder to staff and residents of what the hostel was about and what it hoped to achieve. The interview had been agreed to on the basis that it would be a positive piece demonstrating to the local community the benefit of having a secure facility on their doorstep. Jeanette didn't trust Sloane, but for some reason, the journalist went easy on her and to this day, she still doesn't know why. She read the article as, right now, she needed something else to focus her attention on.

RIPLEY HOUSE: FRIEND OR FOE?

By Sloane Armstrong

Senior Probation Officer Jeanette Macey has worked for the probation service for just over 20 years, but she's been in the role of hostel manager for the last three years. Prior to this, Jeanette spent three years managing the sex offender unit and four years managing a field team. The first 10 years of her career were spent managing her own caseloads in various teams as a probation officer.

When asked to explain the role of hostels, Jeanette informed me that 'Offenders are usually sent to live at an Approved Premises because their probation officer decides they need extra monitoring following their release from prison to protect the public. Within the hostel, I have my own team of officers: probation service officers, or PSOs and residential staff who co-supervise those who come to live at the AP.' The SPO went on to explain that the offender's home probation officer maintains overall responsibility of the case with Jeanette's staff responding to daily tasks and key-work session on the premises. But is rehabilitation of these dangerous offenders really possible?

Through my own research I learned that before an offender arrives at their Approved Premises, their probation officer (sometimes referred to as an offender manager) provides the hostel with information about them as well as what time and day they'll be arriving. The officer also provides a risk management plan which identifies what level of supervision they will need and any licence conditions. I asked Jeanette to explain a little more about this.

'Licence conditions are like rules – it's what offenders need to follow as part of their sentence. Some of the more common conditions include weekly drug or alcohol tests or a curfew. Ripley House already has a curfew of 11pm – 6am but the individual's additional curfew may require them to sign in at the AP reception at specific times. This might seem quite restrictive to some of the residents but a lot of them find it helpful. It puts distance between them and the behaviours that might lead them back to offending.' I think my face *told Ms Macey that I wasn't convinced but I promised to let her have her say.*

Jeanette went on to explain that, 'having intensive supervision is important to ensure the person is properly supervised and monitored. That's the purpose of the Approved Premises, but whilst the offender is in a hostel, there may be other issues that have never come to light before – for example, a learning difficulty or a mental health condition. So, whilst they are living in the hostel environment, staff can begin to unpick those issues and help them to get the relevant referrals they need. Some hostels also have clinical psychologists who do 1-to-1 work or wellbeing groups once a week with the residents, but I haven't been able to secure that option yet.'

Perhaps there wouldn't be a murder investigation happening right now, perhaps the hostel wouldn't be a crime scene, and everyone in it wouldn't be a suspect, if she'd been able to get a psychologist, Jeanette thought to herself before she continued to read the remainder of the article.

'Despite that, there's a lot of support offered at the hostel, and this is a huge factor in keeping the public safe.' Jeanette and her team claim their main goal is to help offenders reintegrate and transition back into society, but I wondered how many have successfully been able to do this? The residents are usually at the hostel for three months; however, some will be there less than that, others for longer. My first thought was, how can effective work be done in such a short time?

In my research for this article, I learned that when a prisoner who has been given a hostel placement is released, they arrive at Ripley House and are inducted. Jeanette or someone from her team will show them around, inform them of the rules and procedures, and then take them to their room. Within the settling-in period, the hostel staff work with them to help set up universal credit, set up bank accounts, and sign on with a GP surgery. Their allocated officer will also help them to engage with all their appointments and set up a support network for them. The public are told that all this work helps to reduce the risk of them reoffending and is a key part of how the probation service keeps the public safe.

What do you think?

I think I know the answer.

When news reached the local community that Ripley House was opening, you all spoke up and protested. I asked Jeanette her view on this. She said she believed 'the biggest misconceptions came about because people weren't really aware of the intensive supervision that's provided' and she had wanted to set the record straight at the time but was met with deaf ears and large mouths.

Jeanette said that in her experience, offenders need to be ready to make a change; probation could motivate them and help them, but they need to be willing to change themselves. The longer you can keep people out of prison, the more they won't want to go back.

Although it had happened occasionally, Jeanette never believed that *she* would get a call to tell her that one of the offenders in her hostel had been murdered. On the premises. And possibly by another resident. How would she explain *this* to the local community?

A tap on the shoulder pulled her out of that thought.

'No time for reading, Ms Macey.' DS Brady tapped the frame. 'Bet *she'd* have something to say about all of this.'

FIVE

Jeanette

Jeanette took her glasses off and wiped them with her sleeve. She returned her gaze to the T-shirt again. She must be mistaken, but on closer inspection, she realised she wasn't.

'Interesting, isn't it? Claims it's his own blood – from a cut on his arm. But we'll be taking his shirt and doing the usual tests to verify his story. We'll need you all to clear out so the CSI can do their thing.'

'That could take a little bit of time, detective. It's not like we can just stick them all in a B&B.' She instantly regretted the sarcasm, but stress often brought out that side of her.

'Yes, Ms Macey – we are well aware. That's why we're sealing off the living room area and part of the top floor while you find appropriate accommodation for these lads. A few hours should do it.'

'I can stay with my girlfriend,' one of the residents called out. Jeanette glared at the man and resisted the urge to smack the smile off his face. He was on licence for murdering his wife

20

and daughter and was required to inform staff of any new intimate relationships.

'Well, that's new information. Best I inform your probation officer, so they can get a warning letter sorted. Anyone else have any secrets they wish to share?' She turned back to the detective. 'One of my team is looking for openings now, but this will only be for the daytime. The men will have to return to the hostel to sleep. Of course, we'll do everything we can to keep out of your way.' In situations such as this, there was an understanding between agencies that workarounds would be required. Jeanette was pleased that DS Brady didn't kick up a fuss. The detective thanked her and returned his attention to the room. Jeanette leaned against the wall in the corner as she listened to him stressing that he would find the culprit and make sure they never saw the light of day again. The detective was looking at everyone and she couldn't gauge whether any specific resident had been identified as a suspect, but given what they were saying about Danny Wells, they all could be hauled down to the station and questioned formally.

There had been seven residents present and none of them were angels. Jimmy Ludlow was a registered sex offender with a history of rapes against both men and women. He had some convictions of violence against men, all relating to random drunken fights. They had another registered sex offender, Brian Caldwell, but he'd been recalled the previous evening after a room search found a contraband laptop stuffed in between his mattress with images of children on it. Jeanette shuddered. There had been no evidence to suggest any contact had been made with children directly and his recall to prison had so far appeared to fly under the radar in terms of local and national papers; however, whether this would remain the case once the press got a hold of the Danny Wells murder was another matter.

The remaining five residents all had convictions for murder, rape, and/or violent robberies. All were on life licences – Jack Campbell, Ray Southwell, Devin Murphy and Mark York; Danny Wells, of course, was no longer a risk.

There was nothing more for Jeanette to do here, but as she turned to go she felt a hand on her arm. The detective was too touchy-feely for her liking. She looked down at it before raising her eyes to the detective. He held his hands up and backed away slightly.

'Sorry. I didn't want you to leave without finding out when we could look at Wells's records?'

'Actually, you can't. They're still confidential. However, we can share his OASys with you.'

'O what?' The DS scratched his chin.

'Offender Assessment System – we record all pertinent information relating to the index offence – family, housing, and the like as well as a detailed risk assessment. I can find out when his full record can be released, but given he's the victim, there will be some hoops to jump through.'

The detective shook his head. 'Whatever you can share with my officers now would be great. I take it the same applies to this lot's records?' He waved his hand around the room.

'More so. OASys is OK but for anything else I'd need their permission or a warrant.'

'Well, I'll give you my answer now: the pigs can fuck right off. Why's the finger pointing at us? We was all asleep when Frank yelled out – it's fucking discrimination if you ask me.' Jack Campbell nudged the guy next to him. 'Am I right?' The men around the table nodded in agreement.

The last thing she wanted was a riot on her hands. The

volatile energy in the room was rising and made Jeanette feel uneasy. 'Calm down. This is not the first time you've been on licence – you know the score and you've just heard me explain everything so wind your neck in.' Jeanette turned to the detective. 'I'll be in the main office; perhaps we should have this conversation privately or send one of your officers in and I'll update them and my team at the same time.'

Jeanette left the dining room with the detective at her heels and returned to the front office. Irene was sitting at one of the desks, writing notes and squinting as she stared at her monitor and tapped her mouse.

Jeanette turned to speak to the DS but he wasn't there, and she hid her annoyance when she spotted him talking to Frank on the far side of the room. He must have brushed past her when she was focused on Irene. The detective waved her over.

Frank leaned in to Jeanette. 'This detective wants access to our computers but I've tried to tell him I can't allow that.'

'Thanks, Frank. Can you do me a favour and print out a copy of Danny Wells's OASys as well as those of the remaining residents – apart from Caldwell, as he was returned to custody last night.' Jeanette waited until Frank left before speaking to DS Brady. 'There was no need to sneak past me. I've explained the process and we're both on the same side. Is there anything else I can help you with?'

'I won't need Murphy's records either. We had to drag him out of bed – apparently Irene gave him a prescribed sleeping tablet at 10.30pm and he was out for the count. Could barely keep his eyes open when questioned. Of course, we'll have to confirm with his GP but...'

'That's fine. His medical information is included in his assessment so that should assist.' That explained why Devin Murphy had been dozing in the dining room. 'He's due to move to another hostel closer to home in the next few days, so you'll have those contact details too. Was there something else you needed?'

'Do you have time to answer a few questions for me?'

Jeanette looked at her watch. The kitchen crew would be arriving soon if someone didn't call them. 'Yes, but let me just take care of something first. If you'd like to wait in my office...' She pointed to a door at the back of the room which led upstairs to her office, before realising it would be locked. 'Come.' Her finger waved and the detective followed her. She turned on the light and pointed up the small stairwell. 'If you head up there, you can grab a seat and I'll be two minutes. Can I get you anything?'

'No thanks.'

Jeanette watched as he stomped up the staircase before heading back to Irene's desk. 'Sorry to interrupt but would you be able to call the manager of the kitchen staff and advise him that they can't come in today? Let him know I'll contact him as soon as I can later today to explain. Don't give him any more details. Oh and one more thing. Can you just pop your head into the dining room and make sure everything there is OK?'

Irene looked up at Jeanette with puffy eyes. 'Sure.'

The PSO was exhausted, and Jeanette made a mental note to see when she could release the nightshift so they could get some sleep. They'd be no use to anyone at this stage. The other probation staff – Steph, Amy, and her deputy manager, Anwar Hussain, would be arriving shortly and she'd have to deal with them; it was going to be chaos for the next few hours.

Jeanette jogged up to her office and sat at her desk. 'Before we start, can I just check whether it would be OK to send Frank and Irene home once the day shift arrives? They're both exhausted and won't be of much use in terms of questions...'

'Not my decision, Ms Macey.' He pulled a radio out of his pocket and spoke. It crackled as he listened and the detective nodded in response, as if the person was in the room. 'They'll be needed for a formal statement. Looks like that's going to be arranged shortly. Now, if I could just ask you a few questions?'

Jeanette realised that the police were going to be as tight-lipped as she and her team were being, and she didn't have the energy to argue. 'What would you like to know?'

He flipped open a notebook and positioned his pen.

Very old school, Jeanette observed, though it seemed to fit the aging detective's image.

'Had anyone expressed any dislike or ill feelings towards Mr Wells in the last few days?'

She had to hold in a laugh until she realised he was being serious.

'Danny wasn't a favourite amongst the residents. He'd been accused of bullying, been abusive to staff, could be a right pain in the arse, so the answer is yes. But that's quite common in Approved Premises.'

'Uh-huh...' When he raised his eyes to look at her, Jeanette frowned.

'And did *you* ever say that one day Mr Wells would meet someone who would put him in his place' – he turned back a few pages in his notebook and stopped, tapping the paper before he continued – 'permanently?'

'What the hell are you implying, officer?' Did he think she was responsible for what happened?

'I'll just come straight out and ask you: did you threaten Danny Wells?'

The colour drained from Jeanette's face as she tried to think of her response.

Who had told him?

SIX

Killer

O
h my God. I can't believe I did it. I actually did it.

I take in a deep breath to curb the excitement I feel. With the police and CSI moving about the hostel, I can't draw any attention to myself. I need to behave like it's any other day.

'Do you know if there are any other exits out of the building?' a young officer calls out to me.

Shit.

'I've no idea. You'll probably have to speak to the manager.' He follows me into the dining area and I take a seat at the back.

'Where have you been?' Irene eyeballs me.

'Bathroom. Think that police officer wants a word with you.' I point behind her.

My heart's racing. *Do they suspect me?*

For now, I need to blend in and keep my mouth shut even though I want to scream from the rooftops.

I did it!

I killed that fucker and it won't be long until I'm gone.

SEVEN

Sloane

W hen she wasn't writing the news, Sloane was watching it or attending court – she never sugar-coated anything she learned and believed the public respected her for that, based on the numerous letters she received on a weekly basis.

She had worked her arse off over the last fifteen years, getting to know all the ins and outs of the criminal justice system from the professionals, and this was what brought her stories to life for her readers.

Sloane had been bitten once before, after taking the word of a criminal as the truth and she had ended up with egg on her face; now she was twice shy. She had learned the hard way. Luckily for her she had worked with some of the best editors in the business – Finn Morgan and Bethan Cotton – and still called upon them both when she was unsure of the integrity of her article or story. They held nothing back and challenged her to do her best work.

She had built her career reporting on character-driven narratives about the criminal justice system, and quickly learned that some crime and court topics demanded a deeper sort of training. Now a more experienced freelance journalist, and a regular contributor to the crime section of the *North Warwickshire Herald*, Sloane often relied heavily on police accounts, but she was careful about how she used the information, asking herself why the police had provided that information and what they stood to gain from sharing it. She wouldn't be their voice but she couldn't ignore them either.

Sloane was well aware of how the police could be using the media to apply pressure to a suspect, and there was no way she was going to face a lawsuit or credibility crises because she published false allegations. Her checklist of questions was something she either voiced or asked in her head as she was getting the information. Why are they giving me a perp's name if they don't have enough to actually charge? What's in it for them? How are they trying to use me?

She preferred to rely on the vetted information that authorities publicly shared on their own social media accounts and had no problem using her contacts in the CPS, Social Care, or emergency services to substantiate any information. Publishing additional information that these agencies might dangle could mean beating the competition, but she'd rather be right than first.

Separating fact from fiction was easier said than done, and always depended on the perspective of the person doing it. In court, Sloane knew that she might hear two completely different narratives from the CPS and the defence and she would have to try and present her version in print in a way that was both fair and as close to the truth as possible.

One thing Sloane always kept in the back of her mind when deciding on what story she would write about was the danger of writing on every crime. The last thing she'd want to do is stoke fear of a crime wave or of crime increasing when it wasn't. In her opinion, that kind of coverage could have negative repercussions and should be weighed against the news value of the story. When you have a house full of killers on your doorstep though, all rules went out the window.

The moment she'd heard that Ripley House Approved Premises was opening only a few streets away, she'd made it her business to ensure the local area was informed in order to protect themselves from the criminals on their doorsteps.

She'd forged a strange but useful relationship with the local busybody – Helen Burgess – who fed her information she used in her articles in the *North Warwickshire Herald*.

Always in the back of her mind was the thought that if her sister had known about the predator who'd been stalking her for weeks, she might still be alive today.

The alarm bleeped and Sloane moaned, groggily reaching across the bed. She smacked her hand on the nightstand until she found the button and switched the noise off. Stretching her arms, she stared at the ceiling until her eyes focused in the darkness. She threw off the duvet and sat on the side of her bed.

She was not a morning person.

From the corner of her eye, she saw the screen on her mobile light up.

A text message.

She stood, grabbed her dressing gown, and wrapped it tightly around her before picking up her phone and unlocking it.

It was from Helen Burgess, and it was something she'd hoped she'd never see again.

A body had been found at Ripley House. The police had blocked off the area. There was no time for her caffeine fix – she needed to get over there and see what she could find out.

Sloane dressed as quickly as she could. Jeans, a hoodie, and her trainers. Being freelance had some advantages – she could dress how she liked and save her suits for court. Looking at the time, she guessed she could be at the hostel in twenty minutes if she ran – which would count as her regular jog of the day – but she needed to do something else first.

Sloane scrolled through her phone and pressed *call*, resting it between her ear and shoulder as she pulled her trainers on. She didn't have to wait too long for the phone to be answered.

'Oh my word! What took you so long? The whole street is cordoned off. It looks like they are— Oh, hang on, I need to move to another window.'

Sloane waited as she listened to the older woman shuffle across the floor.

'That's better. Yes. They're definitely taking out one body. I wonder if there are any more.' Helen's voice rose an octave.

Sloane could just imagine the woman standing on her tiptoes to take in as much as she could.

'I'm just out the door. If I have any trouble getting through the cordon, I'm going to tell them you're my aunt and you called me because you were scared. OK?'

'How exciting. I'll get the biscuits out.'

Sloane ended the call and raced out the door. The cold air smacked her in the face, and she regretted not putting a coat on. She picked up the pace to keep herself warm.

When she arrived at Ripley Avenue, she stopped to catch her breath and take in the scene. There were lights flashing from the police and emergency services vehicles, neighbours milling about on their front lawns and paths, each one trying to get information on what was happening, and officers stationed around the perimeter to keep people getting too close to the hostel. The air buzzed with both fear and anger, and Sloane knew she'd need to be clever to get anywhere near Helen's home.

A young officer was coming towards her, and she switched on the tears, waving him over. 'Officer! I need to get to my aunt's house.' She pointed in the direction of Helen's home. 'She's just called me crying and I'm worried something may have happened to her. You see, she's not well.' A white lie. No harm to anyone in the long run.

'I'm sorry, miss, but I can't let anyone through. I can send someone over to see if your aunt is OK though.'

'Please let me through. She won't open the door to anyone but me. I don't know or care what's happened here, I just need to make sure she's OK – she rang me very upset.' Sloane showed the officer her call log which detailed the time, hoping it added some authenticity to what she was saying.

She was a good actress – she noted his features softening – and after looking around, he let her through, and she squeezed his arm. 'Thank you.'

Sloane's eyes were glued on the hostel as she walked up the pathway to Helen Burgess's front door. Sloane spotted Jeanette Macey standing in the window and their eyes locked before Helen opened the door and let her in. Helen pulled her by the arm into the living room where she had set up two chairs by the large front window. Sloane smiled when she saw the pot of tea with Penguin biscuit bars on the side table.

'Sit. Sit. I haven't seen any other bodies coming out, but it doesn't mean there aren't any. Could be they solved the problem themselves and got rid of each other, right?' A glint in her eye told Sloane that Helen genuinely was hoping for a slaughter to have occurred.

Sloane placed her bag on the back of the chair and reached in to take out her notebook and pen. She sat down. 'What do you know so far?' She unwrapped the chocolate biscuit and nibbled while Helen spoke.

'Well, you know how bad my sleep has been lately, what with all that negative energy next door.' Helen rubbed her arms. 'It's unsettling. So, at about 1am or thereabouts I heard shouting. Then, within twenty minutes the police and an ambulance was there. I went out back – the men like their fags, you know, and they can't go out front – something to do with those tags some of them wear on their ankles. A few were outside, and I overheard one saying that Danny had been stabbed to death. Blood everywhere apparently.' She rubbed her arthritic hands together.

Sloane was fascinated by the twinkle in Helen's eye as she relayed the information. She had questions but didn't want the woman to stop. They were kindred spirits when it came to their goal of shutting down Ripley House.

Helen turned towards her and grabbed her knee. Sloane shifted in the chair, unsure of what to expect out of her friend's mouth next.

'We were right all along. You can't place a bunch of killers in a house together and think there won't be trouble. When I saw all those lowlife druggies out front every day, I used to think those guys got away with murder – looks like one of them might not this time, right?'

Sloane scribbled everything in her notepad. 'Uh-huh. Did

you hear anything else? Did they say anything about a suspect or whether more than one person was involved?' She stared out of the window as Helen took a sip of her tea before continuing.

'No. Nothing of that sort, but I can find out for you.'

'How?' Sloane presumed she would have a hard time getting any information from the probation staff or hostel residents, so she could use any help offered by Helen.

'I volunteered to work in the kitchen. They're always looking for part-time help, and you know the saying: keep your friends close but your enemies closer. I never liked the idea of having so many horrid people living next door to me, so I figured the best way to protect myself was to know what I'm up against.'

'But they know you run the neighbourhood watch and protested against the hostel when it first opened. How in the world did you manage to get a job there?'

'Oh, that was easy. I stay mainly in the background now for the neighbourhood watch stuff – Gladys has taken the lead. I told them that I had seen what good work they were doing and that everyone deserves a second chance.' A sly smile spread across her face. 'They ate that up; I can be very convincing, you know. The only thing is… we all got a text cancelling our shifts for today – but I'm an old woman.' Helen winked. 'Never really got the hang of using those mobile things.'

'Helen, I don't know whether to hug you or fear you, but I will say that you're an absolute genius.'

EIGHT

Jeanette

'Are you taking the mick?' Jeanette tilted her head, trying to read the detective's face. 'I'm a probation officer – do you really think I'd threaten one of the residents I'm responsible for?' She was surprised by the detective's accusation.

DS Brady paused. He was playing the silent game, but Jeanette had been trained in that interview technique too. She stared him out and eventually he cracked.

'So, are you denying that you said something about Mr Wells getting what's coming to him? Or words to that effect? Think carefully – we have someone who says they overheard you say that.'

Jeanette stood and looked down at the detective, taking back the control in the room. This was her territory, and she wouldn't be intimidated, especially when she knew she had nothing to hide.

'You must be kidding me. I may well have said something like that – I can't remember – but my meaning would have been related to a warning letter or recall, not that I was going to kill the guy! This is a hostel for rehabilitation, something I firmly believe in, detective.'

She happened to glance out of the window and caught sight of Sloane Armstrong.

'Great – just what I need…' She dropped like a dead weight back into her chair.

DS Brady looked up. 'Problem?'

'Nothing I can't handle. Is there anything else? Let me assure you – I didn't have anything to do with this. I was fast asleep at home when I got the call. Have you checked the doors? How do we know we're not dealing with a break-in? The back door sometimes doesn't close properly. The estates and properties team haven't been around to fix it yet.' Jeanette should have thought of this earlier, but she'd been too focused on everything else to think straight when she arrived.

'Our initial observations conclude that this was an inside job. No evidence to suggest the locks were tampered with, but thanks for the update on the back door. I'll have them check it out again. We'll need your CCTV as well.' He was blunt, not offering any hints as to the direction of the investigation other than that they wouldn't be looking outside the hostel for suspects.

'You'll have to request it through the appropriate channels.' Normally Jeanette might have been a bit more forthcoming, allowing the police to have a quick look before directing them to request the information through the Comms Department as part of the local Service Level Agreement (SLA) in place. But the detective had rubbed her the wrong way from the get-go, and she wasn't going to make his job easy. She wanted to review the CCTV before she had to hand it over; they had been having issues with it, but Anwar had assured her the cameras had been fixed. She was under no illusion that her own line manager would be expecting answers after the phone call she had coming this morning.

The detective took a deep breath and glared at Jeanette. She didn't care and wouldn't be swayed into bending the rules. She'd eventually have to hand over the footage, but it would only be what was directly related to the incident, and she'd leave it up to her manager and the Comms department to decide.

'If that's all?' She raised her left brow, hands on hips, waiting for the detective to take the hint.

'For now.'

He left the room and mumbled something into his radio, but Jeanette couldn't make out what he was saying.

Fifteen minutes after logging in to her computer, muffled shouts and some sort of a commotion from downstairs caught her attention. She ran down the narrow staircase, glad she had decided to wear flat shoes as there could have been another death had she been wearing her heels. The stairs were steep and sometimes the frayed carpet got caught in her heels. Another thing the properties and estates team had failed to rectify, despite numerous complaints. It's like they forgot... or didn't care about the health and safety of staff.

'What the hell is going on?' She walked into the main office and Irene pointed at the plexi window, designated as the reception area. Jeanette recognised Helen Burgess from next door. 'Why is she here? I thought I asked someone to contact the kitchen crew.'

'I did call.' Irene shrugged and returned to working on the list in front of her, leaving Jeanette to deal with the situation.

Jeanette walked out into the corridor. Helen was trying to shove her way past the two officers who held her loosely by the shoulders.

'Get your hands off! I can have you both done for manhandling me, you know. Just because you're police officers doesn't mean you can get away with assaulting me.' Helen huffed and Jeanette noticed her straining her neck to see what was happening just a few feet away from her.

'I'll talk to her, officers. She volunteers here.' Jeanette stepped in.

The officers let go of Helen and Jeanette took her into the main office. 'Why are you here so early? Didn't you get a text from your supervisor? As you can see, we've had an incident and you won't be required to work today.'

Helen ignored her. 'Was that blood I saw in the living room?'

'I'm sorry but I can't discuss any of that with you. You'll have to go now.' Jeanette directed the woman back to the front door. She didn't trust her after seeing the journalist walking up her path. 'By the way, you do know that you can't discuss what happens in the hostel with friends, family, or members of the public. It's in your contract. Confidentiality is part of the job…'

'I may be old, but I am not an idiot. I don't think I like what you're implying.'

The fact that the woman wouldn't look her in the eye as she made the remark told Jeanette all she needed to know. 'Go home, Helen, and don't go telling that journalist I saw sneaking into your house earlier anything about what you may have seen or heard just now.'

Jeanette watched as Helen Burgess stomped off. She needed to make a call and try to implement some damage control, as she suspected Helen would be gossiping within seconds of being back at her house.

Once back in her office, she closed the door. Picking up the desk phone handset, she dialled and waited for the grumpy greeting she expected to be met with from down the line.

'We might have a problem.'

NINE

Sloane

S loane watched as Helen trotted up the path and burst through the front door. She waited for her to catch her breath before launching into questions.

'You weren't long – what happened?'

'Ugh – that snooty manager wagged her finger at me and told me to keep my lips zipped before shoving me out of there, but I don't remember signing any non-disclosure. Who does she think she is? I mean, I don't even have access to records; I cook meals and leave.' Sloane watched as Helen fixed her hair. Her hand was shaking. She was either angry or scared. If Sloane had to guess she would say the former as Helen's cheeks were flushed and her jaw was clenched tight.

'There was blood all over the living room floor so whatever happened, it had to be pretty big, that's for sure.' Realising how that sounded, she added, 'Might have been a struggle… so much blood.'

'Can you describe exactly what you saw?' Sloane guided Helen back to their front-row seats by the window so she could still observe any comings and goings as she wrote down what Helen told her.

'Hmmm. I only caught a quick glance, as there were a lot of those CSI people around. Almost felt like I was right in the middle of filming one of those TV shows – you know the ones I mean. I can't imagine they love their jobs. All that blood, and the smell...' Helen visibly shivered.

Sloane nodded. She didn't want to dismiss Helen's feelings but needed to bring her focus back to the discussion before she went off on one of her tangents. 'OK, so, ignoring the people, what else did you see?'

Helen closed her eyes. 'OK, I can do this.' She drew in a deep breath. 'I saw a couch. It looked like there was some blood on it, but most of the blood I saw was pooled on the floor. *Big* patch. But it was hard to see much with all the people and Jeanette standing in my way.' Helen's hands were waving about. 'Wonder if that's where he was stabbed? On the couch. There was too much blood for him to have been beaten to death and I didn't hear a gunshot so he must have been stabbed, right? Oh. I could also hear a bit of shouting from the back room.' Helen turned to Sloane. 'That's the dining area – if I'd been allowed into the kitchen, I could have heard more of what was going on, but the police wouldn't let me past the front corridor before Jeanette pulled me into the main office. Oh! Oh! I remember something from there – one of the probation staff had a list of something on her desk. She pulled it away when she saw me looking but I bet they're trying to find places for those other lowlifes while the police search their premises. Damn! I should have tried to get a picture on my phone.'

'No, that's great information. They probably would have confiscated your phone if you did that, and anyway, we'd never learn where they placed them because if that information was leaked they'd move them out as quickly as they moved them in. You've done brilliantly.'

Helen's eyes brightened. She'd once told Sloane that she had become like a daughter to her. Helen was childless and Sloane didn't want to pry but suspected it wasn't by choice. She was lonely and Sloane tried to keep her company as much as she could, not least because of the information the woman seemed to be able to gather. Helen's husband had died just when the hostel had opened two years before and Sloane believed that was why Helen focused so much time and energy on making sure everything was above board within the neighbouring property. Apparently, Malcolm Burgess had died of a heart attack, and although the doctors had told Helen that it was an underlying medical condition, she refused to believe that. She blamed the stress of having what she called 'vile human beings' moving into their nice neighbourhood for causing her husband's heart to shut down. Sloane noticed Helen's eyelids were drooping as she rubbed her hands together.

'You haven't had much sleep. I should go and let you get some rest. I don't think we'll be finding out much more, but you've been a big help as always, partner!' Sloane winked.

'Are you sure? I can keep watch for a little while longer, you know.' Helen let out a big yawn. 'Or maybe not. OK, well, if I see anything else, should I call you? I can just grab a blanket and have a nap on the couch.' Helen pointed to the floral-patterned settee behind her.

'You can call me any time. Now go and get some rest. I'll let myself out.' Sloane waited for Helen to go upstairs before she pulled her phone out. She scrolled through her contacts and hit *CALL*.

'Conrad? I've got a story for you. I just need to finalise some details but expect it in your inbox within the next few hours or so.'

She listened for a moment before responding.

'The headline? How about: A Licence to Murder – Body Found at Ripley House? Gotta go. Watch your inbox!'

TEN

Jeanette

Jeanette watched from her office window as Sloane Armstrong left Helen Burgess's house. The spring in the journalist's step was unnerving. She needed to find out what the nosy neighbour had said. It still bothered her that Helen had been able to fool the interview panel into letting her volunteer for the kitchen staff post. Jeanette had done everything in her power to block it but had been overruled; she reiterated this to the area head in the call she'd just finished but he was having none of it.

She returned to focusing on the journalist, who was now talking to some of the officers outside, no doubt recording them without their knowledge. Jeanette's jaw clenched. She was only winding herself up and needed to concentrate on something else before she did or said something she would later regret. But after a final glance at Sloane, Jeanette knew she wouldn't relax until she had spoken to the woman herself – but that could be tricky. Stepping away from the window, she stomped downstairs towards the front door, ignoring the looks she received from her staff as she passed through the main office. She was just about to open the front door and call out to Sloane when she felt a hand on her shoulder.

'Don't make it worse by saying something that will end up splashed all over the front page.' Frank dropped his hand to his side and Jeanette turned to face him.

'You know she's going to have a field day with this, right? I can just imagine the clickbait headline she's concocting now. Who knows what bull Helen has told her...' She ran her fingers through her hair. 'We're screwed this time, Frank. I may as well bend over now and take it.' Jeanette wasn't referring only to the murder but all the internal investigations that would come with it. 'Serious Further Offence, Death on Probation Premises...' She shook her head. 'The forms and interviews that will take place, turning colleagues against one another so they avoid the finger of blame... The stress... Why did this have to happen here?'

'No matter what you do or say the press will turn it around. We've seen it before – the only time probation appears on the news is when something bad happens, but we'll get through it. You've a more immediate problem to deal with though. Irene is having a bit of a meltdown. In fact, she's been a bit off for weeks, but I didn't want to stick my nose in. You should probably speak to her.'

Jeanette snapped out of self-pity mode and nodded. 'Righto. I'll have a word. Are you off now?' She noticed the backpack in his hand.

'Yeah. The police want to take a formal statement at the station and have asked us all to leave. Irene has found day placements for the residents and the rest of the team have been told to go to other offices but will pop in here to speak with you or you'll contact them. You're going to have a crazy busy day. I got an email informing me I'll still be required here in the evenings so I'm going to get some sleep while I can.'

'OK. If anything comes up or changes, I'll be in touch.' Jeanette returned to the main office, grateful to Frank for the update. She made a beeline for Irene. 'Hey. How are you holding up?' Jeanette reached out and squeezed the woman's shoulder.

When Irene looked up, her eyes were puffy and bloodshot. She shook her head. 'I just want to go home now. I've done all I can. The community payback team are sending around someone with a van to drop the residents off at their temporary placements.'

'That's unusual. How'd you manage that?'

'I didn't. The CP manager reached out to me. Looks like they were contacted by head office and it was all arranged to ensure no one goes astray while all this is going on. They've given us day placements for two weeks and the residents will return here in the evenings, with limited access to the house.' Irene's voice quivered and her eyes looked everywhere but at Jeanette.

Jeanette agreed with Frank that something was definitely off with Irene. 'Are you really OK? I'm sensing there's something else, other than what happened here tonight… What's bothering you?'

'Can we go into your office for a minute?' Irene whispered.

'Of course,' Jeanette stepped aside to let Irene go ahead and when they were both in her office, she closed the door behind them before taking a seat. 'What is it?'

'I know I shouldn't be telling tales, but Frank should have been watching the CCTV and he wasn't. It's not the first time either. He brings his iPad into the office and watches films – and I'm pretty sure he lets some of the residents get away with coming in later for their curfews. I called him out on it once and he threatened me, Jeanette…' Irene's body shook. 'Said he'd get me fired if I said anything and you know how much I need this job.' She tugged at her sleeve.

Jeanette did know. Irene's husband was a useless twat who drank all day, and the couple were in a lot of debt. 'You should've told me about this sooner, but better late than never. Did you tell the police?'

'No, do I have to? I kinda hoped you could tell them maybe. That way it wasn't coming from me.' She looked down at the floor.

'I'm afraid you do – now that you've shared this information with me, I'll need to include it in my reports and the police need to know this for the investigation.' Jeanette sighed. This would complicate things. Frank was a good officer but if he had been actively abusing his power to make his job a little easier, it would need to be looked at further.

'Fine.' Irene stood. 'Can I go now?' There was an iciness in her voice and the tears that had earlier been threatening to escape now seemed to be gone.

'Uh… yes. I'll let the detective know what you've told me and I'm sure he'll be in touch. You and Frank will both have to give a formal statement at some point. Probably sooner rather than later, so get off home and get some sl—' Jeanette looked up from where she had been taking notes when she heard the door click.

Irene had left.

That was strange. Was Irene pointing the blame at Frank because she was trying to deflect suspicion? Rubbing the goosebumps that had crept onto her skin, she could hardly bear to think of it.

Jeanette looked at her watch. She needed to find the detective and let the residents know what was happening. This incident could mean a loss of jobs – or worse.

Her work mobile was ringing again. Frank had been right, this was going to be a crazy day.

ELEVEN

Sloane
_____

With the sunrise, there came a bitter chill in the air. Before heading back to her flat, Sloane stopped to talk to some of the officers outside Ripley House. She wasn't convinced they'd help her, but it was always worth a shot.

'Any suspects yet?' She casually pressed the record button on her phone, holding it down by the side of her leg.

'The public will be informed of any developments in due course, ma'am.' He didn't even look at her as he rambled off the standard line.

'What about the press? It would be great to be able to put a positive spin on this, don't you think? The police and probation services will be massacred in the national press. How about getting your version out before that happens?' Sloane didn't really care how either service came out in the press as it would be down to their own failures, but it never hurt to show concern.

His eyes narrowed as he looked her up and down. 'Nice try. I've said my piece and I suggest you move along now. Do you live on this street?'

That was her cue to leave, otherwise he might decide to use force to make her go. 'I'm leaving, but don't say I never gave you the opportunity.' Sloane shrugged her bag over her shoulder and when her tummy grumbled, she took a detour by Gregg's for a coffee and croissant before returning home.

At her house, she kicked off her shoes and dropped her bag by the door. When she had a good story on the go, she often neglected to eat, so having the Gregg's around the corner was a godsend. She wasn't much of a cook either and the croissant would tide her over for a bit. She wanted to research who else resided at the hostel and see if she could speak to some of the local drug users who hung around the area like a bad smell. They might be able to give her some information to help narrow down anyone who might have had a reason to get rid of Danny Wells. But first, she had to whip something together to send over to her editor, Conrad, as he would only hold the spot for so long.

She sat on the couch, pulled her laptop onto her knees, and began typing.

A LICENCE TO MURDER:
RIPLEY HOUSE – ARE LOCAL RESIDENTS SAFE?

By Sloane Armstrong, Investigative Crime Journalist

In the early hours of this morning, I discovered that Ripley House, a probation hostel that houses some of the UK's most dangerous offenders, was the location of a grisly murder. One of the residents was slaughtered in cold blood right under the noses of probation staff. My sources tell me that there are no identified suspects at the moment and the remaining residents will be temporarily supervised in other undisclosed locations while the investigation continues. If the police and probation can't keep the public safe in a hostel that is supposed to be secure, how safe are the rest of us?

(Note: Conrad, if you could insert a picture of the hostel attached here – I think I got a good angle – bit menacing, isn't it?)

Sloane attached the picture from her files.

When the hostel, more commonly known these days as Approved Premises, opened two years ago, local residents were up in arms, concerned about the increase in crime and risk to the public that such an establishment would bring to the area. With the incident that occurred in the early hours this morning, it's safe to assume those concerns were not unfounded. What happened? Did someone snap or was the murder premeditated?

Statistics from the council indicate that burglaries, substance-misuse-related offences and car crime have steadily increased in the area since the doors to Ripley House opened, and although there was no hard and fast evidence of a direct correlation, it seems that with the horrendous crime – a murder – this can no longer be ignored.

Local residents can rest assured that I will keep pressing the police for details to make sure we're kept informed. In the meantime, I urge you to remain vigilante, but don't take matters into your own hands and keep safe.

If you have any knowledge of the residents of Ripley House or any information relating to this shocking crime, you can contact me anonymously at the North Warwickshire Herald.

Sloane re-read the article before pressing send. She lay back and closed her eyes, mentally listing everything she needed to do for the rest of the day. After a few moments, she opened her eyes, stretched her legs and went to the kitchen where she put on a large pot of coffee. She'd make up a flask to take with her as she went out to speak to people about the crime, Danny Wells, and the hostel.

But first, a shower.

The hot water felt good against her skin. She squirted a small amount of shampoo into her palm before rubbing her hands together to lather. Running her fingers through her short hair, she gave her scalp a quick massage before rinsing off. She soaped up a loofa and ran it over her body, a moment of sadness coming over her as she traced the outline of the black rose tattoo she'd had done on her thigh after she and Noah had broken up. She'd always wanted one and after some persuasion from her friend, and a few tequilas, the deed had been done at a friend's party, and she had no regrets. She could still see that tattoo artist's face as he inked her thigh. He'd warned her that the alcohol would have diluted her blood so if the ink didn't take, he wanted no come-back. Thankfully there were no problems. For her, the rose symbolised grief and loss, and that was how she had felt after she and Noah had split, despite her being the one to end it. It also symbolised rebellion and strength, so it was a constant reminder of how far she had come since her sister had been murdered, though her friend had joked that it was also a perfect reminder of the darkness in her heart. Sloane smiled.

After drying herself off, she felt more awake. She went into her bedroom and looked at the pile of clothes she had thrown on the chair a few days ago. They'd do. Sweater and jeans on, she searched her closet for her combat boots and headed downstairs, spotting her leather jacket on the coat rack.

Sloane grabbed her bag and slung it over her shoulder, locking the door behind her as she left. She'd head out to

Hartshill Park where she knew many of the local heroin addicts hung out. She needed to stop by a bank machine before she got there, knowing that the information would not be free. She didn't like the idea that any money would be spent on gear, but she wasn't stupid either. Needs must. She'd been down that road herself before. If it got her a break in the story, it was something she could live with. Better that than robbing some poor old lady, right?

She stopped again at the Gregg's and picked up a few sandwiches – sometimes food went a long way in getting what was needed. It was a long shot, but it had worked in the past. It depended on the person. The girl at the counter eyed her up and down before there was a glint of recognition.

'You hungry today?'

She stuffed the sandwiches into a paper bag. Sloane forced a smile.

'Yeah. Long day ahead.'

She paid the cheeky cow and left the shop, feeling the woman's eyes on her back before hearing her say to a colleague, 'Weirdo. She's been in already – how can she stay so thin when she eats so much?'

———

Despite the cool breeze, Sloane's pace kept her body warm. At least it didn't look like it was going to rain. She pulled her jacket around her, catching a scent of vanilla which always reminded her of her sister.

She wasn't prepared for the flashes of her sister's murder as they came flooding back. Lately they seemed to be triggered by anything at all and she was struggling to suppress them. She'd tried counselling when she was younger but instead of dealing with the trauma, it had brought it bubbling to the surface and she hadn't been able to cope, so she'd stopped. A few years of drugs and alcohol had helped keep the memories at bay until she got clean. Her family and friends still tried to get her to return but she found that writing about crime, helping catch the perpetrators, and keeping the community safe by spreading awareness went further in helping her heal – better than any counselling or grief therapy she'd attended.

Sloane was startled out of her thoughts by a hand around her ankle and she had to work to regain her balance.

'What the hell?'

Looking down, she saw a middle-aged woman with unkempt greying hair, her thin frame layered in old sweaters that had seen better times and wrapped in sleeping bags that had a strange odour emanating from them. She couldn't hear what the woman was saying as she was speaking in a low voice, so she bent down, subtly holding a hand over her nose.

'Are you OK? Hungry? I've got a sandwich if you want it.'

Sloane started to open her bag when the woman grabbed her wrist – much tighter than Sloane would have expected.

'Be careful. A pretty girl like you could get hurt out here.' The woman spat the next words: 'They're not finished yet…'

TWELVE

Sloane
_____

Sloane stumbled back and shook her wrist free from the woman's grasp.

'What do you mean?'

The sandwich she was holding dropped to the ground, landing at the woman's feet, and Sloane rubbed her wrist, hoping for an explanation. The woman ignored her and picked up the sandwich, tearing it open before holding it to her nose.

'Egg salad. Pffft.' The homeless woman shoved the bread into her mouth and stared at Sloane.

After the initial shock of the woman grabbing her, Sloane realised how she must be coming across and sat down next to her.

'Do you ever hang around Ripley House? You know, the hostel a few blocks away?'

'Alcohol is my crutch – not drugs. Why you asking?' The woman's lips pursed. Sloane noticed her eyes attempting to focus on her. She sounded more lucid.

'I want to talk to people who may know some of the hostel

residents.' Sloane doubted the woman even knew about the murder – it was only a few hours ago after all.

'This about Danny? Heard he was killed last night. That true?' The woman finished off the first half of the sandwich, bits of egg salad flying out when she spoke.

'It is.'

Word travels fast then.

Sloane shouldn't have been surprised, especially if Danny Wells had been involved with drugs in the community.

'No need to be afraid anymore if that arsehole is gone. Got what he deserved, if you ask me.'

Sloane's eyes widened. The woman might be more useful than she first thought. 'Afraid? Why?'

'Nothing good about Danny – he was a bully and a tosser. Threw his weight around like he was something special, but he was worse than anyone round here' – she waved her hands around her head – 'ripping people off, threatening them. I knew one day someone would make him pay. You mess around with people and one day they'll just snap, you know?'

'Did you hear anyone threaten him?'

'Are you the police or something?' The woman sat up and eyed Sloane.

'No, I'm a journalist. I'm writing a story about the murder and wanted to speak to people who knew Danny or may have information on the hostel.' Sloane shifted in place as her arse was beginning to get cold from the concrete beneath her.

'I told you all I know, and don't go telling people you heard anything from me – I may not have the best life in your judgey eyes, but I still have a few years left to live.' She reached into the makeshift pillowcase and pulled out a bottle of vodka. The woman took a long slug. 'I'll tell you one more thing though' – she gestured for Sloane to come closer – 'for a fiver…'

Sloane reached into her pocket and pulled out some change. 'I have £4 here – will that do?' Always negotiate, she had learned early on, as people would more than likely take what they could get.

The woman snatched the coins from Sloane's hand. 'It's the druggies you want to speak to. They was pissed at Danny for a real bad batch of gear he sold them. Wouldn't surprise me if they did something…' The woman turned her back to Sloane and nestled down for another kip.

Sloane thanked her as she stood up. She took one more look over her shoulder as she walked away, realising that her life could have ended up the same way, and headed to the underpass in Hartshill Park, where she knew many of the local drug users hung about. It was close enough to the pharmacy for their methadone and the local Drug and Alcohol Agency for their appointments, but there was also a more sinister reason for pitching up by the underpass. They'd wait for someone to make the mistake of walking through so they could rob them. She tucked her bank card and the cash she had taken out into her bra – if they took her bag, they'd get nothing – and placed two five-pound notes in her back pocket in case she needed them.

It took her just under twenty minutes to arrive at the park's underpass and Sloane was disappointed to see only a handful of people hanging about.

Three males of mixed ages and a youngish female were sitting on the wall. Sloane approached cautiously but was spotted right away.

'Hey lady! Spare some change to feed the poor?' A man with a black knitted hat wiped his mouth.

'I can do better than that – I've some sandwiches.' Sloane cringed at how condescending she sounded in that moment and quickly blurted out the main reason for being there. 'My name is Sloane and I wondered if I could talk to you guys about Danny Wells – I heard you might know him?' She saw the group look at one another before the hat man answered for them all.

'Let's see those sarnies before we say anything…'

Sloane reached into her bag, but it was snatched out of her hands by the hat man. 'Hey! There's no need for that.' Sloane grabbed a handle and pulled it towards her – it was a tug of war she didn't plan on losing. She may have wanted information, but she wasn't going to let this group of lowlifes do what they wanted. She tried another tactic, letting go of the bag. 'OK, I'll come clean. I'm a journalist and if any of you fancy talking to me, I'll see if I can do a bit better than some sandwiches if your info turns out to be useful.'

The man moved closer and squared up to Sloane but before she could put all her self-defence moves to good use, the young woman in the group intervened.

'Don't be a prick, Jay.' She pulled him away from Sloane. 'Sorry, he sometimes gets a bit savage when he's hungry, don't you, babe? What did you want to know about Wells?' The young woman stepped in front of the man she had called Jay, but he'd already lost interest and was tearing open the plastic bag, choosing his food first before sharing out the rest with the others.

Sloane shot him a look and turned her attention back to the female. 'I heard he was selling dodgy gear, pissed a few people off, and now he's dead.'

'I know you're not accusing any of us of killing that cu—' Jay's sentence was cut off by the woman.

'He means arsehole, don't you, babe? No need to be rude.' The female of the group glared at Jay; she seemed to have an influence over the others.

'No, I'm not accusing anyone of anything. I'm writing an article about his murder – maybe you've heard something?'

The woman let out a screechy laugh that made Sloane's teeth hurt. 'If someone killed that bastard, you won't see any of us shedding any tears. Have you spoken to Roddy? He despised Wells. Wouldn't surprise me if he did the deed.'

Sloane wrote down the name – she thought he might be one of the residents of the hostel. 'What did Wells do that pissed Roddy off?'

'Stole his gear, mixed it with shit, and then sold it on for more money. Roddy was swearing blind that he'd sort Wells out. Looks like he actually made good. He's usually full of shite but maybe he grew a pair.' The woman leaned against the wall and grabbed one of the remaining sandwiches.

The teenager, who had been very quiet, suddenly spoke up. 'Ha! I bet it—'

The woman hit him in the leg with her arm and glared at him. 'That's all we know.' Her jaw clenched. Sloane wasn't sure what she had said to shift the woman's attitude, but it was becoming clear none of the group had anything more to offer.

'Could I leave you my details? I wouldn't name any of you in my story… unless you wanted me to.' Sloane pulled out one of her cards from her inside pocket.

The woman took the card and nodded. Sloane locked eyes with the teenager and smiled. He knew something. She decided she'd come back later and try to get him on his own.

He was a lot younger than the rest of the group and might be known at the Drug and Alcohol Agency in town.

Whatever he knew, the others didn't want him sharing it with Sloane.

THIRTEEN

Jeanette

W hen her deputy manager, Anwar Hussain, had arrived, Jeanette filled him in as best she could on the situation. She'd leave him to update Amy and Steph when they got into work.

'Murdered here? Was it caught on the CCTV?' Anwar's eyes shot up to the camera above them.

'Seems that once again our systems may have failed us. Did you really log it with maintenance?'

Jeanette had asked Anwar to follow up on the camera faults after the last incident a few weeks back when a resident had accused another of breaking into his room. This was nothing new – they always seemed to be accusing each other of something – but when it had been discovered that the camera on the landing was faulty and not recording as it should have been, the situation had escalated and one of the residents had been forced to move.

'I asked Frank to do it. I'm sure I checked that he did...' Anwar scratched his head.

The look on his face made Jeanette question the truth of that statement and she was annoyed that he would pass something as important as security on to Frank.

'Can you check, please, as I told the police that it had been, and they'll need to know if it wasn't.'

That was all she needed. She waited as Anwar logged in and when he rubbed his chin, she knew the answer.

'I don't know what happened – he must have forgotten. I'll log it now.'

'Don't bother. The Estates team will be coming out and it will be sorted then. What's going on, Anwar? You've been all over the place recently. Next time, when I ask you to do something, I expect that *you* do it.' Jeanette had raised her concerns with him in their last supervision session, but he had assured her that it was just a bit of friction at home and was on the way to being resolved. Now she wasn't so sure. 'Can you come up to my office, please?'

His head dropped as he nodded. 'I'll just finish up here and be with you in a sec.'

Jeanette logged in to her computer and opened Anwar's last supervision notes while she waited for him. He'd been a probation officer for fifteen years and had worked in a variety of roles in the service before he joined her at Ripley House. Jeanette had heard some rumours about his hot temper but in the time he had been in the hostel she had never witnessed anything other than a dedicated and calm member of staff. In fact, he was often called in to the group sessions to calm situations due to his conflict resolution skills. People change, Jeanette thought to herself, and perhaps it was just the previous work environment...

Anwar closed the door behind him and before Jeanette

could ask him anything he blurted out, 'None of this is my fault. If Frank wasn't so useless, we wouldn't be sitting here right now.'

'I don't know what your problem with Frank is, but sort it out. We don't need any more finger pointing. We're all on the same side.' Jeanette hadn't realised how much tension there was between the two men but she'd need to keep an eye on it.

'Fine.' He sighed. 'Look, things at home are still tough. My wife and my mother are not getting on and it's just caused a lot of stress with me being put in the middle. My eldest boy is off to university soon and this is worrying because we're waiting to hear whether he can get a student loan or not, but it's not looking good. I know it's no excuse, but I promise things will get better.'

Jeanette put her hand up. She was sympathetic to his situation but, like he said, there was no excuse and if problems at home were affecting his ability to do his job, he should have come to her again. 'I really want to let this go but I can't because this isn't the first time something like this has been brought to my attention. Did you contact the Employment Assistance Scheme like I suggested the last time we spoke?'

He shook his head and looked down at the floor.

'I'm afraid that I will have to speak to my line manager and see where we go from here. It isn't just about the cameras, is it, Anwar? I see that from our last session, you still haven't signed off on the OASys assessments in your inbox and they are now sitting in *my* inbox to do. Your colleagues are growing impatient with the delays. Why did you think I wouldn't notice that?'

Jeanette's eyes caught sight of one of his fists clenching and that surprised her.

'Can you look at me please?'

He lifted his head and stared straight into her eyes.

'I accept that I've fallen behind a bit, but my workload has become a bit overwhelming, and I did tell you that it was too much to do by myself. I can't be expected to manage this place on my own when you're at meetings all day for weeks on end. It's just too much. We're short-staffed and that leaves me screwed – half the team is lazy and I'm tired of covering for them, so if you need to put me onto work improvement measures, go ahead, but I won't keep quiet about my feelings anymore.' There was venom in his voice.

Jeanette sat back in her chair and took a moment before responding. 'I'm a little surprised at your attitude. It's like you've had a total personality shift, Anwar, and I'm seeing a side of you that I don't like one bit. I thought we had a reasonably good working relationship and I appreciate that you, perhaps, have had more put on you with me attending MAPPA, DV Forum, and other meetings, but let me remind you that some of those meetings were ones *you* should have been attending but you convinced me that you needed to catch up on a backlog of work so asked if I could step in... or have you forgotten?' If her deputy manager was going to try and drop her in it, Jeanette was going to make it clear that he was messing with the wrong person.

'I don't have anything more to say.' His lips were pulled tight and his fisted hand unclenched. 'If we're through, can I go back to my desk and get on with finishing those outstanding tasks?'

Jeanette nodded. She didn't want to say anything she might regret so she let him leave without having the last word herself. The tension in the room dissipated as soon as he left, and Jeanette waited as she heard him stomp back to his desk and slam drawers. It just seemed so out of character for him, and this concerned her. Maybe she had been wrong about him all along. She'd speak to other members of the team to see if they knew more about Anwar's situation. She had a feeling there was more to his story than he was letting on and she was going to get to the bottom of it.

FOURTEEN

Helen

Helen hadn't had much sleep with all the noise from next door. The quiet street made the voices echo and this had kept her awake for the hours she did try and drift off into the land of slumber. She chose to put a more positive spin on the situation, realising that rising early meant she had the opportunity to head into town before the crowds and get her shopping done.

She did a quick check of the weather by opening the window and sticking her hand outside. A cool breeze on her hand and a glimpse of sunshine told her that a thick cardigan would do.

She went around the house and made sure the doors and windows were secure before she grabbed her buggy and stepped outside.

'Bloody police cordon...' she mumbled to herself as she pasted on a smile and waved at the two officers out front. Her walk to the bus stop would take a bit longer, but she was early enough, and the extra few steps would do her some good.

Thirty minutes later she had arrived in the centre of town.

Helen strolled slowly, looking in the windows as she headed towards the Tesco Express. She was so engrossed in a gorgeous window display that she was startled when someone tapped her shoulder.

Helen jumped and then turned to see Sloane. 'Oh my word! You shouldn't sneak up on the elderly.'

'Elderly my arse. You may be nearing seventy but you're sharper than I am! I didn't mean to scare you – I called out, but you didn't hear me.'

'Maybe I'm going deaf.' Helen pulled on her ear. 'What has you in town so early? Working on your story?'

Sloane nodded. 'Actually, I'm glad I bumped into you. I wondered if you knew anyone named Roddy. I was speaking to a few people, and they mentioned that he and Danny had been fighting recently?'

'Shall we go and grab a cuppa in the café over there?' Helen pointed across the square. 'It's getting nippy standing out here and I'm sure my brain would work better with a hot tea in me.'

'Good idea.'

Helen grabbed a table while Sloane placed the orders. She did know a bit of gossip and though she was unsure whether it would help Sloane or not, the company would be nice. After Malcolm died, Helen realised she hadn't many friends or associates to socialise with, so she grabbed moments like these when she could.

Sloane returned to the table with a tray and Helen smiled. 'Cakes at this hour? I guess I could force myself. So, what is it about Roddy that you want to know? His real name is Ray by the way. I've no idea why they call him Roddy, nor do I care.'

'I'd heard that there was a bit of animosity between him and Wells at the hostel. Did you overhear any arguments or see anything that made you think there might be trouble?'

Helen sipped her tea. 'Funny you should say that. At the time I didn't think anything about it, just boys being boys, but there was an altercation a few weeks back. The pair of them were arguing in the back garden. A bit of a shoving match and some choice words but I don't know exactly what they had said. By the time I cracked the window open, one of the probation officers had come out and broken it up. Do you think Roddy had something to do with Danny's death?'

Helen watched as Sloane scribbled in a notebook.

'I'm not sure but he could have. Do you know what he's on licence for?'

Helen shook her head. 'I don't have access to that information. Don't you have any contacts who could tell you that? Or that goggle malarkey.'

'Goggle?'

'You know, where you search things on the internet...'

Sloane smiled. 'Oh, Google. Yeah, I'm sure I can find it out.'

'He's always been polite to me, but I don't trust any of them. I mean they wouldn't be in a hostel if they were nice guys, would they?' Helen bit into the cream cake.

'That's true. OK.' Sloane looked at her watch and Helen hoped it wasn't the end of their chat – she liked the journalist's company.

'Uh, I forgot to say, I saw that Anwar showed up to work. I wasn't sure if he would...' Helen hoped it would be enough to keep Sloane talking. 'He's a funny one, you know. Very sneaky – talks to the offenders like they're bosom buddies. And I overheard some of the officers outside saying that Harvi had called in sick. He's a PSO on the nightshift. Little bit convenient, don't you think? Always on the sick, that one.'

'Oh really?' Sloane leaned in. 'Have you heard anything I might be able to use?'

Helen hadn't thought that far ahead. 'Well, nothing specific about Harvi, but Anwar does seem to go out with them quite a bit. He's really rude to his colleagues. Acts like he's above them all. I don't see any of the other probation officers doing that... even Jeanette, and she's the boss!'

Sloane looked at her watch again and Helen got slightly annoyed as she was sharing stuff she didn't have to.

'I'm really sorry. That's all great info, thank you. What would I do without you? Finish up and enjoy the cake – I'd love to stay a bit longer but I need to dash.' Sloane got up and squeezed Helen's shoulder as she left the café.

Helen looked around at the remaining people and realised how alone she felt sometimes. 'No good dwelling on things you can't change...' She realised she had said that out loud when a few of the other patrons turned to look at her.

Helen finished her cake and set off to do the shopping she had come out for. If Sloane needed information, she'd make sure to get some – no matter what it took.

FIFTEEN

Jeanette

J eanette had to admit that having thinking time during the days that the residents were in temporary placements had made the world of difference, but the air within the hostel was eerie and full of tension. Every creak and crack from the building had her on edge. Due to the nature of the situation, the residents were being monitored closely in their temporary placements while the police and CSI finished gathering the evidence. Normality was returning and Jeanette felt relieved.

For the last two weeks, Jeanette and half of her team remained working at the hostel to ensure that the day-to-day management continued, while the other probation staff were dispersed to various offices. They had been running on a skeleton crew and everyone was exhausted. After getting the go-ahead from the police, Jeanette was given permission and additional funding from the area head of probation to call in a specialised cleaning team to make sure the communal areas were returned to their pre-incident condition.

One of the cleaners had confided that a journalist had been

snooping around and Jeanette hid her annoyance, knowing full well that it had to be Sloane on her mission to place her and the hostel in a bad light. She needed to do something. What that was, she didn't know. It wasn't that she had major concerns at the moment, as everything she had read in Sloane's articles so far showed minor errors in judgement from her staff, but her years in probation meant she had seen many times when the press had twisted situations to mislead the community, and with the murder she was already on thin ice as it was. It had happened on her watch, so no matter what was found in the internal investigations or via public scrutiny, Jeanette had overall responsibility and could find herself out of a job when this was all over.

Her line manager had confirmed that new CCTV cameras were being installed and that the locks and security pads would be changed. Even though there was no evidence to suggest that the killer had entered the premises through either entrance, despite the malfunctioning back door, they wanted to be safe rather than sorry. Probation had begun their own internal investigations and Jeanette had used some of the quiet time to complete the appropriate paperwork relating to a death on probation premises. She was still going through her officers' files to make sure that everything had been recorded and wouldn't be flagged up during the Serious Further Offence (SFO) investigation. They would all be questioned, of course, but she would be held to account for any errors her team might have made.

The PSOs on the day shifts kept immaculate and concise records, but she was disappointed to read the records kept by her night staff – Irene Watkins, Frank Brown, and the always poorly Harvi Gates. She needed to follow up on his absences. She brushed her finger over the sick note that had arrived on her desk – *off with stress* – and shook her head. This was becoming a regular occurrence with Harvi and Jeanette wondered if he was up to the job any longer. What she also found disturbing was that some incidents recorded by the daytime staff seemed to have been second-hand information from other residents which should have been dealt with and recorded by her night team.

It could be difficult to get decent and experienced evening staff – not many liked doing the nightshift in a hostel – but this didn't excuse the poor record keeping and dismal lack of action, which should have been shared with the home probation offender manager. All of this would come out in the probation investigation and although it wasn't the first one she'd been involved in, it was the first murder. She wasn't looking forward to the shitstorm that was sure to follow.

How could she have missed seeing any of the red flags? She'd always been a hands-on manager, getting to know the offenders that her officers were supervising, observing the group sessions when she could, and being overly cautious when signing off risk assessments. What else had she missed?

'You look stressed.'

Jeanette looked up from her computer to find Irene staring at her. She immediately noted something different about her colleague: she was back to wearing jeans and a baggy sweater, with her hair pulled back in a loose ponytail. It was then that Jeanette had realised that Irene had been dressing up more to come in to work – skirts, make-up, and her hair down. The strain of everything must be getting to her.

'There's a lot going on, and I'm finding things I really... never mind.' She needed her team to be focused so adding to the pressure they were already under wasn't what was needed now.

'Am I too early?' Irene looked at her watch.

'A little, but that's fine. Would you mind making a coffee and I'll just pull out your supervision notes. We can get started then.' Jeanette didn't want to admit that she had forgotten about the meeting.

Irene nodded. 'I'll grab a few biccies too – I think we could both use some.'

Jeanette grabbed Irene's notes from the filing cabinet behind her. She had refused to give them up when the service had gone paperless. As much as she loved technology, she never completely trusted it and made sure to keep printed copies of her supervision notes. She would have them on the screen as well and turn the monitor towards Irene so she could see what Jeanette was referring to.

Irene returned to the room and placed the mugs and a packet of chocolate Hobnobs on the corner of the desk.

'Have a seat. I'll just explain what you can expect from the investigation process, what I'll be doing, and then if you have any questions, you can ask them. Does that work for you?' Jeanette noticed Irene's hands shaking.

'Yeah. I read the probation circular about these sorts of things, but I don't think any of it sunk in. I'm not going to lie, I almost went off sick – it's all been too much. But I would've been more worried staying at home with my husband so... here we are.' Irene bit her lip. 'And I want you to know that I honestly have no idea who could've done this. I mean, none of the residents are angels, but other than the little spats now and again, I couldn't tell you who hated Danny so much that they would kill him and risk going back to prison.'

'Noted – but let's not get ahead of ourselves. Sometimes we forget significant things because they seem small at the time. So the first thing I want to go over is that I noticed in your case records for Danny that he had made complaints against quite a few of the residents but I can't find where any action was taken. Can you tell me a little about the complaints and then we can look at why no warnings were given, or contact made with the relevant home offender manager?'

'Danny was making complaints daily but none of them had any substance. He accused Jack of having drugs in his room, but when a search was conducted, no drugs were found. Then there was the time he accused Ray Southwell of stealing from him, but again a room search found nothing. Ray even allowed Frank to check his pockets and personal belongings. It began to feel a bit like the boy who cried wolf and the only thing that was happening was a lot of bad feeling getting stirred up amongst the residents. I did call their home probation officers and thought *they* would record the information...' Irene bit her lip. 'But clearly they didn't and now it feels like I'm going to land in a heap of shit over all this.' She slumped back in her chair, shoulders hunched and hands across her lap.

Jeanette held her hands up. 'No one is pointing the finger at you, Irene. Regardless of what happens within the field teams, you're still responsible for recording everything you do relating to the individuals in the hostel. You've been here long enough to know that...' Jeanette's head tilted. She could understand why Irene felt the way she did.

Despite having only been working in hostel environments for a couple of years, Irene was an experienced PSO and knew the correct probation processes. She had come highly recommended by her previous line manager.

'Frank said we were just wasting time recording all the minute details because Anwar wasn't checking anything anyway. Since he's been working in hostels longer than I have,

I trusted his input but obviously that was wrong. Anwar still hasn't countersigned my assessments either. It's not all me...'

'Mmmmm.' Jeanette jotted down a note in her book. She'd already had a go at Anwar so she'd see what Frank had to say on the matter. Irene couldn't look her in the eye, and she wondered if she was just blaming Frank to deflect any further attention from herself.

'I swear, if I had known anything like this was going to happen, I would've recorded when they took a piss.'

Jeanette's eyes were drawn to Irene's hands. They were now clamped tightly around the arms of the chair, so much so that her knuckles were turning white.

'No need for sarcasm. Did you ever challenge Danny about his constant complaints?'

'Are you kidding me? Have you read his case file? He was a monster and had no problem pummelling a woman. I didn't want to be next!' There was something in her tone that made Jeanette question whether Irene believed what she was saying but it still shocked her. They dealt with offenders like Danny on a regular basis, so why would Irene feel this way?

'Did Danny ever threaten you?'

'Uh. Well... not exactly...'

Jeanette didn't like where this conversation was going. Irene fidgeted in her seat. 'There's no room for being vague. What aren't you telling me?' Jeanette tapped her fingers on the desk.

'The man was an animal. I don't know what happened to him but—'

'Spit it out, Irene!' Her patience was growing thin.

'I wished he was dead, OK?' Irene's shoulders shook. 'I told him in his last supervision that he deserved anything that came his way.'

Jeanette's eyes widened as she watched the woman sob uncontrollably. 'I think we can stop here for a break. The group will be starting shortly. Do you want to go out and get a coffee... clean yourself up?'

Irene nodded.

'Ok. We'll pick this up later.' *Shit*. With that loaded comment not being recorded and occurring just before Danny ended up deceased during Irene's shift, the PSO could most certainly be looking at a disciplinary hearing.

What the hell had she been thinking?

Irene left her office and Jeanette put her head in her hands. Could she have snapped? Did Danny say something to push her over the edge? She didn't want to think the woman was capable of murder, but she couldn't shake the feeling that there was more to Irene's story than the PSO was sharing. After all, she was one of two staff members in the hostel at the time and her whereabouts were sketchy.

SIXTEEN

Killer

Everyone in the hostel is walking on eggshells and I have to do the same or they might become suspicious. I sit on my bed, amazed that no one seems to have any clue who killed Danny. Admittedly, it could have been anyone as he was such a dick.

I need to see the items again. I got such a buzz after the murder, and I want to feel it all over again. I walk around my room, tapping the floor as I go.

Ah… here we go.

The floorboard creaks where I stuffed the bag of evidence. It's so well hidden that even I have trouble locating it but for the creak. I pull the boards up and look at the bloody baseball cap, knife, and hoodie.

I'll have to do something to make sure the police don't put me on their persons of interest list.

I look around my room and spot a Tesco bag. I empty the contents and with gloved hands, I shove the baseball cap inside.

Now, who's pissed me off enough to deserve a bit of bad luck?

SEVENTEEN

Jeanette

After making sure that Irene's notes were securely locked away, Jeanette eased back in her chair. She needed to process things before she decided what action she'd be taking. The drug and alcohol keyworkers were already on the premises – Jeanette had spotted them in the camera while Irene had been crying. The random drug and alcohol tests would be completed and, according to the schedule, it was time for the first of the twice weekly group sessions on addressing the residents' issues; they usually focused on things like looking at how certain events in the offenders' pasts were linked and what could trigger their offending behaviour. Ironic considering the circumstances.

The sessions were always recorded for training purposes, and Jeanette sat back in her chair to observe. As they were not allowed to record the offenders' faces, all she could see was the wall at the front of the room.

With everything that Irene had disclosed, Jeanette decided that she would attend the session and observe more closely. As soon as she walked into the group room, all eyes were on her, and she ignored the whispers as she made her way to the free seat at the back.

What did they know that they were keeping to themselves?

She listened as the two keyworkers did the usual introductions – going over the rules, expectations, and reminding the attendees that all sessions were recorded.

'Don't you get bored of repeating the same shit each day?' someone called out.

Jeanette understood where the man was coming from, but it had to be done in case any action relating to breach or recall was required. That way, the offender hadn't a leg to stand on if they moaned that they weren't aware. It happened so often.

The keyworkers glossed over the remark and started the session by asking the group to discuss and disclose any relapses. The purpose of this was so that they could explore and challenge each other, but Jeanette was distracted when something a group member said caught her attention. One of the group members had just admitted to using a hit of heroin and his justification was not surprising when challenged.

'What do you bleedin' expect when all eyes are on us for this murder? Wells had his throat slashed. Who's to say he didn't do it himself? Wouldn't put it past the attention-seeking prick.' Ray Southwell looked around the room, waiting for others to agree.

'Did Danny ever mention harming himself or ending his life to any of you?' The high-pitched tone of Becca, one of the keyworkers, made Jeanette cringe. Her voice was like nails on a chalkboard and by the looks on the group's faces, Jeanette could see she wasn't the only one who thought this about the young woman.

'Wasn't his style. He'd love seeing us get recalled for

something he done to hisself.' Ray seemed to have appointed himself the voice of the group.

'Those are the types of concerns that you should be speaking about to the police or to your offender manager. Let's dig a little deeper and why don't you all tell us how you felt when you heard about Danny. Then let's examine how those feelings could have manifested in negative thoughts leading to your decision to use drugs again.'

Jeanette made a note to speak with the managers at the Drug and Alcohol Agency. Becca's tone was condescending and blaming. That wasn't what these sessions were about. Even though she was right in what she said, the silence from the group made it clear they didn't appreciate it either. Becca's delivery needed to be addressed. It wasn't Jeanette's place to do that.

The session carried on for another twenty minutes before they took a break. Jeanette caught a glimpse of Helen Burgess carrying in the large pump-action thermal coffee flask and a plastic bag, which Jeanette presumed contained the usual cheap biscuits supplied by probation. She had asked her line manager to suspend the nosy neighbour's volunteering at the hostel, but he said she was overreacting. She would confront the woman herself if need be; she had a bad feeling about Helen Burgess and didn't like the way she injected herself into the residents' lives – or the hostel's business for that matter. For someone who had been dead against the hostel opening in the first place, the busybody had sure made a quick turnaround.

Jeanette didn't like it one bit. Could *she* have got into the hostel that night?

'Right, I've had enough of this. If no one else is going to do anything about it, I'll do it myself,' Jeanette mumbled to herself before she stood and straightened her blouse.

She headed towards the front of the group and just as her eyes locked with Helen's, her name was called out from down the hall.

'Looks like you're needed. Wonder if there's more trouble? Do you ever question why your staff is so… friendly with this lot?' Helen looked at the group.

Jeanette didn't have time to deal with the old woman's snarky remark now. There was a sense of urgency in the voice calling her. With one more sharp look at Helen, Jeanette turned abruptly and walked towards the main office.

I'm not through with you, Mrs Burgess.

EIGHTEEN

Helen

Feeling satisfied with herself, Helen couldn't help the smirk that planted itself on her face as she watched Jeanette stomp out of the group room. The manager's attempt at keeping Helen off the premises permanently hadn't worked but she needed to remember not to openly step out of line and give the woman another excuse to try and get rid of her. She'd just have to be more careful; a remark or two to plant a seed would do the trick...

Her heart raced as she thought about the snippets of conversation she'd overheard earlier as she prepped the coffee and biscuits, first about flirty Irene – that was a bit of a shock – and then about the outside cellar. Playing the old fool sometimes had its benefits, but one thing she wasn't was a fool. She had to fight the urge to call Sloane there and then but realised that there was no way the journalist would be allowed on or anywhere near the property, so she needed another plan. The last thing she wanted was for Sloane to be caught trespassing, and what if what she'd heard were something else entirely? She didn't want to waste Sloane's time if it came to nothing, but she'd have some fun finding out for herself.

An unexpected surge of excitement brought a tingling sensation to her body. She had to act normal or people would become suspicious. In that moment, Helen felt like a private investigator going undercover. At her age, the most excitement she got was when Amazon had delivered a package she forgot she'd ordered. She jumped when she felt a tap on the shoulder.

'You gonna stand there all day or can we have some of those biccies before you crush them?'

'Of course. There you go.' Helen gave the man a false smile as she laid the biscuits on the tray and then quickly made an exit. She needed a plan. She couldn't just go to the cellar – that would raise questions for which she did not yet have answers.

The cellar at Ripley House could only be accessed from the outside and needed a key but she'd noticed the gardener was on the premises today and if luck was on her side the door would already be open. For some reason, perhaps security, the kitchen staff had a key for the bottom door but not the initial door. They had to ask a member of the hostel staff to open that one for them. It was used for storage space – there was personal property down there for the offenders who were returned to custody. Helen had learned that those items were only kept for thirty days and then discarded if no arrangements were made by the prisoner. She'd also seen the police and outside probation staff collecting the property but that was rare, and she had no idea what they did with it. Perhaps they searched through it for evidence or maybe they were just nosy buggers. That would make sense. Old furniture also found a home in the outdoor pit and because it was a cool area, they often stored the vegetables which were grown on the premises down there too.

When Helen got back into the kitchen she looked around. She only had two more hours left on her shift and the other volunteers were busy making sandwiches for those residents who had paid extra for an evening snack.

That's when it came to her. *A stew! I could make a stew for tomorrow.*

She glanced out of the window and saw Pete, the gardener, at the far end of the property. He looked to be doing a bit of weeding – and as there were a lot of weeds to pull up, he'd be occupied for some time.

'If anyone needs me, I'm going to have a mooch in the cellar. I think there are some veggies that will go off if we don't use them. Thought I'd make a stew which we can freeze. Save us a bit of work tomorrow for the meals.' She was pleased with herself, but no one even looked up or acknowledged her, except for one other woman who was close to her age. She got a scowl from her and gave one right back in return.

Miserable cow.

Helen grabbed a crate from the stack by the back door and went outside. A few of the men from the group were still smoking so she brushed past them and walked slowly towards the rhubarb patch, stumbling to her knees and then cursing herself when she heard cracks and pops as they hit the ground.

'Like it on your knees then, do ya? I can find something for you to do if you're stuck,' one of the smokers leered.

Helen looked over and gave him an icy stare. She wouldn't give him the satisfaction of responding. They always wanted an audience. She pulled her pocket-sized notebook out and jotted down his description. She'd report the savage to the staff.

Cheeky git. Rehabilitation my backside.

Although none of the other smokers challenged the man, one grabbed his arm and mumbled, 'Leave it. Time to go back now anyway.'

Helen waited until they were all inside before she pushed herself up and brushed the dirt off her knees. She picked up the crate and reached into her pinny, pulling out the keys. Every member of the hostel staff was allocated a specific set depending on their job. She had to return the keys at the end of each shift, and they were always checked so it was now or never – she couldn't be sure when or if she would get this opportunity again. Whatever was in that cellar could be gone by tomorrow. The outer door to the cellar was wide open but there was an inner door at the bottom which staff were told must be locked at all times. She looked over to the gardener and he still had his back to the house; he hadn't even noticed her come out. Helen often wondered if he was partially deaf because he shouted when he spoke.

She paused at the top before descending the dark stairwell. There was a light switch at the bottom, but enough light from the outside to at least let her get down without falling. Her hips cracked with each step taken so she held the wall for support. Helen flicked the light on and as soon as her eyes adjusted, she used her key, applying a little force to push it into the rusty lock. It was tricky, but using all her strength she managed to pop the lock and open the door. After a quick glance behind her to make sure she was still alone, she stepped inside the room, closing the door behind her. Her eyes scanned the room, trying to spot anything that seemed out of place. She didn't regularly come down to the cellar, but it was always in the same order.

The men she had overheard earlier had been whispering

about an old barrel; something was inside it that they wanted to keep hidden. One of them had obviously stolen a key to the lock as there was no other way to get inside the cellar, as far as Helen was aware. She walked over to the barrel and tried removing the lid. It was stuck but there was an odd fermenting smell wafting through the air. She needed something to pry it open and her eyes locked on a screwdriver on the workbench.

That should do.

Her skin tingled. What if she were to find the murder weapon? It could be the final nail in the coffin for the hostel and Helen would be the one to close it down once and for all.

A loud bang caught her off guard as the door hit the wall with force.

'What the hell do you think you're doing?'

NINETEEN

Jeanette
___

'I really need you in here.' This was the second call-out from the PSO, and Jeanette picked up the pace.

'I'm coming, Amy! Give a gal a chance. What's so important?' Jeanette waited until the main office door swooshed closed behind her. 'I was right in the middle of something.' She took a moment to catch her breath.

'Danny Wells's brother has been on the phone. He was fuming – said he learned about the murder on the news.' A look of concern washed over Amy's reddened face. Jeanette knew she didn't like being the brunt of other people's anger, but they had been working on that as the PSO would never carve out a career in probation if she couldn't handle conflict.

Jeanette rubbed her temples. 'Shit. Notifying the family was the responsibility of the police but I was supposed to write them a letter once I got the thumbs-up that they were informed. I never followed up on that with everything going on here.' Jeanette took a deep breath and thought about the best way to handle this. 'OK. Give me his details. I'll try and smooth things over and then find out how this slipped through the cracks.'

Amy handed Jeanette a soggy Post-it note with the information she needed. 'Sorry. I spilled some coffee as I was writing.'

'No worries.' The team were already anxious enough about what the future could hold so there was no point in picking on the small things. 'Make sure you record the call in the case records, please.' The eyeroll from Amy was not missed.

Generally speaking, probation and the public ran smoothly alongside each other without any cause for concern – until something bad happened and then the only thing ever said about probation was how incompetent people were, causing an unnecessary and false fear of crime and mistrust in the agency. Jeanette was going to do everything she could to keep that criticism to a minimum, even if it meant pointing out the obvious to her officers.

It was also at times like this that Jeanette questioned whether she should pursue other avenues in her career, but probation had been her calling and she shook the thought out of her head. It wouldn't help anyone if she was distracted, daydreaming about how easy things could have been if she'd become a lecturer or worked in a shop. She headed upstairs to her office, stopping at the water cooler to pour herself a drink. Once back at her desk, she played with the Post-it note, a hand hovering over the phone receiver. *What would she say?* After a few moments she picked up the handset and dialled the number, preparing for the onslaught of abuse that she expected would be coming her way. She was surprised, however, when a meek voice answered after the third ring.

'Hello?'

'Hi. Can I speak to' – she looked down at the name – 'Mr Colin Wells, please.'

The man cleared his throat. 'Yes. That's me. Who's this, please?'

The man was polite, but she wouldn't let her guard down. 'My name is Jeanette Macey. I'm the Senior Probation Officer at Ripley House Approved Premises. My colleague advised that you rang, understandably upset when no one had been in contact about your brother, and I can only apologise for the miscommunication.' She didn't want to play the blame game, although it danced on the tip of her tongue to point the finger at the police for this failure.

'I appreciate that, Ms Macey. I also need to apologise as I had quite the rant at the poor woman who was only trying to help me earlier. I'm glad you understand my frustration. Learning my brother was murdered on the news was bad enough, but to have had no contact from anyone since, well, that was a bit of a shock.'

'I totally understand. Was there something we could help you with while you wait for more information from the police?'

'I've been away on holiday with my family and returned to find reporters camped outside my house. I live in London – that's where we're from. Danny moved to the Midlands on release as I suspect there were no hostel vacancies for him here. We didn't have the best childhood so I couldn't blame him for wanting to get out as soon as possible, but what he went on to be... well, there's no excuse.' His thoughts were disjointed, but under the circumstances, Jeanette felt it was best to just let him speak.

'That must have been a shock for you. Danny was a resident here with us for only a few months and I'm not going to sugar-coat things for you – he was a handful, to put it mildly.'

'I work for the Crown Prosecution Services, Ms Macey – I know what Danny was like. Pure evil. So yes, there's no need to protect my feelings. Danny and I were never close, and, in all honesty, I was relieved when I learned he had left the area. We both chose different paths – he chose to hurt people, and I chose to prosecute people like him.' He sighed.

Jeanette knew little about Danny Wells's childhood as he had never shared much about it when asked and his case records were limited to what he had told his supervising officers both inside prison and out. Probation was aware he had a brother and that both his parents died when he was in prison – his father due to liver failure after years of alcohol consumption and his mother from a stroke.

'I can provide you with the details of the detective leading the investigation, if you'd like?' Jeanette shuffled some papers around her desk until she found the card from DS Kurt Brady.

'No, thank you. I'm calling because I was just going through the mountain of post that had built up while I was away, and I came across a letter from Danny. I'm not sure how he managed to get my address but the fact that he did... I'm actually relieved he's dead. I wouldn't want him showing up on my doorstep, if you know what I mean.'

'I do but I'm a little confused. If the letter contains anything of importance, it's probably the police who need to see it.'

'Yes, but I thought it was important to contact you – or rather the hostel, as the last part of his letter was very cryptic and concerning. Hang on and I'll read it out to you.'

Jeanette bit the skin around her nail – a bad habit that had left her with open wounds and made her fingers unpleasant to look at.

'Sorry about that. You may want to sit down.'

'I'm ready…'

'The majority of the letter was him being crude, a bit of guilt tripping about how I had it easy, and he also talked about a woman in the hostel, suggesting but not saying outright that he was working his way… uh… into her favour, if you know what I mean, and this was the curious bit…' Jeanette could hear the paper rustling. 'He said, and I quote, "Sometimes the places where you are meant to be safe are the ones you should fear the most." Any idea what that could mean?'

Jeanette felt her chest constrict as a thought invaded her head. One that she wouldn't share with Colin Wells.

Had Danny known he was going to die?

TWENTY

Danny

THE NIGHT OF THE MURDER...

D anny Wells was sick of their directions. You must do this. Be home by then. Fucking licence conditions on top of the hostel rules. He should have stayed in prison until the end of his sentence – at least he would have no one to answer to then.

When the note was slid under his door, he hadn't been able to resist.

I've got what you want. Meet in the communal room in fifteen minutes. This ends now.

He hadn't used Class A drugs since he was released from prison. Instead, he was robbing others and dealing the gear to his fellow residents and outside users for a significant profit. He patted the mattress he had cut open to hide the notes until he had a fair wad to deposit into the new account he had set up. The staff at the hostel were incompetent twats, lazy in their room searches, and the ones that weren't... They only needed a bit of flattery and they were like putty in his hands. He lit a match and set the note alight, chucking it in a cup of cold coffee before it burned his fingers. He'd learned his lesson about leaving any evidence.

The moment he'd been released, Danny had promised himself he wasn't going to end up like the rest of the losers in here. He was saving for a flat – and using his dole money to pay the hostel fees. He'd find himself a decent job... maybe even start a family. Would be nice to have someone carry on the Wells's legacy. They thought he was a dumb fuck all along, but he'd learned a few tricks inside and it was about to pay off.

Lately though, he'd been getting bad vibes and even though he wasn't one for all that karma bullshit, something hadn't been sitting right with him. Funny looks, whispers behind his back, talk on the street. He didn't want any fucker getting their hands on his money should something happen to him, so he'd written his brother a letter and on the outside back flap he'd printed 'If I die, you need to read this letter. If I live for ever, you can watch it burn.'

He chuckled to himself; his brother would understand the reference. It was a play on the words that their pisshead father used to say to them as he made them watch him beat their mother. *'Boys, this is what happens when a woman disrespects her husband.'* The words were always slurred while spittle dripped down his chin. *'If she dies, well, I'll be fucked, won't I, but I plan to live for ever as there's no way any of youse are going to get the satisfaction of seeing me burn in hell.'*

It never made any sense, but neither did half the shit that spewed from their father's drunken mouth. When their father did die, Danny didn't even shed a tear; same when he learned his mother had had a stroke – good riddance to the bitch. She should have left their dad before he turned his hands to her two sons.

Danny laughed to himself and looked at the fluorescent lights flashing the time on the cheap alarm clock he'd purchased at the market. It was time.

He stretched before grabbing his hoodie off the floor. He thought about what he could say to fob off payment. That bitchy prick couldn't keep a hold over him for ever. Maybe another threat to the family was needed since the last one didn't seem to have any effect... If he wasn't careful though, *he* would be the one to suffer the consequences. He'd wanted to use his fists but that would end with him being recalled and he was done with prison. He needed something different, something permanent, that wouldn't lead back to him.

He cracked open the door to his room and looked out into the hall. The corridor was dark. The probation nightshift were useless fucks at the best of times. They'd either be asleep or watching TV. He'd learned their habits early on, as did others in the hostel. Evenings were the best times to get away with something if you were so inclined – and he was. If he was caught on the CCTV, he could always say he needed the loo, but he had overheard the staff complain numerous times about the faulty cameras, so he wasn't too worried about that either. With the closest toilet being two floors down after some eejit on this floor blocked the one he normally used, it was almost as if fate was intervening.

He pulled the door closed behind him and locked it. *Can't trust anyone in this place.* There was the faint sound of music coming from the room to his left. He crept by the door, careful to avoid the creaky floorboard, and made his way downstairs.

He stopped at the bottom of the landing. To his right was the door to the main office, and to his left the door to the communal living area. He spent as little time in the living room as possible. That's where the scroungers hung about, and he had more important things to do than bitch about how hard done by he was. There was a second door just down the hall that led into the adjoining dining area – he'd use that door in case anyone happened to be watching out of the large Plexiglas window where the part-time receptionist sometimes sat during the day. He'd once seen one of the nightshift staff sitting there reading, but it looked like the coast was clear.

When he finally made it to the living room, he spotted a few baggies on the table. He looked around the room.

'Hey! Who's there?' he whispered but no one replied. The hairs on his neck stood on end.

Is this a fucking set-up?

He probably should have been more cautious but the cocky side of him took over and he sat down on the stale-smelling second-hand couch. A further look around the room confirmed he was alone, and he pocketed the drugs.

He started to push himself up off the couch to leave when he heard a familiar voice.

'I see you found the packets. How much will you give me for them?'

'Hah! You're having a fucking laugh now, aren't you?' Danny eased back into the couch and put his arms behind his head. He wouldn't give any power to the arrogant twat by acknowledging their presence in the room and looking at them. The fucker could come to him, look him in the eye and see that the only exchange happening here had already been done.

'Sorry you feel that way…' the voice whispered in his ear.

'What the actual fu—'

Before Danny had a chance to turn around, there was a sharp jab in his neck, and he knew instantly as his body tingled what was coursing through his system. How the dickhead had managed to get a vein was the least of his worries now.

'If that doesn't kill you, this will…' Danny felt woozy as a hand came from behind and held his chin firm. They were stronger than he had given them credit for. He couldn't even fight against it as the heroin kicked in and his eyes rolled back into his head. Something cold ran across his neck and his head lolled forward.

Opening his eyes, he saw the blood and knew he'd be seeing his father soon.

TWENTY-ONE

Helen

'**O**i! Are you deaf? What are you doing with my tools?' Broken lines etched the man's features, giving him a hardened, sinister aura.

Helen exhaled. 'Goodness. You gave me a fright. I'm just looking for the veggies and this lid was stuck.' She tapped the barrel. 'I picked up the screwdriver to pry it open.'

'Course it is.'

He rolled his eyes, as if Helen should have known the lid would be stuck.

What kind of muppet was this guy? She didn't have to wait long as he continued with his lecture.

'There's no veg in there – look behind you. Or are you blind as well as deaf?' He stood firm with one hand on his hip while the other wagged in the direction of the shelves attached to the back wall.

Helen bit her lip to stop herself from giving the grumpy sod the mouthful he deserved. How dare he talk to her like that! 'Hmm…' She pulled her glasses from her top pocket and rested them on her nose before looking at the back wall. 'Ah yes. That's what I was looking for.' She turned back to the gardener. 'What's in here then? If you can give me a hand, I might find something I can use—'

The gardener walked towards her, snatching the screwdriver from her.

'Hey!' Helen rubbed the palm of her hand. 'There was no need for that. I could report you.'

'Go ahead. You shouldn't be touching things that don't belong to you. Nothing in that barrel that concerns you. Now get the veg and be on your way. I need to lock up here.' He pointed at his watch. 'I gotta leave soon.'

Helen had always had a bad feeling about him. Never went above and beyond. Probably did the bare minimum all his life. He was shifty.

'Hmmph. No need to be rude – kindness, they say, costs nothing.' But Helen's words fell on deaf ears.

He snapped his fingers as Helen gathered some onions, potatoes, and carrots. She noticed some were rotting and left them where they were. It would give her the excuse to come back after the grump had left and check the barrel if she got the chance. She picked up the crate and stared him dead in the eyes. 'Next time you speak to me like that will be the last time. This cellar belongs to the hostel, not you, so I'll use whatever I like, when I like.' She pushed past him and made sure she banged his shoulder with her own.

He mumbled something under his breath as she climbed the stairs out of the cellar. Helen was tempted to lock the old bugger in, but that would only bring more attention to her. Little did he know but his performance today placed him on her list. He was going into her little black notebook. The one she filled with information and details for the neighbourhood watch scheme.

She was curious as to why he was so adamant that she shouldn't look in the barrel.

It only made her more determined.

The kitchen was quiet when she returned. She dumped the crate of vegetables onto the counter and began chopping the veg. She pulled the stockpot out from the lower cupboard, filled it with water and a few Oxo cubes, and placed it on the hob. She began to chuck the chopped veg into the pot but stopped when she felt her phone buzz in her pocket.

Hi Helen! Just checking in – are you back at the hostel? If you're free this eve, I can pop by on my way home. Sloane x

Ever since the journalist had learned that Helen shared the same view of the hostel as she did, they had become close. Sloane would stop by at least once a week for a natter and text her every other day to check in. Such a nice girl. It helped fill the void of losing Malcolm.

Helen tapped the keys on her phone. She really didn't have much to tell yet, but the company would be nice. Sharing her concerns about the gardener with Sloane would pass a few hours in the evening at least but she didn't want to annoy her friend if it turned out to be nothing. It might put her off visiting if Helen was just rambling – better to have something solid and worthy than guesses. She quickly changed her mind and declined the offer. Best to wait until she had some real information that Sloane could use.

But then, what if the murder weapon was in the barrel? Or

drugs? Or money? Why would the gardener care? He couldn't have killed Danny, could he?

The police and newspapers had all stated that there had been no evidence of a break-in, but the gardener had a key to the back gate. Maybe someone let him in through the back door, or he could have just pushed his way in as she recalled the door having been on the fritz for some time – no one had been out to repair it. He could be working with one of the lowlifes staying here.

So many possibilities. She should blow the whistle on all the failing systems she knew about, but would anyone take her seriously?

She pulled out her mobile and sent another message.

Changed my mind. I may have something. Come by any time after 5.30pm. x HB

Within seconds her phone vibrated again and some of the other volunteers gave her a look. She wasn't supposed to have her mobile while working but had lied to her supervisor and said she needed it as she was waiting for an important call from her GP. One of the benefits of being elderly was that people took her at her word. For now anyway.

Great! I should be there by 6pm and I'll bring cakes! Sloane x

She smiled.

Out of the corner of her eye she caught some movement in the garden and spotted the grumpy git.

There was something in his hand.

The screwdriver.

Now, why would he be taking that?

TWENTY-TWO

Sloane

As she walked through the doors of the Drug and Alcohol Agency – Recovery Starts Here (RSH), a non-residential rehabilitation centre that enabled ex-addicts to sustain abstinence and rebuild their lives – Sloane put a reminder in her phone to pick up some cakes to bring over to Helen's. Her mind was like a sieve at times, and she had to rely on technology and notebooks to be her brain.

The building set her on edge. The smell reminded her of her own time in rehab and the demons that taunted her when she tried to bury her grief. Sloane pulled her jacket around her and a shiver crawled down her spine. She'd once done an article on RSH after they had noticed an increase in the number of 'second generation' addicts coming through their doors. When she had dug deeper, she'd learned that children who grew up with one parent or both with a severe alcohol and/or drug problem often suffered extreme neglect and, in most cases, severe trauma. Ripley House had cited this as one of the reasons it needed to open in the area as it partnered with RSH and could offer enhanced services. Sloane had never seen any evidence of a reduction in substance misuse since the pairing and, in fact, felt the opposite was true. Her suggestion that out-of-area offenders being housed at Ripley were bringing more drug and alcohol use to the area did not go down well with the council, who had partially funded the partnership. She was only reporting the facts though.

There was a big poster on the wall to her left explaining the nature of the work that RSH did. Sloane sniggered; it felt a bit out of place to her. The picture showed a family reunited with a paragraph below saying that the recovery agency hoped to reduce the chances of issues becoming triggers for relapse, with the end goal of assisting individuals to be able to rebuild their lives with the skills and self-belief they were not provided with as children. But Sloane knew first-hand that the user had to help themselves first and want to make that change. Given the people Sloane had spoken to at the park, she questioned this agency's success rate.

A bell chimed as she stepped through a second door and made her way to the reception desk. She had to bend over to hear through the small holes in the plastic screen separating her from the young man behind the counter.

'Do you have an appointment?' He eyed her up and down, probably wondering whether she was a client or a visitor. It had happened to her before given that she only wore suits to court and not as standard while investigating or writing her articles. She had once been mistaken for an offender when she visited a probation office in the West Midlands. She had misplaced her ID and had to wait while they contacted her editor to verify who she was. She laughed to herself at the memory. The man had a confused look on his face.

'I'm not an addict if that's what you were thinking?' Sloane regretted the sharp tone she had used when the man leaned back and frowned. 'Sorry. That came out wrong.' She was, in fact, a recovering addict but given the memories that time in her life evoked, she refused to think of herself that way; she certainly wouldn't admit it to this guy. She reached into her pocket and took out her card, passing it through the open slot. 'My name is Sloane Armstrong. I'm a freelance journalist and I wondered if there was someone I could speak to about Danny Wells.'

The young man's eyes twitched when she said the name, confirming that he knew who she was asking about.

'If you'd like to take a seat, I'll just see if anyone is available to talk to you.' He pointed to the chairs behind her.

Sloane declined the offer of a seat and instead looked through the various leaflets scattered about the reception area. Five minutes later she heard the click of a door and a woman with a tight bun and glasses gestured to her.

'Ms Armstrong. I'm one of the managers here. As I'm sure you're aware, with an ongoing police investigation, no one from RSH is allowed to speak to the press. In fact, due to confidentiality, we wouldn't be allowed to speak to you at all without the client's permission. I'm afraid you've wasted your time...'

'I don't want to know any specific client information; I just want to talk to anyone who may have heard rumours or expressed fear to their keyworkers about Danny. Perhaps they felt threatened or were actually threatened by him?'

'My answer remains the same. We have your card; if circumstance change, we'll let you know.' The woman nodded towards the exit and Sloane knew she wouldn't be getting any cooperation from the agency.

'Thanks for your time,' Sloane mumbled through gritted teeth.

Once outside the building, she stood and used the time to think of her next move. She had known it wouldn't be easy getting information out of criminal justice agencies, but she could usually sniff out a weak link. It was then that she spotted the receptionist standing at the opposite end of the block having a fag. When she caught him looking at her, he quickly looked away. She took a chance and walked over to him.

'I know what your manager said, but I get the feeling you have something to say. Am I wrong?' She kept her tone soft. She'd already pissed him off to the point that he clammed up earlier, and she wouldn't make the same mistake again. She noticed his name tag said Marcus Webb.

He looked up and past her. Sloane followed his gaze. There was a CCTV camera pointed right at them. He shook his head in an exaggerated fashion and as Sloane turned away he mumbled, 'I can't talk here, but there are some things you should probably know. Drop your card on the ground and I'll text you when and where we can meet.'

Sloane didn't look at him as she followed his instructions and walked away. Something told her that what Marcus had to say would be important. He was nervous as he spoke. Did he know something that could identify the killer? Were the RSH staff covering something up? Whatever the case might be, she would push this guy to get the information.

She happened to glance at the clock tower in the town square and then her phone beeped – her reminder to pick up cakes.

Sloane smiled as she walked to the bakery. She was pleased with the progress she was making even though there were still more unanswered than answered questions. Now wasn't the time to dwell on that though – cake was occupying her brain. At the bakery counter, she selected a couple of Victoria slices and some chocolate eclairs – her favourite – and then walked to Helen Burgess's house, avoiding the underpass.

The fresh air filled her lungs as her breathing increased with the pace. But when she strolled by a newspaper stand, the front page headline caught her eye. A quick scan of the byline made her blood boil.

What the hell?

TWENTY-THREE

Helen

Helen watched the grumpy gardener bend over and place something beneath one of the larger rocks outside the cellar door. He looked around, pocketed the screwdriver, and she averted her eyes, pretending to be scrubbing at an imaginary spot on the window. Someone coughed behind her.

'It might work better if you had a cloth.' The hostel manager cocked her head to the left and pointed at Helen's sleeve.

'Erm. Of course. Silly me.' Helen reached across and picked up a shammy from the box beside the sink. 'The garden is looking lovely, isn't it? How long has he been working here?' Helen pointed at the gardener. He was now dusting off his overalls and heading towards the house.

'Pretty much since we opened. Quiet fellow… unlike some.'

Helen ignored the snipe. 'Is he allowed to keep his own tools in the cellar?'

'Technically, no – anything in there is the property of the MoJ – sorry, I'm so used to acronyms, the Ministry of Justice –

but I suppose he may bring in his own things and just leave them here for convenience. Why are you asking?'

Helen hid her annoyance at Jeanette's assumption that she wouldn't understand the language used. There was no need to dumb things down for her; she had done plenty of reading when she was protesting against the hostel opening. 'No reason. I'm just a curious creature by nature. I see things and then have to ask about them.' She hoped she sounded convincing.

'Well, if you know something that I should be aware of, I trust you'll tell me. We have to ensure that all staff and residents are safe in order to keep the community safe – and I know how important your neighbourhood watch scheme is to you.'

'You know I stopped being involved in that—'

Jeanette held up her hand. 'Save it, Mrs Burgess. You may not be leading the scheme anymore but I'm well aware of your behind-the-scenes involvement. There's nothing wrong with that – we're all on the same side. We all want to keep the public safe. But if you see or hear something that's concerning, you really do need to let *me* know... and not that journalist friend of yours.'

Helen smiled and nodded. 'Of course. Same page and all that.'

Jeanette stood for a further minute before leaving.

What did she want in the first place? Is she spying on me? Maybe she was checking on the gardener too. I could be on to something.

Helen's imagination was running away with her again. She found this was happening more and more since her husband had died. When she had spoken to her GP about it, he had said that it was natural and all part of grief – but was it?

'Time to go, Helen,' her supervisor called out.

She looked at her watch. It was four o'clock already. 'I'll just put these things back and be away.' She glanced again at the rock outside the cellar door – she wouldn't be able to get to it now but if she started work earlier tomorrow, she might get to check it out.

Helen handed her keys in to the main reception and headed next door. Sloane would be arriving soon. She'd have enough time for a quick sandwich and a nap. She was tired. She didn't know how the police coped with investigations; they wore her out.

The bang on the door startled Helen awake. Everything was blurry and as her eyes focused and adjusted to the room, she saw it was 6pm. She hadn't meant to sleep so long and glanced at the half-eaten sandwich on the table.

'Just a moment!' she called out. Helen cleared away the sandwich and popped the kettle on.

One of her slippers nearly came off and she stumbled her way to the front of the house. She slid the bolt and unlocked the door, pulling it open for her visitor.

'Sorry, did I wake you?' Sloane stepped inside.

'No, not at all. Why?'

Sloane pointed to Helen's head and when she looked in the mirror on the wall, she saw the tousled mess of her bun and patted it down. 'You caught me. I just had a little catnap – time ran away with me. Come in. Kettle's boiled. Coffee or tea?'

Helen walked behind Sloane and watched as the woman put her bag down and sat on the oversized leather chair her husband had loved so much.

She gasped as her chest tightened.

'Coff— Are you OK?' Sloane turned and made a move to stand up.

'Yes, I'm fine, dear. Sorry, it's just Malcolm was the only one to have ever sat in that chair. Caught me off guard is all. Please, sit. I'll go and get the coffee.'

'I can move if you'd like?'

Helen shook her head. 'No, it's just me being silly. Sit. Sit. I'll be back in a moment.'

'Do you need a hand? I can grab a plate and set out the cakes,' Sloane offered.

'Ah yes. The cakes. I have the perfect thing for those.' She could use the big tray her sister had bought her last Christmas. It had a handle which helped when her arthritis was playing up.

When Helen returned to the room, she was surprised at the number of pastries that Sloane had brought. 'Oh, that's way too many – take some home with you.' She placed the tray on the table.

'It's fine. Maybe you can take the leftovers into the hostel tomorrow as a treat?'

Helen didn't miss the glint in Sloane's eyes. Might make people more open to speaking with her. As they sat and ate, Helen updated Sloane on what she had witnessed at the hostel.

'What are you saying? You think the gardener is involved? Maybe he's just precious about his space. You know what men can be like with their sheds.'

'That's true. He was really aggressive though. I mean, all I did was touch the barrel – you'd think I had my hand in his wallet the way he reacted – and then I saw him hide something under the large rock by the cellar door. They let those people get away with murder in there.' Realising what she had said, she covered her mouth to hide the smile and explained to

Sloane, whose brows had furrowed at the implication, 'The way they're so overly… friendly, well, it doesn't seem like they realise the people that live there are dangerous. Jeanette was right behind me when that gardener pocketed a screwdriver!'

Sloane perked up then and leaned forward. 'Really? Can you see the area from your garden?'

'I think so. If we go out back, I can show you where. Follow me…'

Helen led the journalist to the back door. 'Mind those boxes. I'm still going through Malcolm's things. Probably time for me to let go.' She felt a hand on her shoulder and Sloane gave her a gentle squeeze. The two women stood at the corner of the back porch and Helen pointed over the fence. 'Ah, that tree's blocking the way now. It isn't usually that high. But there's only one large rock by the cellar door and I'm sure that grumpy git put something under it. Maybe he's covering for one of those scumbags who live there.'

'That's a possibility. Are there cameras in the back?'

'There's a camera over the back door. It looks straight down the garden. Why? What are you thinking?'

'I'm thinking your fence isn't that high and maybe I could check it out?'

Sloane helped Helen drag the lawn chair against the fence. 'If you just hold it so it doesn't tip over, I think I can get myself over.' She climbed onto the chair and steadied herself while looking around the back garden. She clocked the CCTV. With the hedges and trees not yet having been trimmed, she was reasonably confident that if she stayed close enough to the ground, she might be able to avoid being seen on camera.

Sloane wasn't sure whether the motion detector lights worked or whether they were just there for show. She turned and looked down at Helen. 'How sensitive are those lights?'

'Well, they can't be too sensitive as I've often spied some of the men walking in the garden smoking that smelly, skunky stuff…'

Sloane laughed to herself. 'Hmmm. OK.' She'd have to try and avoid being too close to the building as well. The lights might be the kind that are only alerted when someone approaches the back door.

She jumped over the fence and crouched down.

TWENTY-FOUR

Jeanette

The light from the day had disappeared and when Jeanette moved her eyes away from the computer, she had to readjust her vision to the enveloping darkness. Either the days were getting shorter, or she was spending more time at the office than she normally did. Her head throbbed and her brain couldn't face any more. She began to pack up to leave.

The call with Danny Wells's brother earlier had been playing on her mind. She'd urged Colin Wells to contact the police with the information he'd disclosed and wondered why he, as a prosecutor, hadn't done that in the first place. What really disturbed her was the implication that members of her team had been behaving inappropriately. Why hadn't she noticed and who had Danny been referring to? Was this why Irene's appearance had changed? She shook her head. It couldn't be Irene… it just couldn't.

A tap on the door pulled her out of her thoughts. 'Hey, Frank. How are you doing?' Jeanette had suggested to Frank that he think about taking some time off after being the one to discover Danny's body, but he'd declined. She could've enforced leave, but knew if it had been her, she would've done the same thing. Sometimes, despite where they worked, the job could be an escape. She'd monitor the situation and if anything of concern reared its head, she'd act on it immediately. 'Have a seat.'

'Sorry, are you leaving now? This can wait…' He flicked on the light switch by the door.

'Thanks. I hadn't realised how dark it was in here until I stopped staring at my monitor. I'll be going shortly but I have a bit of time.' She rubbed her eyes. 'Take a seat and tell me what's on your mind.'

Frank closed the door behind him and sat down in silence for a few minutes. Jeanette didn't try to fill the space.

'I probably should have said something about this a while ago, and since everything that has happened I wondered whether it would even do any good, but I wanted to speak to you first.'

Jeanette leaned forward. 'If this is about Anwar, I know things are tense right now, but I've had a word with him already.

Frank eyed her suspiciously. 'Uh… it isn't exactly, but thanks. He's been a real pain in the ass. You'd better be careful – I think he wants your job. It's actually about—'

Jeanette interrupted him. 'Can I just say that you do know that I can't promise to keep anything confidential so if I feel I need to go to the police or my line manager then I will.'

Frank nodded. 'Yeah, I know. Listen, I've suspected for a long time that someone has been dealing inside the hostel – and I don't mean the residents, though I'm pretty sure some of them have been involved in using and dealing.'

'Someone who works here? Dealing drugs?' Jeanette's eyes

widened. 'Who? And why didn't you say anything sooner?' Jeanette's leg shook under her desk.

What the hell had been going on right under her nose? It was the last thing the hostel needed, since they were already under an intense level of scrutiny. Another incident would surely see Ripley House closed for good. Jeanette wasn't worried about her job or most of her team – they would just be placed elsewhere. But the situation with Approved Premises and lack of housing meant that it was just one fewer place for high-risk offenders to be safely monitored. She had to stifle a laugh at her last thought. Given the murder, was the hostel even safe at all?

'Thing is, I don't know for sure, and I haven't been able to pinpoint one person but... maybe I'm just being paranoid because of what's happened.' Frank rubbed his head. 'I mean, I don't want to point the finger at anyone and be wrong – that would be just... well...' He was getting lost in his words and Jeanette took the reins for a moment.

'How about you tell me what evidence you have and then we can talk through what to do next.' She poured him a glass of water and pushed the glass towards him. Her mind jumped to the conversation she had had with Irene; she needed to speak to Frank about those allegations, but they might have to wait for the time being. This was far more important.

Frank gulped the water down as if he hadn't drunk for a week. He wiped his mouth with his sleeve and then reached into the pocket of his hoodie, pulling out a small notebook. 'I've kept some notes...'

Jeanette watched as he turned the pages.

'I record the date and time – and...' His lip twitched.

'Why don't I ease some of the stress you're obviously

under? Give me the notebook and I'll have a look?' She held out her hand and he reluctantly passed it over.

Jeanette thumbed through the pages. Not only had Frank made detailed notes of times, dates, and incidents, he'd marked certain parts for special attention. 'What are these?' Jeanette pointed to the highlighted bits.

'Those are… erm… situations I thought were concerning enough that I informed the home probation officer.'

'And was any action taken?' Jeanette couldn't recall any specific calls or meetings of significance around the dates she was seeing.

'Not that I'm aware of.'

'And was all this information recorded on the system?'

'I left that to the home PO to do. I didn't want to record it if it turned out to be nothing.' Frank's shoulders slumped.

Jeanette sighed. 'You know the rule: if it isn't recorded, it didn't happen.' Jeanette had drilled that into everyone she worked with, repeated the phrase as often as she could in the hopes that it stuck in her team's minds. 'If it turns out that anything comes of even one thing you've written in here, you and I will be held to account.' It frustrated Jeanette when her team failed to follow her instructions. 'If you don't mind, I'm going to keep this and update the records to reflect that we've had this conversation. Then I'm going to pass it on to DS Brady.'

'I'd rather you didn't.' He reached across to take it back.

Jeanette looked at the notebook and realised it came from the stationery cupboard. It was technically probation property. 'This is our stationery and so whether you like it or not, I'm keeping hold of it.' Jeanette looked at the clock on the wall just above the door. 'Curfew checks will be starting soon. You'd better go back and give Irene a hand, don't you think?'

'Yeah, probably best not leave her alone in the company of all those men...' he mumbled.

Jeanette didn't miss the comment or the cold look that Frank gave her as he left her office. She opened her email and sent an update to her line manager, copying in DS Kurt Brady. She knew that neither would respond tonight and was about to place the notebook in her bag so she could go through it in more detail at home when something on the CCTV caught her eye. She leaned in to the screen and was surprised to see someone jumping over the back fence.

Jeanette picked up the phone and dialled 999.

'Emergency. Which service?'

'Police, please.'

'Transferring your call now.'

'North Warks police. How can we help?'

'I'd like to report a trespassing – possible burglary...'

TWENTY-FIVE

Sloane

S loane leaned against the fence and listened for any sounds in the garden.

'It's the big rock by the cellar door – don't forget. And for goodness' sake, be careful.' Helen's voice travelled through the fence slates.

'I will.' Sloane hunkered down and began to make her way towards the cellar. She was careful not to trigger the motion sensor and as soon as she reached the landing which led up to the back door, she lay flat on the ground and pulled herself across the path. Pebbles pricked her body through her thin shirt. She regretted leaving her leather coat at Helen's house now; it would have protected her from the stones sticking into her skin.

She heard something snap just as she passed the back door. She stopped and held her breath, lifting her head carefully and looking around. She exhaled when she saw two eyes staring back at her and heard the hiss. It was just a cat.

Pushing herself back up into a crouching position, she

reached the cellar door and spied the rock. She bent over and tried to pull it up with one hand but couldn't budge it. She rested the tip of her shoe underneath one side of the rock and then pulled with both hands. After a few seconds, she managed to roll it and reveal what had been hidden in the mud underneath.

It was a key.

She reached down and picked it up, placing it in her pocket. Sloane began retracing her footsteps back towards Helen's house when a bright light flashed in her eyes.

'Police! Show me your hands and walk towards me slowly!' a male officer shouted.

'Fuck.' Sloane did as she was asked. 'Sorry, officer. My friend who lives next door launched a… treat at a cat from her porch but her ring flew off with it and it went over the fence. I didn't want to disturb the staff as I'm sure they're busy so…' She shrugged and hoped he wouldn't ask to see the ring.

'Name please?'

She was about to speak when the back door flew open.

'What do you think you're playing at, Ms Armstrong?' Jeanette Macey bellowed.

The police officer approached the manager. 'Do you know this woman?'

'I'm afraid I do. She's a journalist and she's trespassing!' the hostel manager hissed.

'Ms Macey. I really am sorry, only Helen lost something, and I said I'd help her get it back. It's really all been a big misunderstanding.' Sloane put on her most sincere voice.

'Misunderstanding my arse. You were probably hoping to snoop about and overhear something you could include in your next article. I'd have more respect for you if you didn't try and insult my intelligence.' Jeanette stood firm with her arms crossed.

A few of the residents began to gather on the back porch, lighting up cigarettes, probably hoping for a catfight between the two women.

The police officer was walking around the garden, his flashlight flickering as he checked out the perimeter.

Sloane wanted to tell him he was wasting his time but thought better of aggravating the situation.

'Can you all please go back inside until I've dealt with this?' Jeanette called out to the offenders. There were mumbles and curses. 'Now, please!'

Sloane could hear the anger in Jeanette's voice. She wasn't going to give them any leeway. 'You do realise that now I'll have to stay even later to deal with this lot.' Jeanette thumbed towards the men who were taking their time going back into the building.

'What do you want me to do then? Are you pressing charges?' The police officer held the radio on his shoulder ready to inform his colleagues of the action to be taken.

Jeanette paused and Sloane noticed her biting the side of her cheek.

'No. I won't be pressing charges *this time* but if you could escort her off the premises and give her a stern warning? If this happens again, I'll definitely be pushing for charges.'

'Will do. Ms Armstrong, come with me, please.' The officer indicated that Sloane should follow him down the path at the side of the building.

Sloane pasted on her most believable smile and thanked Jeanette, but it appeared to fall on deaf ears. She followed the officer up the path that ran alongside the hostel and out the gate – which she clocked wasn't locked – the padlock was missing... and then she realised Jeanette had probably done this so she wouldn't be alerted to the police approaching.

Well played, Macey.

The officer gave Sloane a lecture, advised her that she could've been facing some serious charges, and warned her to keep away from the hostel. 'I suggest you make your way home now. In fact, I'll drop you there myself.' He directed her towards his car.

'I have to pick up my things from next door.' She knew it was pointless arguing and she didn't fancy a further lecture.

'Make it quick.' The officer leaned against the car while Sloane ran towards Helen's home. Before she even had the chance to knock, the door was opened by an excited Helen, who pulled her inside.

'Oh, my goodness! I can't believe they called the police. What did you find?'

'I'll have to tell you all about it tomorrow as the cops are waiting to escort me home.' Sloane thumbed behind her, and Helen looked over her shoulder.

'Oh, fiddlesticks to that. I won't get any sleep tonight wondering.' Helen moved out of the way so Sloane could get her things.

'It was just a key, so now you can sleep. We'll talk in the morning.' She gave her friend a quick hug and made her way to the police car.

'I'm ready, officer. You gonna cuff me?' She grinned, trying to make light of the situation.

The officer didn't share her sense of humour, just held the back door open and closed it behind Sloane when she sat down.

She pulled the key from her pocket and wrapped it in an unused tissue. Although she had already handled it, she didn't want to ruin any potential DNA or prints if it turned out the key was relevant to the murder investigation.

She tapped the tissue in her hand.

Now, what do you open?

TWENTY-SIX

Killer

T he commotion outside catches my attention. I stop what I'm doing and go to the back of the house when I notice the group of people milling about the doorway. Guess I'm not the only one interested in what's going on. I pat my top pocket.

Shit. I left my fags in the other room.

I could bum one off someone else but I'd rather not. I'd be pestered then for days on what I owed.

Fuck that shit.

The investigation into Danny's death seems to be moving at a snail's pace – as soon as the hostel returned to its normal day-to-day function, it's like nothing happened here and that suits me just fine. Though it's unlikely the police would openly share what they've learned so far with the media, public, or even the hostel staff in order to ensure the perp – I laugh – isn't tipped off. The sooner this is forgotten, the better chance I have of moving on and leaving this shithole behind. If the case goes cold, that would be a bonus.

I bypass the back door, ducking out of sight to avoid any questions. I'll get a better view of outside from the dining area

– so that's where I head. I pull the curtains back slightly but don't want to draw any extra attention to myself so opening the window is a no-go. I can see a policeman walking around the garden. *What's he looking for?*

I'm glad I managed to remove that bag; things could get awkward if I'm not on the ball.

Just below me Jeanette's having what looks like a heated discussion with that fucking journalist. She's relentless; I can see why some people don't warm to her. Sloane is a walking contradiction – portraying herself as the voice of the people but really, it's all about what she can get. Not an unpleasant woman, but once she gets hold of something she's like a dog with a bone. I'm not worried though as I've heard she's talking to a lot of people – users, drinkers, and anyone who'll give her the time of day in the local area, and they're all giving her the run-around. They'll tell her whatever she wants to hear for a tenner. Not the most reliable bunch, that's for sure. Still… she might be smarter than I'm giving her credit for so I should keep a closer eye on her. If she'd risk arrest by hopping the fence, who knows what else she'd do to get a story.

I glance over to my right and notice that old biddy – the volunteer from the kitchen – pacing up and down her back porch before returning inside. *Did she send the journalist over here?* Another one who just can't keep her nose out of things. When the hostel first opened, she was out front with a few other old cronies and their do-it-yourself neighbourhood watch scheme. She was in all the local papers, spewing statistics, handing out leaflets – I heard the place nearly didn't open. That could have ruined everything. If she's not careful, she'll be seeing her husband sooner than she thinks.

Wow. Where did that come from?

I shake my head, surprised at how I immediately came to

that idea. I can't act on urges that could identify me. But if pushed too far…

When someone ruins your life… well, they must pay. Sometimes you have to take matters into your own hands. You have to get your own justice by any means possible.

Danny Wells deserved to die – I only wish I'd had more time to make him suffer. To tell him why and watch him process everything.

The problem with people like Danny Wells is that they never get the full punishment they deserve. People like him commit the worst of the worst and then get prison – a roof over their heads, no responsibility, no accountability – and then they're out on licence by playing the game. Playing the system. He'd do it all again if he had the chance because he was just that sort. A sociopath. No regrets… no remorse. I even heard him bragging about the murder he was on licence for to impress the other residents. If I could have ripped his head off there and then, I would have. Who does that? Everyone else is here to just get through it; prison can be a piece of piss but not something anyone really wants to go back to.

Then he gets placed here at Ripley House. Uses his dole money to pay the rent and uses threats of violence to con everyone else out of money; he deals drugs, and no one will come forward because who wants to be known as a snitch? Who'd want to risk their own liberty and a recall back to custody if they admit to using or dealing drugs? I wouldn't.

It's a no-win situation.

I just keep my head down; do what's expected of me and get on with things.

The police officer is making his way back to where Jeanette and the journalist are standing. A few words are exchanged and from what I can see, the woman is being escorted off the premises.

That's my cue to go. I'll have to wait to find out more. Might be time to do some digging of my own though – see what that journalist knows.

If she gets too close, I may need to take matters into my own hands again.

TWENTY-SEVEN

Jeanette

J eanette stubbed her toe as she stormed back into the main office. 'Fuck's sake!'

'You OK?' Irene asked as she returned to the office, a vacant look in her eyes that Jeanette shouldn't be ignoring. It touched her that the woman was concerned about her wellbeing rather than thinking of her own as Irene was clearly running on auto-pilot. She'd need to have a word as Irene would end up on the sick if the situation wasn't addressed.

'Yeah. I'll be fine. I think that mess was my cue to go home.' Jeanette leaned against the wall and rubbed her foot. 'Everyone in for curfew then?'

'Uh-huh. I think they'll all be on their best behaviour until everything is… sorted. Speaking of which, what *is* happening?' Irene's voice shook.

Jeanette had been planning to meet with all the hostel staff soon to update them but with something cropping up on a daily basis, she'd let that slip. She understood why Irene appeared so nervous. With no arrests made, the killer was still amongst them, and with no apparent motive identified it was impossible to know if anyone else was at risk. Jeanette's manager had given her and her staff strict protocol to follow in the interim – starting with the rule that no one was to leave the main office during the night shift. If any concerns were raised, they each carried a handheld alarm which connected directly to the nearest police station, and the hostel had been flagged so that any calls to the police would be responded to immediately.

'Why does everyone look so serious?'

Jeanette turned to find Frank in the doorway. Irene wouldn't look at him.

'Where have you been?' If the staff were already breaching the protocol, there was no hope. She tried to hide her frustration.

'TV connection was messed up and rather than have a riot on our hands, I thought it was best to sort it out. Nothing a little gaffer tape couldn't fix.' He twirled the tape around two fingers.

'Thanks for that.' Frank was right; it would make the evening shift more tolerable if they didn't have the residents coming to the main office complaining every five minutes. 'Make sure that's the last time you leave this office until the day shift arrives. The CCTV cameras are now fully functional on the front and back doors so when the men sign in for their curfews any breaches will at least be recorded and can be dealt with swiftly. However, with the finger of suspicion pointing at everyone here, it's doubtful anyone will step out of line. I don't want to have to start giving out warnings to you lot – I've enough to worry about. If there are any emergencies, call the duty SPO – details are on the wall. If it's a serious situation, call the appropriate emergency services. Are we clear?' Jeanette looked between the pair with a raised brow.

'Yes ma'am!' Frank saluted and sat down at his desk. There was a joking tone to his reply but the look he gave her did not escape her eyes. Frank was a good officer, but sometimes he thought he knew better than everyone else and that could land him in trouble.

Jeanette looked around. 'Where's Harvi?'

'Think he's ill… again. Not sure why he hasn't been sacked yet. Surely he's on a stage 2 sickness absence by now.' Frank was pushing his luck; Jeanette was in no mood to be challenged.

'Enough with the attitude. We all have to do things we don't like while the investigation is going on. And you don't need to worry about what stage of sickness absence anyone is on but yourself, OK?'

Jeanette guessed that Frank was probably still angry with her about taking his notebook, but when she spotted a new one on his desk, she realised he was just carrying on where he'd left off.

'What was going on earlier? I saw the police with someone out front. Looked like that journalist friend of yours. Took her away in their car.' Frank didn't even look up from his screen in his obvious attempt at changing the subject. Jeanette suspected he'd heard the residents chatting while he was fixing the TV.

'Let's be clear, she's no friend of mine. She wasn't arrested, if that's what you're asking.' Jeanette scratched her neck. She was tired. 'Just keep an eye on the CCTV and rather than repeating myself, I'll update everyone at the same time. Saves me having to go over the same thing a million times. But if either of you see her or anyone skulking about the property, phone the police. Sloane Armstrong has been warned not to return.'

They both nodded.

Irene stood and stretched her legs. 'I'm going to make a cuppa for anyone who wants one.'

'I'll have one,' Frank called out. 'If I'm going to be doing assessments all evening, I'll need something to keep me awake.'

'Nothing for me, thanks. I really am heading home now. I've stayed longer than I wanted to, and I have to meet with my manager first thing. I'll just update my whereabouts on the board for tomorrow's day shift and then I'll be off.' Jeanette wandered over to the whiteboard and amended the weekly schedule. She didn't want a million messages to her work mobile while she had to deal with her line manager and the criticisms he would no doubt be showering upon her tomorrow.

She returned to her office, shut down her computer, and opened her locked top drawer. She was in two minds about whether she should leave Frank's notebook in her secure filing cabinet – the detective was due to come in and see her tomorrow afternoon and it might be easier to just let him deal with it. She held it in her hand, about to place it in the cabinet drawer, when she had second thoughts. Curiosity took hold and she convinced herself that she'd be more prepared by reading it, saving anything coming back to bite her on the arse at a later date. She closed and locked the drawer and chucked the notebook in her satchel before saying 'bye to her team.

On the drive home, Jeanette couldn't get the thought of Sloane Armstrong out of her head. She was convinced the journalist wasn't being honest about why she had trespassed onto the property. Jeanette could tell from her body language – her eyes had been shifty and she'd bounced about like she couldn't wait to go.

Had she discovered something?

The last thing the hostel needed was more bad press. She looked over at her bag on the passenger seat. Maybe Frank had caught something without even realising it. She stopped at the SPAR shop at the end of her street and grabbed some snacks. It was going to be a long night.

TWENTY-EIGHT

Helen

Helen had been feeling anxious since the police took Sloane away. Sloane had found a key, but what did it unlock? Was it the clue to blowing the whole case wide open?

'Oh my word…' If that were true then Pete, the gardener, must be involved… or maybe he was even the killer? And to think, she had been face to face with him, all alone in the cellar. Anything could have happened. Pete Price had been working at the hostel before Helen had got her placement volunteering. He did a few odd jobs around the house too – the perfect disguise. When Helen had first met him, he'd given her the creeps – constant leering, and the white spittle bubbling in the corners of his mouth every time he strung a sentence together was disgusting. He could definitely be a murderer. Maybe she needed to do something to point the police in his direction.

She shook her head. Her imagination was getting the best of her. Malcolm would have told her to stop judging people – he'd been good like that. Never formed an opinion until he'd spent time with someone. Unlike her. She was quick to judge. But sometimes she was right.

She shrugged her shoulders.

Tick. Tick. Tick.

The cuckoo clock that Malcolm had picked up for her on one of his outings some twenty years ago distracted her. She was surprised it still worked but she'd disabled the noisy birdie because it brought back too many memories and it interrupted her naps – she'd been having more and more of these lately. Grief was planted firmly in her soul, and it seemed it would never leave her.

It was getting late and she needed something to settle her nerves. Her husband would have had a whiskey at a time like this, but Helen wasn't one for alcohol. Never had been.

She walked into the kitchen and found the Ovaltine – she'd drunk it since she was a child and it always helped her to sleep. As the milk boiled in the pot she stared out into her garden. Her eyes were drawn to the ornamental angel she'd placed under the crab apple tree her husband had planted when they first bought this home.

'Oh Malcolm. What should I do?'

Helen knew exactly what he'd say. Malcolm would have told her to mind her own business and let the police do their job. He was always having a go at her for being involved in things – *stop being such a busybody, Helen. You'll end up in an early grave.* But it had been Malcom who had ended up leaving first and she was convinced that the stress of all those vile people living right next door had helped put him there. As far as she was concerned, if the criminal justice system wouldn't give them what they deserved, maybe it wasn't a bad thing that they'd started killing each other. Problem solved. Until that wasn't enough, and the community was at risk. The whoosh and splash of the milk boiling over snapped her attention back to the task at hand.

What a horrible thing to think. She immediately regretted it. Maybe it *was* becoming too much.

Helen finished making the hot Ovaltine and poured it into Malcolm's favourite mug. It made her feel close to him. If people knew she talked to him, they'd put her in a home, but she didn't care. Her GP had told her that her grief could last as long as she needed it to – there was no time limit. There were times though that she envied people… people like Sloane, who seemed able to move on after a tragedy. Sloane rarely ever talked to Helen about her sister.

She sat across from his chair, on the new couch she had purchased when Malcom's life insurance had come through. He'd always been at her to get a new one, but she hadn't been able to justify the expense in her mind. Now, money meant nothing – she had enough of it from his life insurance and no one but herself to really spend it on.

Her mind backtracked to the cellar. She needed to know what was in that barrel – it had made the gardener angry to see her near it, and the smell! She rubbed her nose. Maybe Sloane could check it out further, but given what had happened this evening, Jeanette would be extra vigilant in making sure the truth never got out. Was she in on whatever was going on at the hostel? Helen would need to be Sloane's eyes and ears.

Her legs ached and the Ovaltine wasn't having its usual effect. She'd have to take a sleeping tablet. She finished the remaining dregs of her drink and went to wash out the mug. She hated leaving dishes overnight, especially as it was only her she had to clean up after. No excuses.

Helen checked the lock on the back door and pulled the curtains over the window above the kitchen sink. She then went down the hallway and checked the bolt lock on the front door. Malcolm used to laugh at her for being so over the top about the locks. *It's still locked from the first time you checked, silly.* He used to say this to her all the time, but it was a habit ingrained from her own mother and it made her feel secure.

She flicked the hallway light on, grabbing her handbag that hung over the handrail as she trundled up the stairs – another habit she had picked up from her mother. She placed the bag on the floor by the bed, closed the bedroom curtains, and plugged in her mobile to charge.

Helen changed into her nightgown and went to the bathroom to wash her face, took half a sleeping tablet, and brushed her teeth. She put moisturiser on her face. She wasn't sure why she did this anymore because the wrinkles weren't going anywhere, no matter how much Revitalift she used.

Returning to her room, she got into her bed and reached over for her book. Malcolm used to read mysteries in bed, but Helen preferred historical fiction and had just picked up a new book from the local charity shop – *The Orphanage* by Lizzie Page. She lay back and pulled the covers up, opening to where her bookmark was placed.

Twenty minutes had passed, and she couldn't remember a word of what she'd read. Reading usually helped her escape whatever worry had been in her head, but tonight it just wasn't happening for her. She replaced the bookmark and stared up at the ceiling.

Helen had never been so close to a murder in her life. Watching them on the news and reading articles about them in the paper was one thing, but for it to happen right next door… She shuddered. Things like this shouldn't happen here. The street had always been a nice safe place to live until that bloody hostel had opened. She still got angry when she thought back to how she was treated at the town council meetings. Like a stupid old woman.

Well, who was stupid now?

Helen started to cough. Her chest felt tight. She threw the covers off her and went to the bathroom to get a glass of water. She took a few gulps as she looked in the mirror. Her face was flushed. She really should go to the doctor. She'd call and make an appointment tomorrow.

She shuffled back to her bed, the arthritis in her joints making her knees ache, and got herself settled once again. She could think about things tomorrow.

Her lids were heavy, but just as she was drifting off to sleep her phone beeped, startling her.

'Who in the world would be messaging me at this hour?'

If it was an emergency, they'd call surely.

She was about to turn over when the phone beeped again.

'OK. OK.'

Helen removed the charging cable and looked at the screen.

UNKNOWN NUMBER

If this was one of those bloody nuisance texts, someone would be hearing about it in the morning.

She opened the message.

It wasn't a nuisance text.

Her hand shook as she read the message.

TWENTY-NINE

Sloane

S loane stood in her doorway and waved to the officer as he waited for her to go inside.

Bloody cheek!

She was too tired for any further escapades anyway and she had a lot of information from the day to digest. She should've known the hostel perimeter would be closely monitored after everything that had happened – she'd have to think things through more carefully in future.

She kicked off her shoes and before chucking her bag on the chair removed her laptop and placed it on the couch. Her tongue was sticking to the roof of her mouth, so she went and got herself a bottle of sparkling water from the fridge.

While in there, she found a Ziploc bag and carefully pulled the key wrapped in tissue from her pocket. She dropped it, minus the tissue, into the plastic bag and sealed it shut. She wished she'd looked at the lock on the cellar door, as this could just be the key to unlock that. Even if that were true though, she recalled Helen telling her that all staff and volunteers had to hand in keys and passes before they signed out, so why would the gardener hide this? Was it for himself to return later that night or for one of the residents?

Marcus Webb from the recovery centre, RSH, still hadn't been in contact and Sloane wondered if it had anything to do with the newspaper headline she had spotted on her way home earlier that day. The article, from what she could see as she skimmed the paper, seemed to be accusing the drug and alcohol services of encouraging ex-addicts to place their sobriety at risk by mentoring current addicts, thus putting themselves at risk of relapse. The column insinuated that funding was being misspent as crime related to drug misuse continued to climb. Having had her own experiences with drugs in her teenage years, she could understand the logic of this practice, even if she didn't agree with it one hundred per cent. Marcus could well be afraid that if anyone knew he was talking to her, he might be associated with the mentoring scheme article in the rival newspaper. If she didn't hear from him soon, she'd find a way to make contact with him again.

Sloane returned to her living room, placed the key back into her bag, and added 'Reach out to Marcus' to her to-do list. She'd also ask Helen more about the key if she saw her tomorrow. She opened her laptop and began scrolling through her emails. They were mainly junk or random people with conspiracy theories about crimes that they felt were of public interest. Aliens in Devon Stealing Animals was her favourite so far.

Delete. Delete. Delete. And then…

UNKNOWN SENDER

What's this?
Sloane clicked on the email and her brows furrowed.

All it said was:

Leave it alone.

What the hell was that supposed to mean?

She scrolled through the rest of the emails and moved on. Nothing more from her editor, which she took as a good sign – she had been sending him snippets for her Crime & Justice column to placate him. The less pressure she had from Conrad, the better her final article would be when it was submitted.

Sloane needed to know more about the residents at the hostel. So far, she hadn't had been able to learn enough about their backgrounds to formulate a decent theory, so in the meantime she figured the best place to start was with the victim – Danny Wells. She Googled his name and found pages upon pages of newspaper articles about his offending history, the murder conviction he had been on licence for, as well as a few short pieces relating to his parole and subsequent release to Ripley House. Using the touch pad on her MacBook, she scrolled until one heading caught her attention.

LONDON CPS BARRISTER COLIN WELLS CONDEMNS BROTHER'S VIOLENT BEHAVIOUR

So, his brother worked for the CPS. Sloane opened the article and read further.

Mr Colin Wells spoke out against his brother's actions and offered an apology to the family of victim Emily Nash. Ms Nash was brutally murdered, and her body was only discovered after a neighbour became concerned when they heard a child crying and got no response to repeated knocks on the door.

Sloane ran through the rest of what she felt was a poorly written article as the details were vague and left a lot open to interpretation. From it, she learned that the victim had been held captive for days, beaten repeatedly, and then stabbed twenty-seven times. Apparently, Danny and Emily had been in a volatile on/off relationship for several years. A young child had been found in another room, severely dehydrated. Sloane shuddered. What a monster. She started browsing the Google links for more information about what had happened to the child but there was nothing. She picked up her phone and hit the record button.

'Contact social services about archived records.'

She had a few contacts in the agency across the country due to a previous article she had written on a large paedophile ring. She hoped one of them might be willing to help. She'd be interested in finding out how the victim's child felt now about its mother's killer being murdered. She could already see the headline: *CHILD OF MURDER VICTIM CLAIMS JUSTICE HAS FINALLY BEEN DONE.* At least that would be how she'd feel. Sloane looked over at the picture of her sister on the wall. A flash of her sister's killer's face mocked her from the shadows. Danny's murder was opening old wounds and the harder Sloane tried to bury them, the faster they pushed their way to the surface. Although her sister's killer was still serving time and unlikely to ever get parole, she knew she would cheer anyone who served that bastard his just deserts. *He should never have been released in the first place…*

What really got under her skin was the fact that the arsehole still wrote to her. She looked over at the desk drawer where all the letters sat, unopened. When probation's victim unit had contacted her, she had been angry. Why they thought she wanted to hear from him in the first place was beyond her comprehension, although she was glad he directed his writing to her and not to her parents as they wouldn't have been able to cope with the barrage. The probation officer had suggested even though she might not be ready to read them now, she might one day – so she had reluctantly agreed. They'd sat in that drawer for ten years and she'd never once had the urge to entertain him by reading one single word.

Her mobile phone pinged and she welcomed the release from her past. She pushed away from those memories – back in their box they go. She picked up her phone and looked at the screen.

It was Helen.

The message was short, but the words alone were enough to alarm her. She pressed *call* and waited.

Helen didn't answer. Sloane hung up and tried again. Still no answer. Looking at the time on her phone, she noticed it was late – but she wouldn't sleep if she didn't check on her elderly friend.

She never had managed to get her run in today. She could easily be at Helen's in under twenty minutes.

Sloane ignored the warning from the police officer to stay away; she wouldn't go near the hostel. She'd made up her mind and once something was in her head, it took a lot to shift it. Helen could've fallen and needed some help. She laced up her trainers and grabbed her hoodie.

She was only halfway down the road when her mobile rang and stopped her dead in her tracks.

THIRTY

Helen

H elen fidgeted with the sleeve of her dressing gown, checking the clock periodically as she waited in the lounge for Sloane to arrive. It was too late for coffee, but she boiled the kettle anyway in case her friend wanted something. The knock on the door startled her even though she was expecting it.

She looked through the peephole before pulling the bar across from the deadbolt, letting Sloane in. The journalist must have run all the way as she was panting, trying to catch her breath.

'You scared the living daylights out of me!' She brushed past Helen and plopped herself down on the couch, making herself at home.

'Oh. I'm sorry about that. I'd been having trouble sleeping so took half a pill. The Ovaltine didn't work, you see, and then when I got that text... well, I didn't know what to do. The pill kicked in after I texted you and here we are...' Helen tried to steady her hands but to no avail. 'Do you want anything?

There's water.' Helen pointed to the jug and glasses on the table.

Sloane took a biscuit from the plate Helen had put out. 'Water's fine.' She reached over and poured herself a glass. 'So what exactly did this text say?'

Helen reached into the pocket of her dressing gown and pulled out her phone. 'It's there.' She handed the device to Sloane and sat on the arm of Malcolm's chair watching the journalist's face to gauge her reaction. 'Who would send such a thing? Do you think I may have found something at work and now the killer is scared?'

Mind your business or you'll see your husband sooner than you think.

Helen had memorised the short message; it would not be something she forgot easily.

'It's definitely a threat. You need to tell the police. They might be able to install a panic alarm or even find out who sent it.' Sloane took a picture of the message on her mobile before handing the phone back to Helen.

'I was afraid you were going to say that. The police don't seem to be doing much though – maybe *we* should investigate further. What if this is just one of those creeps next door playing about? We could probably figure it out ourselves.' Helen didn't trust the police; they made her feel like she was a senile old lady.

Sloane reached out and placed her hand on Helen's knee. 'You're shaking. I can't protect you from whoever sent you this and you need to take it seriously. Let the police decide whether it's a real threat, and we can take it from there. I should never have got you involved in the first place.' Sloane sighed. 'It wasn't fair and now' – she held up the mobile phone – 'this.'

Helen stood abruptly and placed her hands on her hips. 'You listen here, young lady! I'm a grown woman and I made the decision to get involved. I'll call the police and let them know what's happened but whoever's done this isn't going to stop me from getting that place shut down.' She walked to her front window and looked over at Ripley House. 'There's evil in that house and it needs to be gone once and for all. I'm doing this for the community, for my own peace of mind and for my Malcolm. So, thank you for your concern, but I make the decision whether or not I stay involved and my answer is... what's next?'

Sloane held up her hands. 'OK. OK. You're right. I shouldn't have assumed, but if we're going to proceed, you have to promise me that the minute something feels off, or if another threat comes through, you will rethink your position. I'd never forgive myself if something happened to you. Do we have a deal?'

Helen turned around, one hand behind her back and her fingers crossed. 'Of course. I'm not ready to leave this earth just yet, no matter how much I miss Malcolm.' She winked. 'Where do we go from here?'

Sloane told Helen about the odd email she had received. 'I didn't pay much attention to it until you called. But you see why I'm so concerned?' Sloane leaned forward. 'We've touched a nerve. We just need to figure out who that nerve belongs too.' Sloane reached into her bag and pulled out the key in its Ziploc bag. 'This is what I found under the rock.'

Helen shuffled over to the couch and took the plastic bag from Sloane. 'That's the key to the cellar. We have to hand all keys in at the end of a shift, so how come no one noticed it was missing?' She was talking more to herself than to Sloane.

What if the gardener is in cahoots with someone? Helen kept the thought to herself for the time being.

'Are you *sure* that's the key to the cellar? Could it be for something else?'

Helen examined the key more closely. 'It looks the same but… yes, I guess it could be for something else. But what?'

'Do you have access to where the keys are held?' There was a slight hesitation in the journalist's voice that didn't go unnoticed. It was clear from her face that she was still unsure of Helen being involved.

Helen thought for a moment. Normally she wouldn't have direct access, but she wondered if there was a way she could get into the main office. 'Erm, leave it with me. I can make no guarantees of course, but perhaps…' She tapped her lip with her finger. 'Every office has a first aid kit, including the kitchen. Maybe if I removed some items and then asked to get refills from the main office? I mean, I'm just an old woman, what could I possibly do, right?' Helen smiled.

'I'm not sure I like that idea. The staff know that you were never keen on the hostel in the first place, and with everything going on, I doubt they're going to let just anyone inside the secure areas of the hostel.'

'One of the younger probation officers has a soft spot for me. I'm sure she'll let me in. I can check if there are any keys missing. The cabinet is near the supply cupboard. Or…' An idea popped into her head, and she went over to the antique desk that her husband used for his stamp collection. She pulled the flap down and pried open one of the small drawers. 'Ha! Malcolm was right. He knew they would come in handy.' She reached in and pulled out a handful of various keys. 'If I can find one that matches that one' – she pointed to the plastic baggy on the table – 'I could say I found it outside and they'd have to check then if one was missing.'

Sloane grinned. 'People should never underestimate you, Mrs Burgess. That could actually work.'

THIRTY-ONE

Sloane

S loane and Helen chatted a little while longer until the journalist felt her friend would be OK and decided it was time to leave. Helen needed her rest, and it was late. She still wasn't keen on having Helen so involved, but knew from the determined look in her eyes that it would be a struggle to keep Helen out and she didn't want to fall out with her. She would, however, be sure to keep a closer eye on her friend and be more careful with the information she shared in future. Helen would never know.

She used the walk back to her home to think through everything in her head. Had they really stumbled upon something or was it just a prank? When she was just in the door, her phone beeped. It was probably Helen checking she had arrived home safe – she pictured the woman wagging her finger and giving her a lecture when Sloane refused to grab a taxi.

She rummaged in her bag for her phone and when she saw *UNKNOWN NUMBER*, she quickly turned and locked her door behind her.

Was she being watched?

I told you to leave it alone. What happens next is on you.

The phone slipped through her fingers and bounced off the carpet. Her heart was racing. She ran into her living room and peeked out through the curtains but she couldn't see anyone in the darkness, no shadows lurking; the street was quiet. She ran back to the front door, picked up her phone, and searched her bag for her wallet. She needed the detective's card.

This was getting serious. Someone had eyes and ears on her and Helen and that meant they must be getting close to uncovering the truth.

She rang the number on the card but got an answerphone. What kind of detective was this? Why did he bother to even give her his details if he wasn't going to answer the phone? She left him a message to return her call as soon as possible, no matter what the time.

She should call Helen but when she looked at her watch she realised it was too late to disturb her friend again. At least she was confident enough to know that when it came to safety, Helen was a stickler for double-checking everything was locked – that gave her a bit of comfort, but she thought she'd text her anyway.

I've had another text. Please DO NOT do anything until we've spoken, and ring the police if you need to. Stay safe. X Sloane

Helen was far more stubborn than she was, so she prayed the amateur sleuth took on board what Sloane had said and waited. She rubbed her eyes. She needed to be up early to chase up that lead with Marcus Webb first thing. If he wasn't going to reach out, she'd make sure he knew she hadn't forgotten their conversation. It might just prompt him to come forward.

Sloane went around her house clicking locks, turning keys, and pulling doors before giving in to the exhaustion she felt and crawling into her bed. She hadn't even bothered to get undressed; if she managed a few hours' sleep, that would do her.

———————

A thud on the window had her sitting up in her bed within seconds.

She sat still and listened but there was nothing more. She could hear the wind whistling and raindrops pelting on the glass. Maybe that was what it was. She'd never get to sleep though if she didn't check.

Sloane pulled the covers off her legs and crept towards the window. She was turning the blinds so she could see out when another loud BANG had her stumbling backwards.

What the hell?

She went over to her nightstand and unplugged her phone from the charger before returning to the window. She didn't want to turn her lights on in case anyone was out there. She decided she'd just call 999. Sloane twisted the pole for her blinds and gazed out into the back garden again.

Was this how her sister had felt? Had she heard the intruder in her home? Sweat formed on Sloane's brow and her hands shook. Leaning against the wall she took in a deep breath before forcing the thoughts of her sister out of her head and returning to her own situation.

What was that at the back of the garden? Her breath caught

in her throat as whatever – or whoever – it was moved… She unlocked her phone and was about to dial 999, still staring out at the intruder, when the wind picked up and moved the mysterious object once again. Sloane squinted and realised it was just a black bin bag. Her fear turned to anger as she remembered having a go at her neighbours a few weeks back about leaving empty bin bags on the fence edge. Clearly the arseholes hadn't taken any notice. Sloane felt foolish at the fact that she had been about to call the police for a runaway bin bag, but that still didn't explain the noise on her window.

That mystery was solved a few moments later when another gust of wind shot a tree branch onto the glass. A small crack appeared.

Sloane didn't know whether to laugh or to cry. A bloody branch. Another complaint she had made to her neighbours. Well, if they weren't going to do anything about it, she would. She put a reminder in her phone to call about having the branches that hung over her property removed. Screw them.

Sloane went to the bathroom and splashed some cold water on her face. Now that the adrenaline was out of her system, she felt tired. She plugged in her mobile again and crawled back into bed.

She didn't have high hopes that she'd get much sleep, but even a few hours would be better than none at all. Sloane had touched a nerve with someone, and she'd be damned if she was going to let that stop her.

THIRTY-TWO

Jeanette

Jeanette rubbed her temples, her head banging from the bollocking her line manager had given her at the managers' meeting that morning. The police had been present and had updated everyone on where they were at with Danny Wells's murder investigation. They didn't offer up much but hinted that there were one or two residents they might speak to further. They would be in contact in due course.

Jeanette's manager nodded his head like one of those bobblehead figurines – emotionless, agreeable, and slightly annoying. Sometimes when he spoke she felt like she was being thrown under a bus, like the perfect scapegoat, but if they thought they'd use this situation – as horrible as it was – against her, they had another think coming.

Once the meeting was finished, Jeanette's line manager called her over. 'Can I have a word before you go?'

'Of course.' Jeanette stayed seated while they waited for everyone to leave the room.

'I just wanted to check in and see how things were at Ripley House?'

Was he serious? Jeanette put a hand on her chest and focused to control her breathing to prevent any of the anger she felt bubbling to the surface. 'We're trying to get back to some kind of normality. It was pretty traumatic for everyone involved so I thought it would be best to get the residents into the routine they're used to and keep everything as calm as possible.' She wanted to lay it on thick, to remind her manager of how her staff and the residents had been impacted, but the glazed look in his eyes told her he hadn't registered or cared about a word she'd said.

'Hmmm…'

Jeanette watched him as he bit his bottom lip. He seemed reluctant to say something and she couldn't waste more time waiting for a response.

'Was there something particular on your mind? Only, I need to get back to the hostel…'

'It's just… never mind. Of course, you should get back to your office. We can catch up another time.'

Jeanette wondered if it had anything to do with the probation investigations but didn't push him – she'd enough on her plate trying to manage emotions and risk, and keep things ticking over without further incident. She gathered her things and headed back to Ripley House.

Jeanette sighed as she turned into the driveway. The hostel was becoming like a second home, given the hours she was putting in. It was at times like this that she was glad she didn't have a husband or children to complain about her job. She parked up and headed straight for her office.

All she wanted to do was sit at her desk and catch up on the pile of Risk Assessments she needed to sign off on. Thanks to Anwar, her inbox was filling up with them and it was adding to her anxiety as she never fell behind in her workload.

She was just logging in to her computer when the shrill tone of the panic alarm pierced her ears. Her eyes shot to the CCTV monitors, and she could see a group of men throwing punches at each other in the common room.

Oh for fu —

Jeanette ran down the stairs to the main office. 'Everyone stay where you are!' She wasn't about to risk any of her staff getting injured. She hit the emergency panic alarm by the reception door. Probation had arranged for it after Wells had been murdered. 'The police should be here any minute.' She wasn't wrong as she glanced to her right and noticed two cars pull up out front.

Jeanette buzzed them in and while three of the officers dealt with the scuffle, the fourth came in to the office to speak with her.

'Do you know what happened?' The female officer took out her notepad and flipped it open, her head tilted slightly to the left as she listened to the radio that was strapped on her shoulder.

'I'm afraid I don't. I just got here. I was about to sit down at my desk when I saw it all kicking off on the camera and I contacted your lot right away. I'm not sure if anything happened in this morning's group session, but we can soon find out.' Jeanette walked over to the three PSOs who had been huddled around each other whispering. 'Ahem. This is…' She turned the officer.

'PC Turner.'

'She'd like to ask you a few questions.' Jeanette stayed put and listened in.

'Your manager mentioned there was a keyworker session this morning? Did anything out of the ordinary happen?'

They all looked at each other but remained silent.

'Please answer the officer. We need to get to the bottom of this.' Jeanette crossed her arms.

Why the hell were they being so shifty?

'I wasn't involved in the group and haven't heard anything, so if you don't mind, I have a lot of OASys reviews to get through...' Amy turned to go back to her desk.

'Anwar and I ran the session this morning and it was all fine until after break. Something must have been said amongst the smokers in the group, as when they returned, the atmosphere really changed. Jack Campbell was being more... aggressive – if that's the right word – than he normally is. And he was eyeballing Jimmie Ludlow every time he spoke.' Steph rubbed her arm as she spoke.

'Do you know if that pair have a history?' The officer didn't seem surprised by anything she was hearing. Campbell was on licence for murder – he had murdered a paedophile who had been grooming and assaulting his niece; drugs had featured in the offence. Ludlow was a rapist; young women in their twenties were his interest. The two were at opposite ends of the offending hierarchy.

'Not that I'm aware of. Though with Ludlow being a sex offender, he often gets picked on by the residents, and you know Jack's history. It's never escalated this much before though. I wonder, with everything that happened with Danny... they're all probably still on edge and looking for someone to blame?'

'Possibly.' The officer turned to Jeanette. 'Was it those two involved in the affray?'

Jeanette nodded.

The officer's radio crackled but Jeanette could barely make out what was being said. She didn't have to wait long.

'We're arresting that pair and will keep you updated on whether or not they are charged. They could well be bailed in a few hours – will they be OK to return here?'

'Depending on whether either are charged, their home probation officers may action recall. For the time being, I'll say yes…' It was more than likely that only one, if either, would be returning. If either had noticeable injuries or were charged with affray or assault, they would be recalled. 'Thanks for coming out so swiftly. We'd really appreciate knowing whether they'll be bailed back to here as soon as you know.' Jeanette wanted to reinforce the importance of that to avoid any unnecessary chasing, paperwork, and pressure on her team. In the past, probation and police hadn't had such a good working relationship, and communication had been poor. But with multi-agency working and MAPPA arrangements, this had improved significantly, though there was still always something that seemed to slip through the cracks.

'Will do.' PC Turner smiled.

Jeanette showed the officer out and went into the common room where the remaining residents had been left.

'Right, who's going to tell me what the hell happened here?' The men looked at each other, shrugged their shoulders, and stayed silent. None of them would want to be thought of as a grass. 'You're going to be spoken to individually and I suggest you think long and hard about being upfront with us. Everything was recorded on CCTV so although you may not have been directly involved in the fight, you were all complicit as not one of you' – Jeanette pointed at each of them, letting the severity soak in – 'came and reported the incident. No one is to leave this room. I'll be back in a second.' Jeanette left the room and returned to the main office to pick up a spare notepad and pen. She then informed her team what needed to be done.

There were two interview rooms on this floor as well as the main group room. She'd need one staff member to stay in the office and answer calls as the receptionist normally in the office was only part-time and wasn't in today. Someone would also need to inform the relevant home probation officers of the situation. Since Amy hadn't been involved in the group sessions, Jeanette felt she would be best to stay behind.

'If you two start by speaking to Mark York, I'll speak to Ray Southall, and Amy, you can stay back and take care of things here. Make sure to update the local officers, please.'

Anwar, Steph, and Jeanette left the office and pulled the residents into interview rooms.

Jeanette took the group room. She felt for the personal panic alarm in her pocket before sitting down.

'You won't need that.'

Jeanette was caught off-guard. 'Need what?'

'That alarm you've been fingering.' He licked his lips as he said it. 'In your pocket. I'll tell you what I know and then I'm going back to my room. I don't want to be involved in any bullshit this close to my move-on date.'

THIRTY-THREE

Sloane

B*eep, beep, beep, beeeeep!*
Sloane groaned as she reached her hand across the nightstand, tapping it unenthusiastically in search of her alarm clock. It felt like she'd only been asleep for two minutes when the damn alarm rang out.

Her legs felt stiff as she got out of bed and made her way to the shower. Normally she'd grab a coffee first and flick through the news on the telly but there was no time. Her shoulders relaxed as the warm water beat down on her skin.

Once dressed, she sat down at the breakfast bar in her kitchen and texted the landscape company she had used in the past to come and get rid of those branches. Next, she scrolled through her emails. A message from Marcus Webb immediately caught her attention, setting up a time when he was free to talk today.

Result! She fist-pumped the air and gulped her coffee down.

Sloane sent a quick text to Helen to check she was OK and give her a gentle but firm reminder that she shouldn't snoop around anymore, given the threats. Sloane could find things out herself. She was concerned that she still hadn't heard back from the detective so tried him again. This time he answered.

'Detective Brady. Didn't you get my message?'

'Good morning, Ms Armstrong.' He paused. 'I did get your message but, in all honesty, I presumed you were just fishing for information.'

'What the hell? Why would I do that? Both Helen and I received threatening texts. Who else but the killer would do this?'

'C'mon now. Why didn't either of you call 999 if you were genuinely concerned for your safety?'

'Are you being serious? I went straight around to Helen's house to check she was OK.' Her blood boiled and she struggled to keep her temper in check. 'We both know what the police are like. I mean it's been weeks now – have you even arrested anyone for Danny Wells's murder? Any suspects? Sounds like you need all the help you can get...' Sloane was irked at his 999 comment. Technically he was right, but at the time she had wanted to go straight to the source. She wouldn't tell him that though.

'Whoa. I think you need to calm down now, Ms Armstrong. Those details are not something I or my team would share with the press. If you fear for your safety, I suggest you come down here with your phones and log your concerns. I'm here most of the morning and would be more than happy to speak with you both. Shall we say 10.45am?'

Sloane clenched her hands. The detective was treating her like she was an idiot. But she'd play him at his game. 'Fine. We'll see you soon, DS Brady.' She ended the call.

'What a prick!' Sloane screamed at her walls.

She scrolled through her mobile and called Helen.

'Well, this is a surprise.' The elderly woman sounded more awake than Sloane felt.

'Morning. Sorry for the early call but I just spoke to DS Brady. He'd like us to come in and speak to him about the texts. If I pop around in about an hour, will you be ready?'

'Uh… yes. I'm not needed at the hostel until 1pm. Do you think we'll be back by then?

'I'm sure we will. I'm going to get a taxi and I'll see you soon.'

'I'll keep a look out then.'

Sloane gathered up everything she'd need for the day and placed it in her bag. She booked a taxi and then responded to the message from Marcus Webb confirming the time and location of their meeting.

Her phone rang. It was the taxi.

If nothing else, she was looking forward to putting that detective in his place. She locked up, jumped in the taxi, and gave the driver Helen's address.

When the taxi arrived at Helen's, Sloane had a laugh to herself at her friend's appearance. She was dressed up – hat and all! A hint of sadness hit her then as she realised Helen clearly didn't get out much lately and she felt a little guilty for laughing.

Helen got into the taxi with a few grunts. 'These knees of mine don't always work as they should. They either lock or buckle on me when I need them most.' Her cheeks grew red.

'I'm the same, don't worry.' Sloane didn't want to see the woman embarrassed and it wasn't a lie – her knees could play up due to her years of running.

The taxi driver turned to face them. 'Was it the police station in town you wanted?'

'That's right,' Sloane confirmed.

Helen leaned over and whispered, 'I've made a list of who I think could have sent those texts. I personally think it was that gardener – after all, the texts only arrived after you were escorted from Ripley House. Who else could it be?'

Sloane turned to face Helen. 'It could be anyone in that place. They might have been watching from the windows. It could have been one of those men standing outside having a fag. I definitely think we should tell the police about what we found under that rock too.'

Helen grabbed Sloane's hands.

'Oh no, we can't do that. It's our biggest lead! The police will just make a shambles of it all. I still haven't had the chance to check—'

Sloane raised a brow. Helen quickly turned away; she must have realised she was saying too much because she'd agreed not to do anything further but her job in the hostel.

'I know you mean well and at the moment your Miss Marple skills are on point, but the texts should be taken as they were meant: a warning. That means you keep your promise and don't do anything foolish. Agreed?'

Helen continued to look out of the window and mumbled something.

Sloane tapped Helen's shoulder. 'Sorry, I didn't hear you… I'm telling the police about the key, and you need to stop the sleuthing for the time being. It's getting serious.' Sloane didn't want to sound aggressive, but Helen didn't seem to understand how easily something could turn from curiosity to danger. In her field of work, Sloane knew what she was doing and could handle herself. Helen was taking the neighbourhood watch role a little too far.

Helen turned sharply. 'Fine. But I'll keep my eyes open – you can't stop me from observing things.'

Sloane wasn't surprised by the reply, but she was by the tone. Helen's eyes were cold, and her cheeks red. Sloane could see the veins on her neck bulging out. She didn't want to upset the woman but before she could calm the situation down and soothe Helen's hurt feelings, the taxi stopped and the driver turned around, waiting for his fare.

It would have to wait.

THIRTY-FOUR

Helen

Helen pushed herself out of the taxi and immediately regretted it as a sharp pain shot down her leg. Her sore hips had been niggling at her for a time now, but she didn't want to bother her GP. It was an age thing, for sure. If she kept telling herself that she hoped it would make it true.

She looked around. She'd never been to a police station before and was a little surprised at how ordinary it looked. A large building with lots of windows, surrounded by a few trees, in the middle of town. In her head she had always visualised a prison-like environment – after all, they locked people up in police stations, didn't they?

'Everything OK?' Sloane came over and stood beside her.

'Yes. I'm fine . Quit fussing.' She stepped away from Sloane and straightened her skirt. 'Just give me a minute – my hip is playing up a bit. This is a nice building, isn't it? I'd never have imagined it was a police station.' Helen raised a hand to her forehead as she looked up. The sun was bouncing off the mirrored glass and reflecting right in her eyes. 'I think I'm ready . Shall we go in?'

Helen walked slowly behind Sloane. The journalist held the door open for her and waited as she hobbled in and sat down in the reception area. She watched while Sloane spoke to the young man behind the Plexiglass. Sloane pointed over to her and she waved. A few moments later, Sloane came back and sat down beside her.

'He's just contacting DS Brady to let him know we're here.'

'Do you think we're going to be taken to a room they speak to the criminals in?' Helen wasn't sure why but she felt a little excited at the prospect. Maybe it was because she loved watching those detective shows and now felt she was a part of an investigation. 'Ridiculous…' she murmured under her breath.

'Sorry, what was that?' Sloane turned in her direction.

'Oh, I was just talking to myself. Ignore me.' She waved her hand about.

Sloane stood up as the door directly in front of them opened. Helen recognised the detective. Although she'd only met him once, she had seen him a few times on the news and his face was etched into her memory. He had much more stubble today and his eyes looked tired, almost droopy. Sloane held the door open and let her through first, following close at the detective's heel. Helen took in her surroundings: bright white walls, a few pictures – plain, but inviting – and various instructions. The detective swiped a card attached to a lanyard around his neck against a small black box and led them into a room that had a couch, two chairs, and a low table.

'*This* is where you interview criminals?' Once again, Helen had spoken out loud and felt her neck redden as the journalist and detective looked at each other and smiled.

'Not usually, but we have done. This is a more informal interview room. Why don't you take a seat? I can get you a glass of water or I can call for some coffee or tea if you'd prefer?'

'Water is fine for me.' Helen suddenly felt parched.

'And me.' Sloane took the cups from the detective and handed one to Helen.

'Why don't we get started. I understand you both have received text messages from an unidentified caller which you felt to be of a threatening nature? Do you have your phones with you?'

Helen reached into her handbag and pulled out her mobile. She unlocked the phone and opened her inbox. Normally she deleted messages once she'd read them – she'd seen somewhere that saving them ate up her phone memory if they had pictures attached. How true that was, she wasn't sure, but she didn't want to risk missing a message because her phone memory was full.

Sloane did the same, passing her phone to DS Brady, but she watched him to see what he did with it.

They both waited while the detective looked through the messages. Helen couldn't tell what he was thinking and it annoyed her. Finally, he looked up at both of them.

'I can understand why you felt concerned, but do you think that perhaps this maybe was a prank? Has anything unusual happened within the last week or so that would warrant threats against either of you?'

Helen looked at Sloane and waited for her response. The detective was digging for information. She watched as Sloane reached into her bag and pulled out the key in the plastic pouch. Helen listened while Sloane explained how she came into possession of the key.

'So, you lied to the police officer who came out that evening?'

'Yes. Well, not exactly. I just wasn't forthcoming with everything. Helen had seen the gardener hiding something and before we came to you, we wanted to see if it was worth bothering you with. You're busy. We wouldn't want to waste your precious time.'

The detective scoffed. 'Well, that would be a first, wouldn't it, Ms Armstrong. So have you then?'

'Have I what?'

Helen's eyes flitted between the pair as she observed their banter – neither revealing their cards at once.

'Found the significance. Or is it just what it looks like? A spare key to the cellar. That is what the key is for, right? I think I'll keep hold of this and return it to Ripley House. I need to go by there shortly anyway.'

'Don't you find it odd that it was hidden under a rock when all keys and pass cards are supposed to be handed in? Why wasn't it reported as missing? Have you spoken to the gardener yet? He's… odd… And why hasn't this murder been solved yet? With all those offenders living in that house, surely it isn't difficult to arrest one of them – they're all guilty of something!'

Helen's hands shook as she spoke. The detective's head tilted, and Helen felt self-conscious. Why was he looking at her like she was a crazy old woman?

'Cases don't get solved within twenty-four hours, Mrs Burgess.' The detective's brow furrowed. 'We need evidence before we can arrest anyone. If we don't have evidence, our hands are tied.'

Helen didn't like his attitude. 'It seems to me that you'd have your evidence if you actually looked. I'm just an old woman, detective. I've already found—' She stopped herself when she realised what she was saying. Her anger was getting the best of her once again. 'I think this was a waste of time, Sloane.' Helen stood. 'Are you ready to go? I need to be at work shortly.'

The detective looked at his watch. 'If you two would like to wait a few minutes, I can drop you there. I'm sure Ms Macey wouldn't mind me getting there earlier than planned.'

Helen looked over at Sloane, pleading with her to decline the detective's offer, but her friend ignored what her eyes were saying.

'That would be great, wouldn't it, Helen? Saves us waiting for a taxi.'

The detective led them back into the reception area and although Sloane was trying to make small talk Helen ignored her. See how she liked it.

Instead, she thought about her next move. While everyone was busy talking to the detective at the hostel, she'd do a little investigating of her own.

THIRTY-FIVE

Jeanette

The man sitting directly across from her was one of the remaining sexual offenders they had at Ripley House; the other one had just been hauled away by the police. Ray Southall had been charged and convicted of rape under the Sexual Offences Act 2003, as well as aggravated burglary and murder. All his victims had been elderly females. He would befriend them, offer to do home repairs, drug their tea and then commit the vile act before strangling them. When Jeanette had read his history, she had been sure there were probably more victims that hadn't even been aware of what had happened to them or those who had just not come forward – those who had survived, before he had refined his MO. His case had made the headlines after the daughter of his latest victim had been found hanged. The poor woman hadn't been able to handle what had happened to her mother, had blamed herself for not being there to help, and three months after his conviction, she had committed suicide.

'What are you thinking about?' He leaned forward with a sly smile on his face, almost flirtatious in his manner. His records indicated narcissistic tendencies and Jeanette was witnessing those today.

'Sit back and listen. No BS here, Ray. What happened today was a serious matter and could have implications for everyone – including you.' That made him sit up straight. Ray was fine with pointing the finger at others but if something could directly affect him, he immediately went on the defence.

'What do you mean? I told ya I wasn't involved. If the bloody cameras were working, you'd see that… I stood back and let them hang themselves. Wasn't going to get myself recalled for some druggie twats. Not my circus, not my monkeys… You can't get me for jack shit.' He leaned back in the chair. Confidence oozed from him and Jeanette had to hide her feelings of disappointment. She hated to admit it, but some people just couldn't be rehabilitated, and Ray was one of them.

'The fact you're still here and haven't been carted away by the police should tell you we know you weren't involved in the actual fight – so what happened?' Repeating the question, Jeanette refused to let him think he could deflect her purpose.

'The fucker Jack was getting pissed at Jimmie for some deal he'd promised that didn't go ahead. Sounded like some money got lost and Jack wanted it back.'

'This was over a drug deal?' There had been rumours that drugs were being sold from the hostel but no matter what Jeanette did to try and catch the culprits, no evidence was ever found. It was hard to recall someone on hearsay evidence alone.

'Something like that. I don't do drugs anymore of course, but I was interested in the money bit as it sounded like a lot of dosh. I heard a stash was found in Danny's bed. That true? In your pockets now, is it? You might want to search all their rooms, see what you can find…'

'The police have the money and thanks for the tip, but you don't need to tell us how to do our jobs.'

He leaned forward again. 'You sure about that? There was a murder here a few weeks back so it seems to me like you guys need all the help you can get. I could be your eyes and ears if you'd like… for a fee of course.'

'Rein it in, Ray. You're pushing the boundaries and if you carry on, your home probation officer will be informed. Now, can we get back to what you witnessed?' Jeanette waited but Ray just sat back and crossed his arms.

'Sorry, miss. Don't know what you're talking about.' He licked his lips the same way as he had when he first came into the room. Jeanette's skin crawled. Just because she worked with this type of offender, didn't mean she had to like any of them.

'Can I go now?' He looked past her, straight at the door.

Her hands were tied. 'Fine. But don't think this is over.'

He brushed her arm as he passed. 'I hope not. You're a little young for me, but pretty nice to look at all the same.'

Jeanette shivered once he left the room and made a note to inform his officer. If this was how he treated women in the hostel, she could only imagine what he got up to during the hours he was out of their sight.

A thought flashed in her head. Had Danny witnessed something?

THIRTY-SIX

Sloane

Outside the police station, the three waited for someone to speak. Sloane took the lead. 'I'm going to stay in town – I have a few things I need to do. Why don't you take up DS Brady's offer and get a lift back? I'd feel a lot better knowing you were with him.' It also meant Sloane could save herself some time, but she wouldn't share that bit with Helen.

'You can't be serious.' Helen's lips pursed and her eyes narrowed into slits. Sloane ignored the looks and waved them off as the detective's banger of a car headed in the direction of Ripley House.

Sloane felt a dull thumping in her head – she needed caffeine. Decision made; her first stop was the Costa Coffee just down the road. Inside the small shop, she placed her order and when the Americano was ready, she found herself a seat and took out her laptop. She wanted to find out more about the gardener since Helen was so fixated on him. What was his actual role at the hostel? Did he literally hold the key to this case? No matter how much she tried to reason in her mind why he was hiding a spare key in the back garden, nothing made sense. It was against the rules and he would know that – why risk his job?

She typed in his name in the search bar of Google and was surprised to see two old articles online. She opened the first one, which contained a small mention that he'd found some special piece of silver – an old artefact – when he was out metal detecting in a field about twenty miles outside of Pottersworth. It was said to be valuable, and he'd sold it for a nice price, which made Sloane even more curious as to why he was working at the hostel.

The next article was more interesting. It seemed the gardener had been in custody for eight years following his involvement in a robbery some thirty years previous. It had made the papers only because the main perpetrator had died in prison and the article named the others in the gang. *He obviously feels comfortable around the residents at the hostel*, Sloane thought. This just reaffirmed her belief that leopards don't change their spots.

Sloane went on to search the criteria that the probation service used when hiring staff and was surprised to find schemes that supported ex-offenders being involved, the idea being that they might better relate to those on an order or licence. Given what she knew about the hostel, she wasn't surprised that Pete had found a home amongst his peers.

The reminder on her phone beeped. Marcus Webb had agreed to meet her on the other side of town at an overpriced café Sloane usually avoided. She hadn't been keen on the location, after a bad experience there had left her feeling that the staff were too pretentious to deserve her money. But he'd been adamant as he said he didn't want to be spotted talking to her and figured it was the one place none of his colleagues or clients would be found.

She gulped down the last of her Americano, packed up her bag, and strode at a comfortable pace to the meeting.

Marcus was already there when she arrived, and she hid a smile when she observed his appearance. He had a green hoodie on, pulled tight to cover his face, while he hunched over a cup of coffee, his eyes darting around. If he was trying to look inconspicuous, he was doing a lousy job, as the woman at the counter kept looking over and whispering to her colleague, pointing in Marcus's direction. Sloane dug into her pocket and pulled out a ten-pound note. She ordered a black coffee and croissant.

Marcus flinched when Sloane greeted him.

'Look, I don't have long. I said I was running an errand, but I feel really uncomfortable so can we just get on with it?'

'Of course.' Sloane placed her tray on the table and scooched into the padded seat across from him. 'Do you mind if I record this? Just makes it easier when I'm going over things later.'

'No way. And if you name me in any of this, I'll deny it. I'm only telling you what I've heard, I don't even know if it's true but if it is, I'm not going to risk my life telling you. You'll probably twist everything I say anyway...' He inched his leg outside the table as if he was going to leave. 'If that's not OK, I'm outta here.'

'Hang on.' She held her hand out. 'That's fine. I'll just take notes – no names. You have my word.' She reached into her bag and took out her notebook. Flipping to a clean page, she waited.

'I've heard from some of my clients that drugs are easily available at Ripley House and not only from the residents.'

Sloane's eyes widened. 'What? Are you saying staff are selling drugs to the residents?'

He nodded. 'Not only the residents...' He rubbed his hands. 'To other users who attend RSH. Let me be clear on something: when I first heard this, I immediately went to my line manager. I mean, that's a serious allegation. He said he'd speak to the hostel manager but, without specific names or hard evidence, there wasn't really much they could do.'

'When was this?' Sloane would have expected more security measures to have been implemented or that investigations would have taken place and was surprised the media never found out. In fact, she was a little stunned that Helen hadn't heard anything about this from inside the hostel. Looks like the place could hide things when it wanted to. 'Did your manager ever make that call?'

Marcus shrugged his shoulders. 'Been at least eight months' – he scratched his head – 'maybe longer, so I have no idea. I did what I was obligated to do. Recently the rumours have started up again. I pushed my client for a name, but he was too scared – I could see it in his eyes – and I don't blame him, if it was Danny Wells he was referring to.'

'I thought you were the receptionist. You have your own clients?'

He nodded. 'I'm a recovery keyworker. We're short on admin staff so we each do a round of duty to cover the reception.'

'Is there anything else you can think of that might help me find out more? Do you think your client would speak with me if I promised not to reveal any details?'

'I dunno. I can ask. He's just a young kid – hangs around a group in the park.' He looked at his watch.

'Oh! I think I may have spoken to him – well, I tried but no luck. Anything you could do to help me would really be amazing. You could save a life, you know.' Sloane was making it seem more than it possibly was, but Marcus didn't seem to grasp the importance – a little shove in the right direction might help.

'Look, I need to go. I've told you what I know. The rest is up to you. I'll speak to my client when they next come in and be in touch if they're willing to speak with you. Don't contact me again though, OK? I don't want anyone finding out I've been speaking to you.'

His fear of repercussions was evident. Sloane reassured him. He looked around once more before he left the café, head down and feet moving at a rapid pace. Sloane noticed the woman at the counter relax her shoulders. She felt like saying something but figured she'd only be wasting her breath. They were snobs.

She tapped her notepad as she re-read everything she'd learned today.

Could Jeanette Macey be involved in this?

Sloane shook her head. Sloane had looked into Jeanette's background when the hostel first opened but she was as clean as a whistle. She imagined the manager would be furious to know that drugs were being sold by one of her staff members.

But if it wasn't Jeanette, then who?

THIRTY-SEVEN

Sloane
_____

S loane's phone vibrated in her pocket. Looking at the screen she saw it was her editor.

Shit.

'Hey, Conrad. What's up?'

'I was about to ask you the same thing.'

She heard him suck in air and presumed he must have started smoking again.

'Thanks for keeping your column going but I haven't had any more updates about that murder from you and, excuse the pun, but the story will die if you don't keep the momentum going.'

'Funny you should say that, I just spoke to someone, and this is definitely a story you'll want to run. I can hint at how it's related to the Wells murder and that should keep the readers intrigued for when the big story is published.' Sloane didn't like sensationalistic articles but she knew her editor did, and if she gave him a vague teaser for a larger story it should keep him happy until she could do some more digging.

'Really? What's the headline?'

Damn. She hadn't thought that far ahead. 'I don't know yet – something along the lines of: Is there more than murder going on in Ripley House?'

'Hmm… OK, I'm curious. We can work on the title but fill me in.'

'My source informed me that one of the staff has been dealing drugs, and it may have something to do with why Danny Wells was killed, but I don't yet know who…'

'Is this going to land me in a lawsuit?' Wherever he was standing it was windy, as all Sloane could hear was a whooshing sound.

'*Anything* I write could land you in court!' She laughed and when he didn't do the same back, she changed her tack. 'If I'm not naming names and I can prove that drugs have been bought from someone at the hostel, other than from the residents, I don't see how either of us can be held liable.'

'Weak, but let's see what you can find out. I'll need something by the end of play Friday, if not before, OK?'

'I'm on it.' The call ended.

Sloane needed to talk to someone connected to the hostel – a resident maybe – but it wouldn't be easy.

Over the years she'd learned that sometimes her sources lied to her, and she was always upfront in advising that if she found out they were lying, she'd make sure their name was known. That wouldn't work with the drug users – they'd want money. She knew all too well how addiction takes hold and how a person would say just about anything for their next fix. These were some of the toughest situations requiring persuasion; you couldn't simply tell a person that your story is worth their freedom. For many, prison was a welcome break from the cycle of addiction.

She leaned against the wall and gathered her thoughts,

going through each of her options to figure out what her next steps would be.

Every story involved a range of facts. Some of what she needed might be confidential, but other information might be available in public records. Asking a source to be her guide to what was available publicly was a great way to build trust. If she managed to get her hands on a document – or even just get to see it and take notes – she could quote the document and have no need to use an unnamed source at all in the story. She felt that familiar surge of excitement when she was working on a strategy.

If the story was good enough, Sloane might be able to convince her editor to allow her to write it without identifying her source, and that would go a long way in getting the people she needed to speak with her openly. Without tooting her own horn, she'd always had a way of exploring the possibility of getting some or all of the interview on the record. Sometimes at the end of an interview, she'd pick out a good quote in her notes that wasn't too damning and say: 'Now what about this thing you said here? Why can't you say that on the record?' If they agreed to put that comment on the record, she'd go to another one in her notes and say: 'Well, if you can say that on the record, why can't you say this?' And so on. She'd got an entire notebook on the record this way. If they insisted on anonymity, however, she honoured it.

But there was always a way to get what she needed, even if it was questionable.

Sloane bit her lip. She knew exactly what she needed to do.

THIRTY-EIGHT

Helen

H elen hid her anger as she and Detective Brady drove off. The sneaky way Sloane had arranged this... It made her blood boil.

And this guy – she glanced at the Columbo look-a-like – if he was any good at his job, the murder would have been solved by now and that horrid hostel closed for good! How many times did she need to repeat herself before people would listen? Who else had to die?

As they pulled into the drive of Ripley House and the detective messed about parking his car, Helen decided she would start work early – she might get to overhear something that would be relevant to her own theories. And those she was keeping to herself for now. She touched her pocket and felt the outline of her notebook. She tapped it twice. She'd have more to add to it when she got home.

Once inside the hostel, she clocked a few of the residents in the communal living area. Two were playing pool and mentioned something about being let out of police custody. *Had something else happened at the hostel?* One was watching TV and another one had just left the window and was staring at the reception area. *Was he waiting for something?* There was a stand filled with leaflets just by the kitchen entry and she stood there, shuffling the booklets in the pretence she was tidying the area. Many of the residents would move them about in boredom or just to be a pain in the arse. Today, she was glad they did as it gave her an excuse to hang about.

The door to the reception area clicked open and Anwar bolted out of the office with one hand shoved into his pocket. He danced about from foot to foot like he had ants in his pants – Helen couldn't help but notice the deputy manager as he stood outside the communal living area door.

Helen stood back a bit from the rack and glanced in the direction of the living area. The resident who had been at the window flicked his head towards the main entry door and gave a hand gesture, which Helen couldn't see clearly.

Anwar looked around and Helen bent over to fix the papers on the bottom row, keeping the deputy manager in her peripheral vision, but he didn't take a blind bit of notice of her. Sometimes being invisible paid off.

She rubbed the dull ache in her lower back and as she straightened up, the man who had been standing by the window left the hostel, and minutes later, Anwar followed.

Why would the probation officer be meeting with a resident outdoors? She looked over her shoulder. The interview rooms were empty. This didn't make a lot of sense.

She felt a tap on her shoulder. It was one of the kitchen staff volunteers. 'You're early. We just got an order in if you want to help out with that?'

'Of course. I'll just see if there are any dishes to be cleared away. I spotted a few on my way in – saves someone else a job, right?' Helen had been caught off-guard and she could only hope that the woman didn't stop her. She needed to see what was happening outside.

'I'll grab them. I was going that way anyway…'

Helen grabbed her arm. 'No!' She realised how strange her behaviour was and released her grip. 'You've got so much on at the minute. Please, let me. I noticed they had the news on, and I thought I'd nip through and have a peek while I collected the dishes.'

The other volunteer shrugged. 'Suit yourself then…'

Helen waited until the woman returned to the kitchen before she dashed into the communal area. A few of the residents looked up and stared at her before returning to whatever they had been doing before she interrupted them. She loathed these men and what they had done to their innocent victims, but she needed to forget that and focus on why she was in such close proximity to these monsters.

She walked to the front window and pulled the curtain back, but Anwar and the resident were nowhere to be seen.

'Hey, lady, what cha looking for?'

Helen didn't turn around. The man wanted an audience, and she wasn't about to give him any attention. She heard a few sniggers from the others in the room and her neck became warm. She could just imagine how red it was.

She stood on her tiptoes to try and see further down the street but if the pair were down the road, they were making sure they stayed out of sight.

'They'll be back soon enough.' She could feel his breath on her neck. 'But if you're looking to score, I can sort you out. What is it? Trouble sleeping? A bit of diazepam will help bring the sandman to your room…'

Helen shuddered. 'If you're trying to scare me, I'll save you the trouble. Get the hell away from me!' she snarled through gritted teeth. 'Or I'll make sure your probation officer knows exactly what you've been up to in here.' She turned to face him. He wasn't fazed, and instead leaned in closer to whisper her in ear, 'Don't be such a tease.' He rubbed his bottom lip slowly with the tip of his index finger as he looked Helen up and down before brushing a finger up her bare arm. 'I do like the feisty ones.'

She was about to lay into him when she heard a familiar voice.

'Are you looking for something, Mrs Burgess?'

Jeanette stood in the doorway with her hands on her hips and the detective beside her, his slitted eyes staring at the man who was now backing away from Helen with a sarky smile on his face. The offender stopped when he reached the pool table and whispered something to the other resident. They both laughed.

Helen picked up the empty mug she had seen on the side table and held it up. 'Just collecting the dishes.' She couldn't even bring herself to smile.

'You really shouldn't be in here and...' Jeanette looked down at her watch. 'You're quite early.'

'We're short-staffed. The kind detective gave me a lift back from town and on the way I got a text from the agency asking me to come in.' Helen wondered if the DS would remember hearing her phone. If he questioned it, she could always say it had been on silent. She squeezed through the pair in the doorway and glanced back over her shoulder at the arsehole who had tried to intimidate her. 'I'm glad I bumped into you both actually... Can I have a word?'

She smiled inwardly as she saw the colour drain from the offender's face.

Jeanette nodded but made no effort to move.

'In private? It's a… sensitive matter and confidential,' Helen whispered.

'Come through to my office then. I'll just let DS Brady out.' Jeanette started to walk towards the front door.

Helen touched the detective's arm. 'This might interest you too.'

He raised a brow and followed Jeanette through reception and up to her office, with Helen not far behind. Helen sat and waited for Jeanette to shut the door. The detective remained standing.

'Ok, Mrs Burgess, what's this about?'

Was Jeanette angry with her? Helen knew Jeanette didn't trust her but there was no need for this animosity when she was actually trying to help.

'Two things really. One of the residents was inappropriate with me just now.'

Jeanette's eyes widened and she looked at the detective before looking back to Helen. *That got her attention.*

'Uh… how do you mean?'

'He came up very close to me and caressed my arm with his hand before…' Helen coughed and cleared her throat. Suddenly, she felt quite sick to her stomach as she realised, he must have been one of the sex offenders. She remembered reading about a rapist who targeted elderly victims. She coughed again.

The detective took the seat beside her. 'Are you OK? You've gone very pale. Would you like a glass of water?'

Helen shook her head. 'I'm fine.' She took a moment. 'He offered to sell me drugs. He's a sex offender though, isn't he? Do you think he wanted to knock me out so he could break into my house and rape me?' All sorts of thoughts were rushing through her head.

'I can't disclose anything about the residents here, but I can assure you, a close eye will be kept on him, and he'll be spoken to.' Jeanette was writing something down, but Helen couldn't read what it said.

'Did you see any drugs?' the detective butted in.

'No. Nothing like that. He mentioned dia… something?'

'Diazepam?' The detective queried.

'Yes! That's it. How in the world does he have access to that and how can he sell them in the hostel?'

Jeanette offered no explanation but shifted in her seat. Devin Murphy was the only one prescribed Diazepam but he had been transferred to another hostel shortly after the murder. A look passed between the hostel manager and the detective.

'I'll get Anwar to pull him in and have a word. You can be sure this will be dealt with immediately.' Jeanette stood.

'Oh, he's not here…'

Jeanette was halfway standing in order to communicate that the meeting was over – or at least she thought it was. 'Who's not here?'

'That fellow – your colleague. If I can be honest…' Helen leaned forward and whispered. 'He was acting strangely when the detective and I walked in. I saw him leave with another resident…'

Jeanette sat back down. 'Can you describe which one?'

'Short, stocky man. Shaved head, and one of those ridiculous beards. You know, comes just around the mouth…'

Jeanette nodded. 'A goatee. Erm… thanks.' She looked at her watch. 'The kitchen staff will be wondering where you are, I'm sure…'

Helen tutted once she realised she was being dismissed. She didn't need to be asked twice.

Before she was out the door, she heard Jeanette clear her throat.

'We'd appreciate it if you kept everything discussed as confidential so we can investigate properly without any… erm… prejudice from the press.'

Helen knew she meant her friendship with Sloane Armstrong. 'Of course.' She smiled, picked up the dirty mugs, and left the detective and manager to deal with everything she had shared with them.

In the kitchen, she grabbed her apron and was tying it around her waist when one of her colleagues called over to her.

'You look like the cat that got the cream. What's the goss?'

'Heh, heh. I suppose I might… but you know me – lips sealed.'

The colleague pursed her lips. 'Fine. Be like that.'

Helen placed the mugs she had been carrying into the dishwasher and went into the large pantry. When she was sure no one was paying her any attention, she pulled out her mobile phone and typed a message to Sloane.

THIRTY-NINE

Sloane

Sloane took in her surroundings as she strolled with purpose. The town centre of Pottersworth wasn't large but had nearly every amenity a person could need. It was a market town, as were most in the area, and Sloane smiled as the men and woman shouted out about their wares. She spotted a stall with some beautiful flowers – she'd swing by after her next destination and grab some. Sloane took a deep breath and enjoyed the smell of the greasy burger van as she passed, reminding her of happier times in her childhood. Her stomach grumbled. The smell of burger vans always got her stomach going.

As she reached the edge of town, she debated whether to take a short cut or continue via the longer, more scenic route to the park. Her plan was to have a second go at getting some answers out of the drug users she had spoken to before.

What she saw next, though, stopped her in her tracks. Less than ten feet ahead, down the alleyway to her left that cut through to the RSH building, was Anwar Hussain, the deputy manager of Ripley House and he was talking to a rough-looking bloke who she was sure was one of the residents from the hostel.

Sloane crouched before they could see her and moved behind one of the industrial rubbish bins that lined the side of the alley. She carefully pulled out her mobile phone from her front pocket and checked it was on silent, before opening the camera icon. Sloane peered out and angled the phone to get a good shot of the clandestine meeting. It didn't look like a normal probation appointment... She could feel the tension in the air, even from where she had planted herself.

Sloane watched silently as Anwar reached into the back pocket of his jeans and pulled out a small package. *What the hell was it?* She squinted, hoping to get a clearer image but when that didn't work, she tried to get a close-up on her mobile. The camera wouldn't focus, and the picture was too blurry, so she settled on a few snaps of the exchange between the two men.

The men's voices were raised as they tugged on the package. The stocky man with Anwar was grabbing at the package 'Don't try and get all smart now! I've got enough on you to get you into some serious trouble,' he growled at the probation officer.

Sloane noticed Anwar's body stiffen. 'Threatening me isn't going to change my mind. This is the last time. Remember, you're in it just as deep as I am – and who do you think the police will believe? You or me?'

Blackmail! She was glad she'd decided to take the shortcut today.

Sloane leaned back against the brick wall behind her, taking a moment to digest what she had witnessed and to decide what she should do with this information. She could go to the police – it might well be that both these men were involved in

Danny Wells's murder and were now bribing each other to make sure the other didn't snitch. Or she could write a story, blurring out the faces and highlighting the risk that having the hostel in the community continued to have, first with the murder and now staff in collusion with residents... They would have to close it down while everything was investigated. That would ease the community's minds. Helen would be delighted.

She leaned forward to see what the two men were up to, but they had left. She was relieved they hadn't come her way as she would find it hard to explain why she was lurking behind the bins. She stood up and walked down the alley towards the opening, where the men had been standing. Her eyes were drawn to the ground, unsure of what she thought she might find, when a voice pulled her out of her thoughts.

'What are you looking for, darlin'? Maybe I can lend you a hand?'

She was face to face with the burly resident of the hostel and the hairs on the back of her neck stood on end. She hoped he didn't recognise her from the newspaper, but when she looked into his eyes she noted the pinprick pupils and knew he was off his head. Part of her was relieved but it also put her on edge, as she knew it meant his behaviour could be unpredictable.

'I thought I'd dropped something, but it looks like I was wrong.' She made a move to leave when he blocked her.

'Are you sure?' He scratched at his cheek; his speech was beginning to slur.

Sloane pushed past him. 'Yes.' When she glanced back as she walked away, he was still watching her. She picked up her pace and when she reached the gateway to the park her phone vibrated.

The screen indicated a message from Helen and when she read the text she smiled. She sent a quick text back and then changed her mind about the park.

Sloane turned around, avoiding the alley as the stocky man still stood there, swaying slightly, staring at her. Instead, she took the long way back into town towards the library. She needed to get everything she had just witnessed written down so that she could formulate her story. It could be risky, leading to some severe consequences, but Sloane was never one to shy away from getting a story out if it meant justice would be served.

She found a quiet corner in the library and plugged in her laptop. As soon as the Word document opened, she began to type, the words coming easily. Once she was happy with what she had written she attached the document in an email, with a few of the photos she had just taken, and hit *send*. Sloane waited to see if her editor would respond immediately. When he didn't, she packed up her laptop and sat back in the chair. There was someone who needed to know this before it hit the papers.

She picked up her mobile phone and scrolled through her contacts. When she found the number she was looking for, she hit *call*. Answerphone. She sighed.

'DS Brady. Sloane Armstrong here. I have some information I think you might find interesting…'

FORTY

Jeanette

Jeanette waited for Helen to leave before expressing to DS Brady how she really felt about everything that had just been said.

'Why is this happening? What a bloody mess.' Head down, she rubbed her temples.

'Sounds about right.' The detective tapped his notebook on his knee. 'I should probably have a word with Anwar again, don't you think?'

Jeanette lifted her head slowly. 'What for? There could be a totally innocent explanation for why he went off with Mark York. A little gossip from a woman who's been determined to shut this place down doesn't mean there's any truth to what she said.' Even as she said it, she knew the detective was right. 'Give me a second, I'd like to check something...' She stepped outside her office. Looking at the large whiteboard to the left of her door which updated her staff's daily whereabouts, her heart sank. She popped downstairs and called out, 'Anyone know where Anwar is?'

Heads shook.

'When he returns, can you tell him I need to speak with him right away?'

Heads nodded.

Jeanette sighed as she hurried back up the stairs and returned to her office.

'So...' The detective looked up at her.

'No meetings on the board but that doesn't mean what you're thinking it does – sometimes things pop up at the last minute.' As far as Jeanette was concerned, until she spoke to her deputy manager this conversation was over. In fact, she should direct the detective to speak to the communications department at head office. This was way above her pay grade. 'Don't you have somewhere else to be? I don't want to keep you from any more serious matters.'

'Like I said, I want to speak with Anwar, if you don't mind?' DS Brady crossed his legs and Jeanette hid her frustration at how comfortable he was making himself in her office.

'Actually, I do mind. There's no evidence he's committed any crime and if there are concerns after I speak with him, I'll be sure to contact the police, as per our protocol. He's a probation officer, and he could very well be attending a meeting with someone he supervises. You can't seriously believe he's involved in selling drugs.' She shuffled through the pile of paperwork sitting on her desk. 'I really need to get back to work and won't be able to concentrate with you staring at me.'

'Before I go, is he Mark's allocated officer?' She watched as DS Brady flipped through his little notebook and stopped at a page that looked to Jeanette like it had some sort of list on it. 'Only, my notes show that he isn't.'

Jeanette shifted in her seat. She really didn't like where this conversation was heading. 'I don't think I owe you any explanation on that front, detective. You of all people should know that when a priority pops up, we can't always wait for the allocated officer to respond. This is a high-risk hostel – urgent matters crop up at the last minute on a daily basis. I'll ask you one more time, what exactly are you implying?'

The detective stood. 'Nothing at all. Just trying to figure out why a deputy manager would be running around with a known drug dealer. When was the last time you had the drug dogs around? Given everything that's happened, I think we both know that drugs are connected to the Wells murder investigation. I would've thought that would be... what did you call it? A priority?'

'We have one booked for the end of the week.' Jeanette rubbed her arm. As much as it pained her, a small part of her had the same questions about Anwar that the detective was throwing at her.

'And do your staff know when these visits are scheduled for?'

'Of course.' She had wanted to come back with a clever answer, but she was beginning to feel really drained by it all.

'I'll have a word at the station when I get back. Given everything we spoke about, I think a surprise visit would be best – that way, if Anwar can be ruled out of having drugs in his possession at work, we can cross that line of enquiry off...'

Jeanette got the impression that there was more to this than what the detective was disclosing. Her brain was telling her that even if no drugs were found on Anwar or on the hostel premises, the police might be using this as a way to get probable cause to check other locations. 'What aren't you telling me, detective? I've been very forthcoming sharing information and if there's something about a member of my team that I need to know about—'

The detective held up a hand and Jeanette's cheeks flushed.

'I'm not at liberty to say, Ms Macey. I'll be in touch.' He pushed his chair in and waited for her to let him out of the main office.

Once downstairs, Jeanette stood in the doorway and watched, open-mouthed, as the detective collided in the hall with an out-of-breath Anwar Hussain.

Anwar stumbled back. 'Oops! Sorry. I didn't see you coming.'

The detective looked past Anwar and Jeanette did the same. 'Your friend not with you?'

Anwar's brows furrowed. 'My friend?'

Jeanette interrupted. 'The detective is just leaving. I'd like to see you in my office, if you can spare ten minutes. I'll be in shortly.' She had been curt, but she was only looking out for her colleague. She knew the detective was trying to catch him out and she wasn't going to be a party to that. The whole idea that a member of her staff was involved in dodgy drug deals was ludicrous.

Anwar brushed past her and looked back at the detective before heading in to the main office. Jeanette waved at DS Brady as he got into his car before returning to her office.

Anwar was seated, pulling at his sleeve; a bead of sweat had formed across his forehead.

'What's up? Am I in trouble or something?' He stuttered the words.

'That's what I'd like to know...'

FORTY-ONE

Helen

As soon as 4.30pm rolled around, Helen removed her apron, handed in her keys and pass to the reception desk, and rushed home. There were some perks to living next door – her commute was never difficult. She chuckled to herself.

Once inside, she checked her mobile and opened the text from Sloane.

'Oh Malcolm, Sloane has had an interesting day too! I doubt it was as good as mine though...' She glanced at the photo on the table in her hallway. Malcolm's pictures were everywhere. It made her feel as if he was still with her.

Helen groaned as she bent over to swap her reliable Clarks shoes for her comfortable slippers and hung her handbag over the banister rail.

She did a quick tidy of her living room in case Sloane decided to pop over. She liked everything in its correct place.

Helen pottered into the kitchen and decided on some soup and a sandwich for dinner. She was feeling increasingly unmotivated to make herself a proper meal, having spent most of her afternoon cooking and cleaning up after others. She hummed as she prepared her dinner, looking out of her back window at the angel memorial – another small comfort for her.

She frowned.

The statue looked off. *Had it been moved?* She shook her head. Her eyes were tired, and an early night would probably do her some good. But as she stirred her soup, the statue's position niggled at her.

'I'll just go and have a quick look,' she mumbled to herself.

Helen went to her back door, removed her slippers, and pulled on her wellies, side-stepping the boxes of Malcolm's things which she still hadn't managed to sort through. As she walked down the garden path, she heard a few voices from the hostel next door. Those men would die from cancer for all the smoking they did. She shook her head, tutted and waved her hand around in the air. She'd die of second-hand smoke inhalation at the rate they were sucking on those fags.

When she reached the statue, she realised it *had* been moved and she gasped when she saw that a cigarette had been stubbed out on the polished white head of the statue. Two large footprints were in the ground behind it.

She turned and looked at the hostel and her eyes narrowed.

'Bloody monsters!' She shook her fist at the men on the porch but none of them paid her any notice. Her fury got the best of her, and she stomped over to the front door of the hostel, pressing the buzzer as she tapped her foot. 'Let me in!' Her fists banged on the door.

She heard the buzz and pushed the door open. At the reception window she demanded to see the manager and when Anwar Hussain opened the main office door, she wasn't happy so she pushed her way in to the office.

'Not you! I want to speak to Ms Macey.' She stood firm with her arms crossed.

Two of the probation staff were packing up and Helen noticed them rolling their eyes at Anwar as they said their goodbyes.

'I'm sorry but Jeanette's getting ready to leave. The evening staff are signing in now. What can I help you with?' Anwar was trying to fob her off and she wasn't going to take that from him of all people.

Helen headed to the back stairs, nearly knocking over Irene and Frank as she ran up and banged on Jeanette's door. 'I need to speak with you before you leave, please.' Her voice shook.

A confused Jeanette looked at her through the small glass window and opened the door. Before she could say anything, Helen began her rant.

'I'd like to make a formal complaint and I don't want this to be brushed under the carpet like everything else in this place seems to be.' Helen's blood boiled. 'Those beasts were in my garden and one of them...' She began to cry, overcome with emotions. '...One of those animals used my memorial statue as their ashtray.'

When Jeanette came towards her with a tissue, she snatched it out of her hand. 'Did you hear what I said? What are you going to do about it?' Helen stared at Jeanette, who was pulling out a chair. Jeanette placed her satchel on the floor and sat opposite the vacant seat.

'Have a seat, Mrs Burgess. I can see how upset you are and can assure you that we'll take your complaint seriously. Now, how do you know that it was someone from here that was in your garden?'

'Well...' Helen sniffed. 'It's obvious, isn't it? First the murder, then your dodgy staff...' She looked directly at Anwar who was standing in the doorway listening. 'They all smoke outside with those animals, all pally wally. It has to be someone from here.'

Jeanette looked at Anwar and shook her head. 'Why don't you go and make sure Frank and Irene are set for this evening. I think there's a keyworker due to arrive soon too. I'll deal with this…'

Helen saw the look of surprise on the deputy manager's face and felt a little smug. She knew exactly what he was like – his card was marked.

'And close the door behind you, please. Thanks, Anwar.' Jeanette turned back towards Helen. 'Right then. Do you have any evidence that one of the residents trespassed? I mean real evidence, not just a hunch.'

'Well… no, not exactly, but they left boot prints in the soil behind the statue. Can't you do a comparison of shoes or something? I know they can do those things; I've heard some of the police from that prolific team mentioning it when they've been here before…'

Jeanette's lip curled ever so slightly as if she was holding back a smile and Helen stiffened. *Is she mocking me?*

'Uh, no, we can't. You can always contact the police. In fact, you probably should. Haven't there been some garden shed burglaries recently? Did you check and see that you didn't actually have a break-in?'

Helen froze. She hadn't thought of that. She'd been so angry at the idea that someone had moved the statue, she hadn't considered that her home could have been burgled.

Had the back door been open when she had rushed out to check the statue? Did she unlock it?

Her head spun.

'You look a little confused, Mrs Burgess. Was anything

disturbed inside your home when you got in today?' Jeanette leaned forward. 'I'll make a note of your complaint and speak to my team. Ask them to remind the residents of the rules. Why don't you go home and check that everything is as it should be? I could come with you if you wait a moment. We can call the police if you suspect a break-in…'

Suddenly Helen felt foolish. She stood up and straightened her blouse. 'Just let me out. I'll deal with this myself.' Helen could tell that Jeanette was just trying to placate her.

She followed the manager to the reception door and as she pushed the release button at the side of the main exit out, she didn't even care when she shouted down the corridor at no one in particular, 'I know you're trying to scare me, but I have your card marked and you'll be behind bars soon enough!'

FORTY-TWO

Killer

S he almost deserves a standing ovation after that performance. It would have been even better if the door had slammed dramatically behind her, but she missed that trick because the special hinges prevent heavy slams. Shame really.

Looks like Helen Burgess has set the cat amongst the pigeons and that's a bit unsettling. Everyone will be eyeing each other with suspicion, including me.

So much drama now, and Danny Wells's murder is being pushed into the background. That suits me just fine. The less spotlight that fucker's given, the better. Though I can't become complacent as that idiot detective was sniffing around earlier. I don't rate him as an investigator – he seems to have drawn a blank on everything so far. Of course, I don't know for sure what he's found so maybe I shouldn't underestimate him.

For the time being, I'm playing the fool – just doing what I need to do to cover my tracks. Nothing in the newspapers or on the telly has me worried. I'll just bide my time a little longer and soon enough, I'll be out of this place. Once I am, no one will see or hear from me again. I'm not looking for glory or notoriety. I did what I needed to do for no one but myself. I'm a hero. I don't care if the police see it otherwise.

My hands won't stop fidgeting. I can't relax thinking the old biddy from next door might turn out to be more of a problem than I've anticipated. Old newspaper clippings I came across while doing some research screamed the fact she'd been dead against Ripley House opening because it 'places the community at risk'. She's not going to give up on this.

But something else is causing me more immediate concern. I overheard the detective outside mentioning that two people had been spotted and that he had some concerns. Is he talking about me? I'm pretty sure no one saw me.

I take a few deep breaths. I need to stay calm. Not draw any unwanted attention. I might be able to find out more from the lads, but will they trust me? I'll be able to speak more freely soon – I just need an excuse. But what?

I do a 360 and return my thoughts to nosy Mrs B from next door. It was me watching her when it got dark. Pottering around her house like she's Miss bloody Marple. But I didn't put any cigarettes out on her precious statue. So, who else has been there?

A Tannoy announcement from the Queen B herself makes me put a pause on those thoughts.

Damn it's loud!

I cover my ears while the system crackles.

'I'd like all staff and residents in the dining hall now, please. Anyone who doesn't show or refuses to attend will face sanctions.'

Sanctions? What the hell is she on about? The old system crackles again. A refurb which is probably unfit for purpose –

like most things at Ripley House – signifies the end of the communication.

I head with the crowd into the dining area. It's cramped and stuffy with everyone in there at once – the room isn't made for large numbers, which is why meals are split throughout the day. I walk to the back wall and open a window. My head is down but my ears are open.

'What da fuck's all this about?' one man grumbles.

'Always threatening us with warnings and recall. I was better off in prison. Treating us like fucking animals they are…' another calls out.

'Some of yous are fucking animals, beasts in fact…' The deep growl gets everyone's attention. 'Now shut yer geggy 'fore I shut it for ye.'

I hope Jeanette didn't hear that as it wouldn't go down well. I can't see her as I scan the faces. As if on cue, I look up at the doorway and there she is, hands on hips, skimming the faces through slitted eyes.

Her lips are moving but no sound is coming out – she's taking a head count.

'Before I leave this evening, I want to make something clear. There's been a complaint today about the smokers and an allegation of trespass. Because of this, I've made the decision after speaking to my line manager that there will be no smoking out in the back area after the final curfew check at 11pm each evening. Furthermore, all cigarette breaks in the evenings, after the 7pm curfew for some of you, will be done with a staff member present.'

I look around the room. Fists are clenched. Jaws have tightened. It's all going to kick off…

'You can't fucking do that! It's against our human rights!' one of the men shouts.

'We're not fucking kids, you know. This is bullshit,' another joins in.

It's then I notice the hand-held panic alarm in Jeanette's fist. She holds it up so everyone can see, her hand hovering over the red button – if pushed, it would have the police at the hostel in minutes.

'Watch the language and quiet down! We'll all be here much longer, and no one will be having a smoke break at all, if you don't listen. The police have been here once today already and if I have to call them out again, no one is going to be happy – especially me.'

A vein on Jeanette's neck pulsates. I move closer to the front of the room so I can see it better. This isn't a side of the manager that most people see. She's usually pretty calm, even in the tensest situations. What else is going on with her?

She catches me staring and I return my attention to the room.

'You couldn't smoke in prison and hostel property is an extension of that, so you should count yourself lucky. I could ban it completely, but no one wants that, do they?' She looks around the room again. 'That's what I thought.' Her lip quivers momentarily. She doesn't look too sure of herself, like she's realised that others might see a weakness and pounce.

'This is not a decision I make lightly, but smoking is a privilege, not a right. I'll review my decision in a few days and if new information comes to light that shows something else was at play, you could all be back smoking in the garden as normal. I can't be any fairer than that.' Her confidence is growing – I can see it in her eyes. 'Going forwards, the back door will be locked at 7pm and you will all need to speak to a member of staff if you want a smoking break. I would suggest you go in small groups as my team will be instructed on the number of escorted breaks allowed between 7 and 11pm. If for any reason staff are unavailable, you'll just have to wait. Are we clear?'

'This is utter bullshit! What about during the day?' someone grumbles behind me. I don't acknowledge them.

'Same rules – escort needed unless you are off the property. Any more questions?' It was more of a challenge than a genuine query from the hostel manager. 'Great. My head count earlier confirms you're all present and accounted for. She unfolds a sheet of paper that's been sticking out of her blazer pocket. 'Sign this sheet and pass it back to me.'

Once everyone has signed their understanding, Jeanette leaves the room, but I hang back with the others. This evening could be interesting. I pop my head out of the dining room entrance and see that Jeanette has left her satchel outside the main office door, thereby breaking her own rules of security – guess what's good for the goose is not always followed by the gander. I think about going over and having a rifle through it, but she suddenly appears, picks it up, shoves the curfew sign-in sheet through the opening in the Plexiglass window and leaves the building.

'The bitch gone?' Hot breath burns my neck and I rub it without looking back.

I nod.

'Fancy a fag?' The man roars with laughter then and soon the rest of the room join him.

This new development might be difficult to get around, but where there's a will, there's a way…

FORTY-THREE

Sloane

S loane's movements were sluggish by the time she finally arrived home. She paid the taxi driver, her legs feeling like weights as she got out the vehicle. She yawned and rubbed her eyes once inside the door. She still had a lot she wanted to do after speaking to a few of her sources earlier in the day. A smile crept over her face. It had not been a waste of her time as she had learned that Anwar Hussain was not the angel he appeared to be.

After she had sent her story to her editor, she'd bumped into the young man she'd been wanting to speak to for ages – the one who was with the group of users from the park. He'd told her, for a price, mind, that an acquaintance named Imran Hussain, brother of Anwar, had served some time in prison for possession of a Class A substance with the intent to sell. Although her source didn't want to provide a contact number for Imran initially, he did know roughly where Imran lived as he'd heard he'd been sofa surfing after falling out with his brother a few months back. Sloane had struck gold and after handing him a twenty-pound note, it didn't take long to get the mobile number from her source.

Sloane wanted as much information as she could gather as the police were holding a press conference tomorrow to update the locals on the murder investigation. She had a few questions for the detective, and she wanted to have all her facts straight before she pounced.

She punched Imran's number into her phone and made herself a coffee while she waited for someone to answer.

She was surprised when it was a female.

'Who's this?' The voice was curt and raspy.

'Uh… hi! My name is Sloane Armstrong. I'm an investigative journalist and wondered if I could speak with Imran Hussain?'

'What the fuck you want him for?' Sloane wondered if this was Imran's girlfriend – she seemed agitated.

'I just want to ask him a few questions about his brother, Anwar…'

'He's got nothing to—'

Sloane cut her off before she could finish her sentence or end the call. 'Tell him I'll pay for the information.'

The woman's tone changed. 'Oh yeah? How much? I know Anwar. I can help ya.' There seemed to be a scuffle and muffled voices as Sloane waited.

A man was on the phone now. 'I'm Imran. You said something about money?'

'Yes. I'm willing to pay for any information you can give me on your brother. I've heard a… few things about him, so anything you have could be useful…' She cringed. Had she been too forward? Even though she'd heard the brothers had fallen out, he might still be protective. *Blood is thicker than water after all…*

'I can tell you what I know, but it will cost you…'

Except when it's not.

Sloane straightened up. Drug habits won over family loyalty and even though a part of her felt bad about that, her story had to come first over her morals. 'I can give you £100.'

'Are you shitting me? I was thinking more like £500.'

Sloane wouldn't be able to explain that amount of expenditure, especially if it came to nothing. '£250 and that's my final offer.' She held her breath, hoping her decision to stand firm would pay off.

'Yeah, OK. So where do you want to meet?'

It had. She exhaled and looked at her watch. It was 8pm now and the light outside was disappearing fast. 'The Sleepy Hollow Pub – do you know it?' Sloane chose a pub that catered to all kinds. It wasn't the nicest of places but it was clean, cheap, and always full. She didn't want to be alone if Imran thought she had money on her.

'And how the fuck am I supposed to get there? Fly?' Sloane could hear the woman shouting in the background, telling him Sloane should come to the house.

That was never going to happen.

'Should cost no more than a tenner in a taxi. When you're five mins away, text this number and I'll pay. If it's more than a tenner, you're covering the rest so don't think you can make any stops along the way. I'll be there at 9pm. If you're not there by 9.15, me and my money are gone.'

'Bitch, you drive a hard bargain.' He sucked his teeth. 'Fine. 9pm. On. The. Dot. Will you be wearing a pink rose?' He laughed down the line at his own joke.

She ignored his reference to a date and ended the call. She wondered how Anwar would feel knowing that getting his brother to grass on him didn't take much at all.

She called and booked a taxi for 8.30, then grabbed an apple as she made sure she had everything she needed. She wasn't concerned that Imran would try anything in a public place but just to be on the safe side, she double-checked that her personal alarm was in her bag. It was something her editor had given to all the freelance investigative journalists on his team. She had sniggered at the time, but it could come in handy.

A horn beeped outside indicating that the taxi had arrived. She grabbed her things and was out the door still eating the apple, which only ignited her hunger. She'd grab a packet of crisps at the pub.

Sloane paid the driver and, realising it was just a few minutes before 9, and there was no text, she stood outside. No point going in only to have to come back out. Her phone pinged.

I see you, bitch.

She was going to have to teach this arsehole some manners. She looked up as the taxi pulled in and Imran stumbled out of the car.

Fuck's sake. Was he drunk, high, or both? He swayed as she paid the driver.

'Were you worried, b—?'

Sloane turned sharply and squared up to Imran. 'If you call me *bitch* one more time, we're going to have a problem.'

He backed away, hands up and laughing. 'OK. OK. I'll just call you *miss*.'

Sloane wasn't going to give him the satisfaction. 'Glad we're on the same page. C'mon then. I don't have all night.'

'Whoa. Where's my money?'

'Imran. You don't really think I'm going to give you the money before I get my information? Did you drop off your girlfriend down the road? Think you'd get the money and then be off? I'm not an idiot and you'd do well to remember that.'

He sneered. Sloane had clocked his game and he put a hand up in the air, waving at some trees just down the road. Within two mins, a thin, dark-eyed blonde girl was at his side, out of breath and desperate for something, if the way her body shook was anything to go by.

'What the fuck, Im?' The woman leaned against her boyfriend.

'Get off me, bitch. She's sussed us.' He looked at Sloane. 'So, we gonna do this or what? As you can see, we've other places we need to be.'

Sloane pursed her lips. They'd have the money spent within minutes of her handing it over. She walked into the pub with the two junkies at her heels. 'Grab a booth and I'll get some drinks.'

'I'll have a vodka and tonic and he'll have a pint.' The woman came to life then at the thought of a free drink. 'Keep 'em coming, and we'll tell you more than you need.'

She had no intention of buying either of them alcohol or she'd be there all night, listening to gibberish, and broke. She ordered three large lemonades with ice and a few packets of crisps. The barman said he'd bring them over and she paid. She headed to the booth and sat opposite the pair who had been whispering amongst themselves.

'Let's get started then. I can see the family resemblance.' Imran was almost identical to Anwar – if it wasn't for the sunken eyes and thinner body frame, Sloane would have guessed they were twins.

'Lemme see the money first.' He tapped the table in front of him.

Sloane reached into her bag and pulled out an envelope. She'd cleared it with Conrad before using her own money and he assured her she'd be reimbursed if the story came through. Although her parents came from money, after her sister had died, they had received a large pay-out once they sued the prison service for the wrongful release of her sister's killer. Seems they had confused him with another inmate who shared the same date of birth and the same last name. Incompetent twats. Her sister had also taken out a life assurance policy and unbeknownst to her, had named Sloane as the beneficiary. Her parents had put the money in a trust for Sloane – she would never have to worry about money. She opened the packet and let him see it, before shoving it back into her bag. 'Once I have the info, you'll have the envelope.'

The barman arrived with their drinks and snacks. He looked at Sloane and then at the pair opposite. 'If there's any trouble, you're all out of here. I'll be watching from the bar.'

Sloane nodded.

'He's a wanker. I was barred for two weeks once. Said I caused a fight. Wasn't me though.'

'Course not.' Sloane took a sip of her lemonade and hid a smile as she saw the look on both their faces once they realised there was no alcohol in the pint glasses.

The girl reached into her pocket. 'Lucky I brought my own then.' She glanced towards the bar and when the blonde saw the barman wasn't looking, dumped the contents into the two glasses.

'I've heard some rumours about your brother. Seems he's

been seen associating with some undesirables and selling them gear. What can you tell me about that?'

Imran leaned forward. 'That's nothing. Did you know…?'

Sloane took out her notebook and couldn't write fast enough to keep up with the information that Imran was sharing. He really must not like his brother, and when Sloane was finished with him, not many other people would either.

But it was the last thing that Imran said before she handed over the wad of cash that had her heart racing, and if it was true, Anwar might be more than a drug-dealing probation officer.

He could be a murderer.

FORTY-FOUR

Jeanette

Her body ached when she arrived home that evening; her feet were throbbing and her shoulders were tight. She felt older than her forty-two years. Her flat felt void, the minimalist decor reminding her of how little she had outside of work. Jeanette had been doing longer and longer hours at the hostel, which wasn't unusual given the circumstances, but it made her weary all the same. Her home, where the merest sound echoed off the walls, added to her feeling of unease. Everything just felt... cold.

It's just what's happening that's making me feel this way. When things were running smoothly, Jeanette had always found her home gave off peaceful vibes – it was why she liked it. Food and some chill time would alleviate some of the anxiety. She just needed to keep to her routine. Her brother often mocked her for being so stuck in her ways, but there was no place for chaos in her home or professional life.

After she ate some dinner, Jeanette ran a bath and as she submerged her body into the hot, bubbly water, the heat relaxed her immediately.

Earlier, her line manager had been in touch to advise that the police would be releasing more information to the public shortly and this could have a negative effect on the hostel. She wondered what world her manager was living in. The hostel had always been portrayed in a bad light by the press – no one liked having murderers and rapists on their doorstep. Jeanette was often frustrated by the public perception of probation and approved premises. Rehabilitation and risk management were important, in her opinion, as the offenders would eventually be released and surely it was far better to have them monitored and offered support as they eased back into society rather than allow them to return to the same cycle of offending. Bloody Sloane Armstrong didn't help. She'd heard about Sloane's sister being murdered, so she did sympathise with her, but she couldn't help feeling that if Sloane looked at the bigger picture, she'd realise that life isn't black and white.

Then there were the internal probation investigations and, as far as Jeanette could tell, although there were times that some of her staff members were cutting corners to save time, nothing in the records indicated that they could have known or predicted that a murder would take place on the premises. They'd have to be mind-readers to have foreseen that, not risk assessors.

Jeanette closed her eyes as the hot water caressed her skin. There was, however, one concerning outcome her manager had relayed which stuck in her mind. It seemed the higher-ups believed that, had protocol been followed on the evening that Danny Wells was murdered, the incident might not have occurred. On this basis, the board undertaking the internal investigation were recommending that with immediate effect Frank Brown and Irene Watkins were to be given a formal warning that would remain on their records for two years. Her line manager had also hinted that Jeanette could face consequences but had failed to specify what those were. This had infuriated her. Her team members would have a right to appeal but Jeanette suspected neither would, as no matter how she looked at it, they were blatantly in the wrong. There was just no excuse other than one of them needing medical attention that could explain why they had failed to follow the proper procedures.

As stressful as the in-house investigations were though, it was her deputy manager's recent behaviour that was niggling away at her. There was so much about him that she didn't know, and he wasn't being forthcoming.

When it came down to it, what did she really know about anyone in that hostel, other than what they told her…?

Her head throbbed and she slid deep under the warm water, letting it roll over her body in small waves. The heat soothed not only her aching head, but also her tired bones.

Had she made an error of judgment in backing Anwar in the past, when concerns had been expressed about his lack of concentration on the job? She had confronted him, and he had told her that personal problems at home were the cause – and she hadn't delved deeper to find out more. He'd even improved after their little chat. There had been no issue in any other placement, bar some concerns about his temper that had apparently been addressed, but the rumours that were crawling out of the woodwork now… Perhaps he had fooled everyone. She didn't even want to think about what would happen if that journalist somehow found out.

The probation senior managers knew that Anwar's brother had previous convictions for burglaries and substance misuse, but Imran Hussain's case files were Limited Access Only

(LAO), and Anwar had never protested or asked to view the files.

When Jeanette learned today from her manager that Imran had recently been staying at Anwar's home and that this was the cause of the friction with his wife, she had been taken aback as he should have informed her immediately. She felt like a fool when she couldn't explain this to her manager. What was Anwar hiding?

Looking back now, she realised that only two weeks prior to the murder they'd all had to have their security access reviewed for ViSOR, the Violent and Sex Offender Register database, and now Jeanette was questioning what information he'd disclosed. She'd pass this on to the board and let them investigate rather than look into it herself – otherwise she might be accused of tampering. All access to ViSOR was strictly monitored.

The more she thought about it, the more it worried her. She felt like everything was spiralling out of control at the moment. With Helen Burgess's outburst earlier that afternoon, things just seemed to be going from bad to worse. Could anything else go wrong? She didn't want to tempt fate.

Jeanette looked at her hands – her fingertips were prune-like, and she realised she'd been soaking a lot longer than she'd thought. She reluctantly got out of the tub and, once dressed in her pj's and a fluffy robe, plonked herself on the couch to tune in to the news.

As much as she wanted to think about something else, her mind replayed the morning she got the call about Danny Wells. Frank and Irene had both been frantic, and now it all made sense. Their laziness was about to be discovered. What she couldn't understand was why so many of the internal CCTV cameras had been defective. It was Anwar's job to log the issue, but he hadn't. Had this been intentional? This may be what her line manager wanted to discuss with her. Jeanette sighed.

Had Anwar shared the details of the defective cameras with a resident? Was Frank turning a blind eye? Was Irene favouring some of the men?

Her thoughts were interrupted then. Something – or more importantly some*one* – had caught her eye on the telly and caused her to almost bolt out of her seat. She searched around for the remote and turned up the volume.

'*Police have advised that Mr Anwar Hussain may be a person of interest in the recent murder of convicted killer Danny Wells. Mr Hussain was taken into custody at 8pm this evening to answer questions after an apparent anonymous tip to the police about Hussain's alleged involvement in dealing drugs.*'

Jeanette stared at the screen with her mouth open.

'*According to our sources, the probation officer is in crippling debt and on the verge of losing his family home. He has allegedly been dealing for the last eight months and his employers were not aware—*'

Jeanette flinched when the shrill ringtone of her mobile blasted on the table in front of her. When she saw the deputy director of probation's number on the screen, she was tempted to just ignore it. It was after-hours, and she was not on call.

She hit *answer* instead.

The anger in his tone reverberated down the line and she held the device away from her ear as she replied to his shouty comments. 'Yes, I'm just watching the news now. I wasn't aware of his arrest… or the allegations of dealing.'

His accusatory tone was making Jeanette defensive. Deep down she had to admit that it would make sense if he had become mixed up with dealing, especially after everything that she'd learned recently.

'With all due respect, sir, I wasn't the one to sign off on his application, so this doesn't fall solely on my shoulders.' Jeanette might be a lot of things, but she wouldn't be anyone's scapegoat.

He berated her some more and then ended the call with 'Be at head office tomorrow morning – 8am sharp!'

Jeanette stared at the phone for a few moments while everything sunk in. If she thought things were bad before, this was only scratching the surface of what lay ahead.

FORTY-FIVE

Helen

'H mmph. Why won't you answer your phone?'

Helen paced around her living room. Maybe Sloane had already seen the news and was too busy to chat. Did Sloane think she was she becoming a burden? She had been spending more time in the young woman's life – maybe Sloane was too polite to tell her. No, Helen shook her head, Sloane was anything but polite.

From the moment she'd seen that probation officer scarper as soon as the detective arrived at the hostel, Helen had known there was something dodgy happening. He'd made it too obvious. She momentarily regretted thinking of the detective as ineffective until she remembered that she'd been the one to alert them of the probation officer's strange behaviour. *Maybe they'll pay more attention to me now!*

Helen tried the journalist's number one last time and when it went straight to answerphone, she left a message.

'Have you seen the news? That Hussain fellow from the hostel has been arrested. This is exactly the break we need to get Ripley House shut down for good.' She couldn't help the squeal of excitement that escaped from her lips. 'I don't think I'll get any sleep tonight – call me!'

After ending the call, she placed her phone in her cardigan pocket and made her way to the kitchen. A nice cuppa and something to munch would do the trick.

Helen wasn't the most tech savvy, but her Malcolm had enjoyed browsing the internet and, not long before he died, he'd taught her the basics on the iPad he'd treated himself to. She'd initially thought Malcolm was going through a late mid-life crisis – her feeling was that it was a waste of money for such a small gadget. That was before she'd found some of those game apps and instantly became addicted to *Case Files* – a game that allowed her to catch a killer. It was almost as if the game was coming to life. She fetched the device from the cabinet and sat down at the kitchen table, trying to see if she could find out anything more from that goggles place.

A breeze from the kitchen window sent a chill down her spine. She pulled her cardigan around her. When the window was suddenly blown off the hook and started banging against the frame, Helen went over to close it.

That was when she saw the figure standing right behind Malcolm's angel. She waved her hands. 'Get out of there or I'm calling the police!' She should have called them after the last incident, and chastised herself for not doing so.

Helen pulled her phone out of her pocket and tapped it against the glass. 'Did you hear what I said? I'll ring the police.' Fat lot they would do though…

It was too dark to make out who the person was or what they were doing other than staring directly at her. She had no doubt it was one of the scrotes from next door and wished she had spent the money on a motion sensor light for her garden. She wouldn't be intimidated in her own home though. She flung her slippers off and pulled on her wellies. She could hear Malcolm in her head. *'Don't do anything foolish. Just call the police and let them handle things. You're not as young as you think you are…'*

'Oh button it, Mal!' He was always having his say. Not this time. Where were the police when Mal had had his heart attack? When those nuisances would hang around out front, blatantly dealing their dirty drugs? No, Helen would handle this herself. She looked around for something to use as a weapon but all she could find was her brolly. Everything else of use was in the shed… at the bottom of the garden.

She wrapped her hand tightly around the brolly and flung open the door, stomping her way down the path and then stopped dead in her tracks, facing the intruder, ready to protect herself and her property.

'What are you doing here?' Helen noted the man had a scarf wrapped around his mouth.

'I thought I saw something. Wanted to check it out. Didn't think there was any reason to disturb you…'

She didn't recognise the voice but there was something familiar about the person in front of her.

'That doesn't make any sense. I'm calling the police – you're trespassing.'

The figure stepped closer. 'Don't do that. This is all a misunderstanding…'

Helen stepped back but stumbled over one of the wobbly paving stones, dropping the umbrella as she fell. The figure stood over her as she tried to get herself up. A hand came out. Helen reluctantly took it – all the while ignoring the nagging voice of her dead husband warning her not to trust this person.

As she was pulled up, she gasped when she felt her arm

being twisted and jerked behind her. 'Ow! What are you—?' The intruder didn't let her finish.

'Not one word. Walk quietly back into your house.' She flinched as the cold whisper hit her eardrum

'I will no— Ow! OK, OK. I'm doing what you've asked.'

'Shut your mouth and walk.'

Helen's lips tightened as she felt something sharp pressed against her back. 'There's no need to be so rough.'

The person ignored her pleas, and she was pushed back inside her house.

'I need strong tape. Where can I find that?' Helen watched the knife waving recklessly in front of her face. It crossed her mind that they mustn't want to actually kill her, or they would have come prepared. For a moment she felt hopeful that once they'd got whatever it was they came for, they would let her go. That thought was quickly wiped from her mind after what happened next.

Helen gasped when the scarf that covered the intruder's face fell, and she recognised them. How could she have been so wrong? Her hand shook as she pointed to a drawer next to the sink.

'In there.'

Moments later her hands were taped behind her, and a large piece of silver gaffer tape was crudely placed over her mouth.

She knew that if she didn't do something to save herself, she'd be the next one dead. If she could get upstairs, to her bedroom, and somehow lock the door, she could call the police from the landline in there. When the intruder had their back turned, Helen made her move.

It was the wrong move though, as the person quickly realised what she had been thinking and raced after her. She'd only made it halfway up the stairs when something tugged on her cardigan and pulled her back. She had no way to stop the fall and felt a sharp pain as the bone in her arm cracked. Helen hit her head hard against the marble tiles. She'd told Malcolm those tiles would be the death of her.

Looked like she had been right all along.

FORTY-SIX

Sloane

S loane was pushing herself out of the booth with the intention of leaving the pub and the two timewasters sitting with her when her phone alert went off. She had flagged certain keywords in Google, so she never missed a potential story.

Her eyes glanced over to Imran Hussain, furious when she saw the smirk on his face – like he knew something that no one else in the room was privy to. 'You knew about this?' She shoved her phone in his face, pointing at the screen with the headline that told of Anwar's arrest.

'Get that phone outta my face before I break it.' He shoved her hand away. 'What if I did know? Doesn't make any difference to what I told you though.' He patted the pocket where he'd stuffed the money Sloane had given him.

Yeah. No difference except anything I write now is completely useless.

Sloane resisted the urge to snatch the money back, but she didn't fancy taking on Imran's girlfriend. The woman was scrawny, but Sloane could tell she had a vicious streak, and the background checks she had run before meeting the pair confirmed that.

'Never mind.' Looking down at her phone, she saw that Helen had called a few times and a voicemail had been left. Helen had probably seen the news too. Sloane left Imran and his girlfriend at the table and went outside to call a taxi. When it arrived ten minutes later, she gave the driver her address and sat back in the seat, shaking her head at the time she'd just wasted.

Sloane dialled her friend and was surprised when Helen didn't answer, given her message. She then recalled the last time this had happened, and she had panicked unnecessarily. Helen had taken a sleeping pill and just missed her call. But something niggled at the journalist. Helen had called three times and left a very excitable message in which she'd made it clear that she probably wouldn't get any sleep. Not something a woman who was going to take a sleeping pill would say.

As the taxi was passing Ripley Avenue, Sloane made a snap decision and asked the driver to pull over and let her out. She paid him and walked down the road towards Helen's house. Her eyes drifted over to Ripley House. Every time she walked past the house, goosebumps formed. It was creepy, even though it had a perfectly edged lawn, it was like everything on the outside was beautiful but as you got closer and closer to the building, you saw the cracks – and the people inside were much the same.

Outside Helen's place, Sloane noticed the curtains in the front room were open and a light was on. Helen was nosy, no doubt about that, but she didn't like it when others could see in to her home. It always made Sloane laugh when she said that – only now, it made her worry.

Sloane walked up to the front door and knocked. Putting

her ear to the door, she didn't hear any movement. She knocked again, this time a little harder, and then walked over to the front window. She didn't see anything out of the ordinary when she stood on her tiptoes and peeked in. She kicked herself for leaving the spare key Helen had given her in her office at home.

She pulled her mobile out and rang Helen once more. She could hear the woman's phone ringing... only it wasn't coming from inside. It sounded as if it was coming from the garden. Sloane ran to the side of the house and listened. Yes, there was the ringtone, but no answer from Helen. She pushed the gate, but it was locked from the other side.

'Helen? Are you back there?' Maybe the elderly lady had fallen asleep in one of those big deckchairs she had on her back patio. 'Helen!'

A feeling of unease swept over her. She dragged one of the wheelie bins against the gate. It was unsteady but she managed to get on top and vault over to the other side. She landed awkwardly and sucked air between her teeth as a pain shot up her right leg. 'Fuck's sake.' She rubbed her ankle and stood. It was a little sore, but she could still walk on it.

'Helen? Are you out here?'

The mobile had stopped ringing, so Sloane dialled it again when she saw the chairs were empty. The ringtone blared once more, and she saw the light from the screen near the bottom of the garden.

'What in the world?' She walked across the grass and picked up the mobile phone, along with the umbrella she spotted a few inches away. Helen must have dropped it. She often came out to talk to the angel statue. Sloane headed towards the back door and knocked. 'I've found your phone. Are you in there?'

When there was still no answer, Sloane tried the handle and was surprised to find it open.

'I'm coming in, Helen…' She didn't want to scare the woman if she was just napping.

The kitchen lights were off, so Sloane flicked the switch by the back door. She saw that a chair was overturned but everything else looked to be in its place.

Sloane walked through the kitchen into the living room – nothing unusual in here either. As if on auto-pilot, she pulled the curtains closed, knowing Helen would be mortified if she thought people could see in.

Sloane looked around the room for a sign of what Helen had been doing. Knitting needles were on the coffee table with no yarn. Perhaps she had gone upstairs? 'Helen? Are you upstairs? Your back door was open…' There was no reply.

Sloane walked over to the door and turned the handle. It was stuck. She jiggled the brass doorknob and yanked it hard. The door hit her shoulder and she paused to rub it before reaching around to feel for the light on the wall.

'Hel—' Sloane couldn't finish the sentence. Instead, she covered her mouth to stifle the scream when she saw the blood drops on the marble tiles.

Helen lay on her back, eyes wide open.

Staring at the ceiling.

One of her arms was tucked awkwardly underneath her body and one of her legs was twisted at a funny angle.

Sloane snapped out of the shock that had momentarily stopped her dead in her tracks and dialled 999.

'I need an ambulance,' she stuttered. 'I've found my friend on the floor. I think she may have fallen down the stairs.'

'Is she breathing?' The call handler was calm, and her voice helped Sloane focus.

Sloane walked closer to Helen and noticed the milky whiteness of her once green eyes. Her lips had turned a pale shade of blue.

'I think she may be... dead.'

It took less than ten minutes for the police and ambulance to arrive. An officer took Sloane into the front room as the paramedics confirmed what she already knew. Helen Burgess was deceased.

The world around her became muffled and blurry. She had to brace herself as dizzy spells came and went. She thought she overheard them mention that a sticky substance could be seen around Helen's mouth and there was a slight redness on her wrists; a reference to white fibres on her hand. The officer in the room with her tapped her knee.

'Was that the way you found Mrs Burgess?'

'Uh... yes. I couldn't touch her.' Sloane bit her lip. 'She must have fallen down the stairs. How long had she been there?' A wave of emotions overtook her just then and she began to cry. 'Sorry.' Sloane reached into her bag, pulled out a tissue, and after drying her eyes she blew her nose. 'I guess I'm still in a bit of shock...'

'That's understandable, Miss Armstrong. Can I ask how you got into the property? Do you have a spare key?' The officer inquired.

'I do, but not on me. I actually tried calling her earlier.' Sloane pulled Helen's phone out of her pocket and handed it to the officer. 'I found this out back, next to an umbrella. When I got no response from knocking and calling out her name, I came through the back door . It was... unlocked.' Sloane cocked her head.

'What is it?' The officer leaned forward.

'Helen is... *was* super OCD about security. If she had dropped these things and then come back inside without realising, she would've locked the back door behind her... and...' Sloane paused.

The officer's foot quietly tapped the floor.

'A chair was toppled over in the kitchen...' A cold breeze hit Sloane and she shuddered. 'Something must have happened. A stroke, maybe... I can't believe she died alone...'

FORTY-SEVEN

Jeanette

A ll eyes were on Jeanette as the deputy director of probation read out a series of failures he perceived to be happening at Ripley House. Failures he claimed should have been identified and prevented. It was easy for him to point the finger when the last time he had worked at an operational level, dinosaurs were roaming the earth. His face reddened as he pointed out that under Jeanette's management, the hostel had brought 'Probation's good name into disrepute'.

Jeanette had taken everything thrown at her that morning with a professional attitude until he had said that last sentence.

She slammed her hands on the table and stood.

'With all due respect, a series of failures may be correct, but they started from the top down…' She paused to let that sink in, her eyes never leaving the director. Her body tensed. She had never been so defiant, but she felt strangely empowered as she continued, 'Surely even you can see that there are others who are at least partially responsible for all the scrutiny directed at the hostel and at probation?' She took a deep breath before her next tirade of words. 'That being said, there was no way anyone could have predicted Danny Wells's murder. No way could I have known that my deputy manager was *allegedly* dealing drugs, because at the moment that's all it is – an allegation. I will get to the bottom of this and cooperate fully with any and all investigations, but I will not be used as a fall guy when *you* all' – she glared around the room – 'were told time and again about the problems we had with security; you and other board members hired my deputy manager for the post and when I raised concerns because of his brother's convictions, they were dismissed. Every concern I raised was ignored, and you'd better believe I logged each and every one. I follow my own advice: if it's not logged, it didn't happen. I made a record of every concern of mine that was reported and ignored so that nothing can be brushed under any carpet.'

Her body shook with fury. Her colleagues were speechless, wide-eyed, their mouths gaping open. Up until now she had been second-guessing herself and the work she did, but not anymore. She was a good probation officer, a good manager, and there was no way the buck would stop with her.

'Ms Macey! That's enough. I think you should take some time to calm down. Your outburst is totally inappropriate and unprofessional. I suggest you get back to the hostel and make sure nothing else happens while we discuss and decide what the next steps are… for the hostel and for you.'

Jeanette grabbed her satchel and stormed out of the room. She'd probably be given a warning for insubordination or maybe even sacked – but how bloody dare they!

The receptionist looked at her, her shoulders slumped and her eyes full of sympathy. 'Would you like a coffee?'

Jeanette felt like screaming but the receptionist was only being nice; she'd probably heard every word and suddenly Jeanette felt slightly embarrassed.

'No, thank you. I'd best get back to work.'

When Jeanette pulled into the drive at Ripley House, her eyes were focused on Helen Burgess's home. The area had been sealed off with police tape and officers were at the property. It felt like déjà vu. Jeanette rubbed her arms, goosebumps forming despite every effort to stop them.

She parked in her usual spot and jogged up the back stairs, using her pass to let herself in via the staff entrance at the side of the building.

'What happened next door?' she asked. Her team were huddled together, talking amongst themselves, but they jumped when they heard her voice and scarpered back to their own desks, all talking at once.

Jeanette raised a hand.

'One at a time please. My head is already pounding – someone please explain what's going on next door.'

'It's Helen – from the kitchen. Apparently she fell down her stairs sometime last night. She's dead – or at least that's what we think. Police were round here asking a load of questions. We tried calling you, but it kept going to voicemail,' Steph rattled off.

Jeanette pulled out her phone and saw eight missed calls. 'Oh my God! Poor Helen.' She may not have liked the woman very much, but she'd never wanted any harm to come to her. 'Did anyone see anything?'

'I don't think so. Before Irene and Frank left, they said everything had been quiet. Even the residents – no one even kicked off about the smoking rules. Everything seemed… normal. Then they heard the sirens coming down the road.

Apparently Irene did a check in the back garden – she said she thought she'd heard some banging about next door but when she looked over the fence, she didn't see anything that would cause any alarm. They've both sent you an email and logged the incident. Just in case…'

Well, at least there was that. Finally they were taking notice, even if it was just to cover their own backs.

'That detective wants to speak to you though.' Steph held up a message.

Jeanette nodded. She'd expected that to be the case. 'OK, no more gossiping about this; you've all got plenty of assessments to catch up on.' She started to walk towards the stairs leading to her office.

'Uh… Jeanette?' Amy hollered after her.

She turned.

'We all saw the news. Will Anwar be in today?' Amy looked around the room, asking the question that others dared not.

For the briefest of moments, she had forgotten about *that* situation – must be all the buzz about next door. 'I don't think so. I'll update you with what I can, *when* I can. You can send any countersigning my way for the time being or to whoever is on office duty today. If you could all pitch in and cover any of Anwar's priority work or raise it with me that would be helpful.' Worst case scenario, she'd need to see if she could find some cover from one of the field offices – the hostel was already short-staffed, and Jeanette was worried she wouldn't be able to deal with everything going on without another manager to assist. She'd cross that bridge when she came to it; having someone new at the hostel might only add to the unease.

'But—'

'But nothing. I don't want to be disturbed for the next two hours unless it's an emergency.' Jeanette ignored the grumbles as she entered her office and shut the door behind her. She leaned against it as she took a moment to decide what needed addressing first.

Call the detective.

She could kill two birds with one stone – he might be able to update her on what was going on with her deputy manager as well as Helen Burgess.

Jeanette sat down and dialled the number.

'Brady here.'

'Hi. It's Jeanette Macey. My colleagues said you needed to speak with me?' She was short but polite.

'I do. Do you have time now? I'm next door.'

Jeanette sighed. Best to get it over with and then she could focus on the rest of the tasks she had to complete before the day ended. 'Yeah. I'll see you shortly.'

Her colleagues would show the detective in. Jeanette wanted to read what Frank and Irene had already told the police. She didn't want to be caught off-guard.

Logging in to her computer, she opened her emails and her jaw dropped.

She wasn't expecting that…

FORTY-EIGHT

Sloane

Sloane's neck ached. She stretched out on her couch, not remembering getting home – an officer had taken her despite her protestations. She'd obviously been in shock and more tired than she'd realised – there was a cold cup of coffee on the table and she was still dressed.

She picked up the mug and got rid of the contents down the sink before giving it a rinse and making a fresh cup.

She couldn't believe Helen was dead. Although it was likely an accident, from what she had witnessed, for a moment she wondered if it had been connected to the threats. Warned off of trying to search for Danny Wells's killer, the police hadn't taken them seriously when the pair reported the messages, but it seemed they might now. She didn't want to believe it was foul play.

Sloane grabbed a piece of paper and a pen. She wanted to note down everything she had overheard last night at Helen's. She shivered as the image of Helen being taken out of the property in the black bag snuck into her head.

Sloane wondered if her ex, Noah, would help. It had been

months since they last spoke. He'd wanted something more serious, and Sloane hadn't been prepared to commit. He was a nice guy but could be a little too clingy. She wondered how he would feel about meeting for a coffee.

Only one way to find out.

She scrolled through her numbers and called.

When she heard his voice, her heart skipped a beat for the briefest of moments and she was taken aback slightly. She hadn't expected that.

'Hi, Noah. It's Sloane.' She paused. She hoped he wasn't going to hang up on her.

'Oh hey. What a surprise! Been a while. I actually thought I'd never hear from you again after… well, you know.'

Sloane did know. The last time she'd seen him had been awful. He'd been pushing for her to move in with him and they'd argued. Sloane had said some terrible things. She could still picture the crushed look on his face.

'I know. About that… I'm really sorry. I just felt—'

'I know. I know. I pushed too hard. I'm over it.' And he did sound completely over it. Why did that bother her?

'How have you been?'

'Great actually. I got promoted – I'm a sarge now. Finally got my own place too so no more house full of smelly guys…'

'Congratulations!' She was genuinely pleased for him. He had worked very hard to get a promotion and had been devastated when he'd passed the sergeant's exam but there had been no vacancies. 'I wondered if you fancied meeting up for a coffee… or a drink? Whatever suits you?'

'Oh, I'm seeing someone now, Sloane. I'm flattered but…' An awkward silence followed.

A tinge of anger washed over her. Did he think she was calling to get back together? She'd meant what she'd said months ago: a relationship wasn't on the cards for her. She bit her tongue and held back what she had wanted to say. 'I meant just as friends. You were always a good friend to me and I…' She inwardly cringed before she said the words, 'I miss that.' Would he see through her?

Noah laughed down the line. 'My bad. I thought… well… yeah, I'd love to get a coffee. You can catch me up on everything that's been happening. I still read your articles. You're really growing as a writer – you should write a book.'

He was backtracking now. Trying to hide his embarrassment, she suspected.

'Thanks! How about 2pm? Will you be free?' Sloane checked her watch. Plenty of time to clean herself up and try to hide the bags under her eyes.

'I'm off all day today, so that's perfect. Usual place?'

'Sure. I'll see you then!'

Sloane hung up the phone and jumped in the shower.

Part of her felt bad for what she was about to do but sometimes the ends justified the means.

FORTY-NINE

Jeanette

J eanette couldn't comprehend why she'd been sent the email. She stared at the sender's email address – it was obvious it was bogus – but she had no idea what the actual message meant.

Only Danny was supposed to die. It needs to stop.

What needed to stop? The killings? The person doing it? The police investigation? Who else had died? Was this a confession?

'You're as white as a ghost. What's the matter?' DS Brady stepped into her office, concern etched in the frown lines that were consuming his forehead.

'I'm fine.' Jeanette forced a smile. She felt a little dizzy and she rubbed her head.

'You got a bug or something?' The detective was about to sit down but Jeanette waved him over.

'Look at this.' The date and time indicated it was sent at

11pm last night. Jeanette pointed at the screen. 'What do you think it means?'

She watched as the detective scanned the email. His breath stank of stale cigarettes, and she pulled her chair back to get out of the way of the offensive odour. He didn't seem to notice... or care.

'Looks like the killer's made contact with you. This the first time?' There was an accusatory tone in his question and Jeanette held down the urge to bite back. She'd had enough arguments that day already, and knew which battles were worth fighting.

'Of course it is – I would have told you otherwise. Do you think they're referring to...?' She gestured with her thumb, pointing in the direction of Helen's house. 'She fell down the stairs, right? Did you find anything about the hostel in her house?'

'I can't disclose information pertaining to an ongoing investigation...' He was fobbing her off. 'So you haven't had any threatening, cryptic emails or texts since Danny was murdered?'

'No. Are you saying Helen did?' Jeanette watched as the detective's face reddened. His normally stony grimace was gone, and she was surprised he'd let his guard down. She'd hit a nerve.

'Look. I shouldn't be telling you any of this but if you're now receiving messages, you may be a potential target. Have you voiced any thoughts to or while around others that might lead them to believe you know something more than you do about Wells's murder?'

Jeanette racked her brains. She couldn't think of anything she might have said that would give others the impression that she knew more than anyone else did. 'No.'

'Well, your neighbour seems to have. Between us, it looks like Helen's death wasn't an accident, though that's not how we're going to be playing it to the public for now. We'll know more after the autopsy, but her death is being treated as suspicious. She'd received some texts kinda like that email there, but more threatening in tone. Might be that she and her sidekick, Ms Armstrong, are better sleuths than I gave them credit for – or they're stirring the hornet's nest without even realising. I haven't decided which just yet. They've touched on something sensitive – of that I'm sure. I'll be speaking to Ms Armstrong at some point today if she bothers to return my bloody calls. If these deaths are related, it looks like your deputy manager is off the hook...'

That got Jeanette's attention. 'What? You think Anwar was involved in killing Danny Wells? He wasn't even here that night...'

'We can't be sure. When he was arrested, his mobile phone and CCTV placed him in the vicinity, not too far from here. Turns out he was making a quick but monetarily beneficial drug deal before returning to a family event. His alibi seems solid. He couldn't be in two places at the same time – and other than possibly being snitched on for dealing – there's no convincing motive. He's not off the hook completely in my opinion, but he was in the cells when Helen was murdered, so if the two are connected, he's not in the frame. But maybe he wasn't acting on his own.'

'You think you know someone...' she mumbled. Jeanette felt a headache coming on and rubbed her temples to ease the tension.

'He'll be bailed soon to appear in court. We've charged him with possession with intent to supply. He had some weed and a few pills on his person when arrested – not prescribed to him and in baggies. He didn't even argue or deny anything. Just accepted it...'

'Well, that's his career down the drain.' Jeanette couldn't believe he'd thrown away a good stable income and pension for a little extra illegal income that probably didn't even put a dent in his debts – and may even have added to them.

'Shame, eh? His case is being transferred to the Disruption Team – it's a new police team set up across areas to *disrupt* criminal activity and protect those who are being exploited... clever, eh? Anyway, they'll probably be in contact to speak to your staff and the residents. Your deputy may have been dealing to them or getting his drugs from them. That's really all I know at the moment.' He gave her a look that made her warm to him a bit. She could see that he was genuinely sorry to have had to tell her all this about a member of staff she had trusted.

'I appreciate the info, detective.'

'Kurt. Call me Kurt. I think we're well beyond the formalities now, Jeanette.'

She nodded. 'What happens next?'

'I'm going to get one of the tech guys out here to take a look at those emails. I doubt they'll be able to get anything but it's worth a shot.'

Jeanette raised her brow. 'I'm impressed – you seem to know a lot about that stuff.'

'I did some time in the cyber-crime unit – learned a thing or two.' He smiled. 'Do you have anywhere you can stay this evening? The email seems more like a cry for help than a threat to life, but I think you need to be extra vigilant. At least until we know more...'

'I can stay at my brother's. I'll give him a bell and make the arrangements. It'll be fine…' Her own flat was beginning to add to her paranoia and a change of scenery might be just what she needed.

'Great. If you could text me those details, I'll make sure we have eyes patrolling when we can. My officers have already spoken to everyone here about the incident next door and nothing out of the ordinary seems to have been flagged.'

'You've just reminded me – Frank and Irene have sent me a statement. We'll see what it says. It'll save you having to come back if there's anything not reported.' Jeanette opened the email and scanned the contents. She shook her head. 'You're right – nothing out of the ordinary. Curfew check – no issues. Everyone was indoors and accounted for. Blocked toilet that Frank sorted out. Keyworker session, two hours – no incidents. Irene did a check of the back garden and other than a bit of banging from Helen's which turned out to be nothing – that's it. Then it talks about your lot coming around to speak – '

'Back up a moment. Why was Irene doing a check outside?' He pulled out his notes and scrambled through the pages. 'She never mentioned that. Who else was on duty last night?'

'Frank, Irene, and the two group workers were here until 9pm. We had an evening group – General Offending Behaviour – which the residents must attend.'

'GOB… that's some acronym! Sorry, please continue.' He jotted down some notes.

'Yeah, we've had some interesting acronyms – uh, not really the time to discuss them, is it. Helen was here earlier that day claiming that a resident had allegedly broken into her back garden and stubbed a cigarette out on some angel statue? She made a big scene as she was leaving as well. I don't know if what she said was true or not, but I instructed staff and residents that any smoking outside must be escorted until 11pm. After that, no one is allowed out to smoke. I said I'd review the situation in a few weeks.'

'Hmmm.' He bit the lid of his pen. 'Bit odd about Irene though – you'd think she'd mention that…'

'Irene can be really high-strung at times. I'm a little worried about her, to be honest. She's been a bit scatterbrained recently and on edge. I'm sure she probably just didn't think it was relevant because she didn't see anything.' At least, Jeanette hoped that was the case as Irene shouldn't have been out back on her own…

'That's possible, I guess, but still. If Mrs Burgess was concerned about someone from here being in her garden, we'll have to look into that now, given the circumstances.'

'Of course.' Jeanette took a deep breath. Another mark against Ripley House. 'Looks like Helen is going to get her wish after all…'

'Her wish?'

'She's wanted this hostel shut down from the moment she learned it was opening. Blamed her husband's death on the stress of having *monsters* – her words, not mine – living next door to her. Her death might just be the nail in Ripley House's coffin.'

'Ironic, indeed.' DS Brady stood. 'You've been really helpful. I know our agencies often seem like they're on opposite sides – us putting away the baddies, you trying to *rehabilitate* them – but I appreciate your candour. I'll have the tech guys contact you, but should anything else come to light between now and then…'

'I'll be in touch. I know the drill.' Jeanette escorted the detective off the premises and returned to the main office. She looked at everyone as she passed.

The residents.

Her own team.

Could she trust any of them?

Something was going on at the hostel and she wasn't about to become its next victim.

FIFTY

Sloane

Sloane checked her reflection in the bus window before she alighted at her stop. She suddenly felt foolish. This wasn't a date. Noah was in a happy relationship, and she wasn't *that* type of woman – the type who didn't give a fuck and pursued a love interest no matter the situation. She'd had her chance and made the decision that was right for her. At least it was the right decision back then...

She fidgeted with her top as she approached Café Noir. They'd always liked this one when they'd been dating. It was a café for the most part but later in the day, alcohol was served and music would be played for those who wanted it. Right now, a stiff drink would ease the nerves dancing underneath her skin.

Noah had been sitting outside under a heated lamp and she waved when she saw him. Her smile slightly turned to a frown when she saw the coffee he had ordered for her. He noticed the look.

'Sorry. Don't you drink coffee anymore? I know you're a

stickler for timekeeping so I figured I'd have it here ready for you.'

'Ignore me. That was really thoughtful. Thanks.' She eyed the gins on the table across from them. 'Coffee is perfect and probably the smarter choice.' Sloane pulled the chair out and sat down. A beam of sunshine hit her in the eyes and momentarily blinded her. She put her hand up to her forehead like a visor. Then she saw him – really *saw* him – the guy she knew he was inside – moral, decent, upstanding – and she almost changed her mind about what she was going to do.

Almost.

The first twenty minutes was spent on weird and unassuming small talk – how's work? Tell me about your boyfriend/girlfriend. Any exciting holidays planned? And once the awkward silence kicked in, Sloane cleared her throat.

'And here it is…' Noah sat back in his chair and looked her straight in the eyes.

Sloane was about to protest at being called out, but he raised his hand.

'We've known each other long enough. I can see through your BS, so just cut to the chase.'

Even though he smiled, Sloane could see he was a little saddened that she'd even tried to pull the wool over his eyes. She felt bad; she should have known. He hadn't been promoted because of his looks – it was because that brain of his was constantly picking up the clues that solved a case. It was also one of the reasons they broke up, if she was honest with herself. Noah thought she portrayed herself as a kind, altruistic, and generous person when really she did whatever she needed to in order to get what she wanted.

'OK. I need your help and I feel shitty about asking you,

but you know I wouldn't ask if I hadn't tried every other avenue...'

He nodded and didn't interrupt. This was a good sign.

'The Ripley House murder investigation – do you think you'd be able to get me some information? If I use any of it in a story, I promise to keep your name out of it.'

He took a deep breath. 'Fuck's sake, Sloane. That's a big ask. People know we were together – it wouldn't take a genius to figure out where the info came from. My girlfriend works at the station. How do you think she'd feel if she found out I was involved in anything that led back to you?'

He was right. But...

'That depends on what I use and how I say it. You have my word that no one will know my source was even a police officer.'

Noah looked at the ground. Those cogs were turning, she could see it.

Her mobile rang and she looked at the screen. 'Excuse me. I need to take this... give you a bit of time to think things over.' Sloane walked down the path at the side of the café. 'Any news, detective?' She'd avoided his calls up until now but if she hadn't answered, he'd probably have his colleagues out looking for her.

'Hello to you too, Ms Armstrong. Nice of you to finally answer me. I'd like to ask you a few more questions. Are you free to come down to the station today?'

She was already in town and nearly finished with Noah. 'I can be there in an hour or so?'

'That works.' He ended the call and Sloane returned to the table,

'Work?'

Sloane nodded. She wasn't sure why she felt the need to hide that she'd be going to the police station, but she did.

Noah looked at his watch. 'I need to get going soon too – tell me exactly what you need and why. I'll see if I can help – but no promises. I'm not putting my job on the line.'

She understood his reluctance. They may have once had something special but right now she was just a friend, and the message was received. She rubbed her thigh, the spot where the rose tattoo lay. A reminder that Noah was her past...

Sloane explained the murder investigation, Anwar Hussain's arrest, and the threats that she and Helen had received. She ended with finding Helen dead less than twenty-four hours ago.

Noah shook his head. 'You don't do things by halves, do you? How is it that you always find yourself in the middle of the stories you're supposed to be reporting on? It's one of the reasons— Never mind.' He rested his arms on the table and the look he gave her made her stomach flip. He still cared. 'I don't want anything to happen to you.' He reached out but then pulled his hand away quickly.

The guilt was back.

'Nothing will. I'm just writing the story, but something isn't adding up. Either the police know something that the public need to be aware of or the hostel does. I won't have another death on my conscience...'

FIFTY-ONE

Killer

I can't breathe. My chest tightens as I gulp in air.

Why couldn't she leave well enough alone? I feel guilty even though I only did what I had to do. There is no guilt, shame, or remorse for Danny Wells – he deserved to die. My only regret is that I couldn't prolong his pain. He should have died in prison.

Life for a life…

I didn't mean for Helen to die. It was never what I'd planned. I wanted to scare her enough that she would stop her bloody snooping – one death was easy enough to cover, but two… Bloody woman! I just snapped. Who did she think she was anyway? If she'd stopped sticking her nose in, like I told her, the hostel would have eventually been closed; there's so much shit going on there that would come out if the detectives did their bloody job right. I feel like I have to do everything myself.

Why didn't I run away when she spotted me at the bottom of her garden? She wouldn't have been able to identify me – I made sure of that. I could have got her on my side – if she'd only listened. Convinced her to keep it to herself, not tell that journalist friend and make me do more bad things. We'd have taken the secret to our graves.

Am I losing the plot? She didn't trust any of us – it had to be this way.

I need to think.

Think! Think! Think! My hand begins to hurt from thumping so hard against the wall.

The investigation will be ramped up if they suss that Helen didn't fall down the stairs. I removed the tape from her mouth and wrists... Would she have bruised right away? I wish I'd closed her eyes when she lay dying in front of me.

I shudder.

I take no joy from killing. Not really – I had no choice. I need to protect myself.

I think if I say this often enough to myself, I might even believe it.

I didn't get the impression that the police suspected me when they interviewed everyone at Ripley House.

Did you notice anything or anyone unusual in the area?

This made me laugh at the time. I reminded the officer that everything appeared unusual when you were in the hostel. People were always watching you. Accusing you. Clocking your every move. Finger pointing was a sport.

'No, officer. Nothing at all,' I said.

Had anyone argued or confronted Mrs Burgess. We've been told there was an incident at Ripley House earlier.

I had looked around, trying to think of something believable to say.

'Thought you said she fell down the stairs?' was what came out of my mouth.

Did my voice rise in pitch?

Did my face redden?

I shoved my hands in my pockets, in case the officer noticed they had begun to shake. The more I tried to stop them, the more they twitched.

'Nope. I heard she was screaming about smoking or something, but I missed the whole thing…'

The officer looked up from his notepad then. *Did you see anyone leave or come back to the hostel behaving strangely?*

I remember raising a brow. 'Yeah – everyone. It's a hostel.'

I noticed at the time that he avoided my question about the old woman's fall being an accident and suddenly I was saying, 'So, you think someone pushed her? Old people fall all the time though, don't they?' I regretted the words as soon as they left my lips, especially when the officer frowned.

Not sure where you get your information from, but I wouldn't say it's a normal occurrence in the elderly. We're just exploring all avenues at the moment – not ruling anything out.

He made it clear that he wasn't about to expand on that further and I wasn't about to push my luck.

Something was stuck to the top of my index finger. *It was the tape.* I had stuffed the pieces in my pocket before leaving her house.

Shit.

The officer handed me his card and said the usual: *If you do hear anything else, here's the number to call.*

I had to use my thumb to push the tape off my finger before taking it out of my pocket to accept the card.

'Thanks.'

I shoved it in my back pocket where it sits now, burning a hole in my conscience.

That was close. Too close.

Gossip around the hostel is spreading like wildfire and

everyone's eyeing each other with suspicion, probably wondering if Danny's killer is about to strike again.

It's hard to sleep. The fear I saw in Helen's eyes as I covered her mouth and plugged her nose... I couldn't afford for her to survive the fall. She'd ruin everything.

But her eyes still haunt me.

Nosy bitch.

You! Of all people...

I didn't let her finish what she was going to say – I knew then that she had to die.

I lie in my bed and stare at the ceiling. Every time I try closing my eyes, it's her face I see.

Just think of something else, you idiot. Think about why this had to happen.

The end game.

That should be my focus.

The paperwork was handed in a few weeks before I got rid of Danny. Just waiting for a signature... As soon as a spot is available, I'll be gone.

Long gone.

I can then make my excuses as to why I need to leave the new place. I'm sure I'll be able to think of something believable. It'll be easy to start again. OK, I don't have a lot of money saved up, but I have enough. Work will come.

The hours pass quickly and before I know it there's a tap on my door.

'You getting up?' a hoarse voice calls out.

I roll onto my side and stare at the door. 'I'll be down in a minute.'

I feel sick to my stomach, but I have to push it aside. If people notice, if they start digging… it will all be a waste.

I throw on my jeans, a T-shirt, socks, and shoes. I grab the tape from my other jeans and hide it with the knife and hoodie. I need to get rid of everything before someone figures it out.

A splash of water on my face, teeth brushed, hair combed – and just a smile to finish it off.

A new day. I'm ready.

FIFTY-TWO

Jeanette

J eanette sat frozen in her chair. Up until now she'd managed to keep the investigations – police, Serious Further Offence, Death under Probation Supervision – all separate by working in a complete silo with the information pertaining to the specific investigation, each having its own designated space in her head to be dealt with as and when the need arose. Now they were merging together, overlapping, and it felt like someone had punched her in the chest.

Her breathing was laboured. Her body dripped with sweat. The room was spinning. She recognised the signs immediately. She was having a panic attack.

Breathe. You've dealt with these things before. And she had, though never all at the same time.

Slow, deep breaths. She listened to her inner voice for a change and, ten minutes later, she felt the pressure ease.

Something foul was lurking in this house – she could feel it in the walls and through the floorboards, and no one was close to exorcising the devil from the hostel. *Who were they looking for?* Jeanette's heart was heavy. She and her team worked hard at supporting prisoners, getting them jobs, working with them so they became accepted in the community, and someone had decided to turn all that on its head. She had to separate her personal feelings and focus on what was logical, no matter where it led.

Since Danny Wells had been murdered, they'd already had a recall back to custody and another resident transferred out. That left four others. Only four – so why hadn't the murderer been caught? The hostel had put a hold on any new referrals until the police and probation's own investigations were concluded. *What weren't they seeing?*

The staff? Someone from the outside agencies?

Jeanette didn't want to believe anyone she worked with, anyone she managed, someone she had handpicked to be a part of her team, could be responsible for the death… could be a killer. That was until Anwar Hussain, her right hand, had been arrested for possession with intent to supply. She just couldn't ignore the possibility even though she wanted to.

Who had been acting strangely lately?

Jeanette began to laugh. It was one of those tired laughs that starts out as a giggle and then erupts into uncontrollable bursts of noise, causing tears to run down her face. Her brain was not coping with the situation. A knock on her door pulled her back to the reality of what she had been thinking. She wiped her face with the back of her hand. 'Come in.'

It was Steph. 'We have a supervision session booked for now.' She tilted her head and Jeanette realised she must look a state. 'We can reschedule if you need to though…'

Jeanette waved her in. Routine was exactly what she needed at the moment. 'I'm fine. Just give me a minute to get your last notes.' She swivelled her chair to face the filing cabinet behind her. Finding the notes, she turned and faced Steph. The PSO was crying.

'Oh Steph. What's the matter?' She felt foolish as the words left her mouth. What wasn't the matter these days?

Steph sniffed. 'I don't know how you are OK. I just feel so… paranoid lately. Especially after Anwar's arrest and poor Helen next door. She was annoying at times, but she had her moments and it's just so sad that she's died. She must have been terrified.'

'Afraid? What would she have been scared of?' As far as Jeanette was aware, no one else knew that the police suspected foul play.

'Yeah, falling backwards down a flight of stairs. I can't even imagine.'

'Of course.' Jeanette's shoulders relaxed and she listened as Steph recounted how Helen had helped her when her own mother had died.

'She was still grieving herself after losing her husband. He was her world, you know. But she still took the time to comfort me…'

A lump formed in Jeanette's throat. She felt guilty for all the times she'd cursed the older woman under her breath and, on reflection, she realised that she hadn't handled Steph's situation well. Jeanette had followed probation policy – she'd allowed Steph the few days' compassionate leave she was entitled to and had checked in on her once while she was off – but she'd distanced herself from the emotional support aspect and it was clear that was what Steph had needed most.

'I didn't know that. It's awful that something like this had to happen for me to learn what you've just shared, and for that I'm sorry.'

Steph blew her nose. 'S'OK. I wasn't having a dig. I'm fine

and I knew if I needed you, you'd be there. I just didn't really know how to ask, with you being so busy and all. You gave me the time off... Anyway, I just have a few things I'd like to discuss today.'

Jeanette opened the supervision template on her computer and typed in the basics – name, date, and time. 'Do you want to start with the priority and risk bits and then we can move on to the other aspects?' While Steph was looking through her notebook, Jeanette filled in the personal info she'd just been told. She made an action point for herself to be more available to staff and find out their needs when they brought personal matters to her attention.

'Can we talk about Ray Southall? There've been a few things bothering me lately and I just couldn't put my finger on why – that is, until Anwar was arrested.'

Jeanette stopped typing. 'Oh really? Why's that?'

Steph shifted in her chair, and she played with the loose papers in her notebook.

'Don't feel nervous for speaking up now, Steph. I think we're all looking back in hindsight and seeing what's been right under our noses. Best to get everything out in the open.'

Steph's shoulders relaxed. 'Anwar spent a lot of time on Ray's case. It was beginning to annoy me. I know he has oversight of many of our cases, but he didn't spend half as much time on my other cases – or anyone else's for that matter. I had thought about coming to you before, but figured you'd just say he was doing his job. Now I wish I'd listened to my gut in the first place.'

Jeanette didn't want to interrupt even though the last thing Steph had said had made her feel like her team didn't find her to be objective or approachable. She had thought she was; but this wasn't about her – it was about the team.

'When Anwar started taking over supervision appointments and rearranging keywork sessions, alarm bells went off in my head, but then I just thought I was being territorial. I'd never felt it on previous cases but on Ray's… well, Anwar seemed to be taking over. And I guess with having so much other work to deal with, I just ignored it when I should have raised it with you.'

'What are you implying?' Jeanette was struggling with the idea that something could have been happening for a long time and she hadn't seen it. She needed Steph to say it though – it was her supervision and Jeanette didn't want to put words in Steph's mouth in case this had to be reported.

'I think Anwar and Ray were dealing drugs together, and I know it may sound a little far-fetched, but what if they were both involved in Danny's murder? It's been so tense in the office – Irene has been so secretive, Anwar and Frank are always butting heads… I think Amy and I are the only normal ones. Oh and you, of course.' Steph's cheeks grew red.

Jeanette took a moment to reflect on what she had just been told. Steph wasn't wrong.

'Well…' She needed to tread carefully. 'Anwar is being questioned but do we really think he could be directly involved in Danny's murder?'

She wouldn't go into the details because she had promised DS Brady, but she wanted Steph to calm down as it wouldn't do anyone any good if Steph started throwing around accusations. Jeanette observed that Steph's leg was shaking and the tone of her voice was rising with each word out of her mouth.

Steph bit her lip. 'He could have been involved in other ways…' Steph pulled out a sheet of paper from her notebook and handed it to Jeanette. 'Look.'

It was a page from Ray's case file record. Steph's initials were at the left side along with the date and details of the session itself. 'Ok. What am I missing?' Everything looked to be in order as far as Jeanette could tell.

Steph pulled out another loose sheet from her notebook and passed it to Jeanette. When she compared the two, a knot formed in her stomach. The dates were the same, but Anwar had deleted some of Steph's notes and replaced them – a breach in practice and a disciplinary offence.

'Did you tell the police when they questioned you? And why am I only learning of this now?' First Mark and now Ray. What was Anwar playing at?

Steph shook her head. 'I hadn't realised at the time and didn't know if I should tell them. I mean, I thought you should know first… I spoke to the union.'

'Why did you decide to print out and keep a copy of your original notes in the first place?' That wasn't normal practice. Case file records were recorded on the system and kept there. The probation service had gone paperless a few years back and no actual paper files were kept on the premises; it was to improve confidentiality and security – though when the system was down, it caused havoc.

'I always print a copy of the things I want to raise at supervision at the time I type the notes, otherwise I'd just forget. I know we're not supposed to, but I do keep them in a locked drawer so there's no way anyone else would take them – and I'm glad I did. As you can see in my original notes, Ray's drug test results came up as inconclusive and he refused to take another test. His home PO instructed me to give him a verbal warning as his previous tests indicated that he was clean. But he'd been erratic in the supervision session, and I wanted to discuss with you whether I should push recall with his offender manager. He was disrupting groups, saying some inappropriate things... well, you can see it all there.' She pointed at the piece of paper in Jeanette's hand.

Jeanette could see the logic in being insistent on a recall. Steph was a good officer, and her assessments were always spot on. 'Where does Anwar come in?'

'He erased my comments, withdrew the warning, changing it to note that there was an error and that Ray *had* attended the keywork session and tested clean. Obviously, because he has an override he was able to do this – I wouldn't be able to without manager oversight. I only noticed this yesterday when I was double-checking in preparation for our supervision today. I had already spoken to the police when I discovered it so it was too late... and I wanted your advice.'

What she meant was, she wanted Jeanette to own the accountability should the shit hit the fan. Steph was on the verge of tears again.

'You did the right thing.' Jeanette remembered that Anwar was due to be released on bail and wondered whether this new information would change things. She needed to speak with the detective. 'Is there anything else you need to discuss? Only I think this needs to be shared with the police...'

Steph shook her head and started to gather her things together when a tap on the door made them both jump.

'Yes?' Jeanette called out.

The colour drained from Steph's face and Jeanette gasped.

'Can I have a minute?'

It was Anwar Hussain.

FIFTY-THREE

Sloane

When Sloane and Noah had parted ways, it had felt like things were back to normal between them – at least on the friendship front – and she was pleased she'd reached out to him. He'd said he could help with some of the information she was interested in, but he wouldn't risk his career or new relationship by disclosing anything that could be misconstrued or that was beyond the scope of what he could divulge from a legal standpoint. She understood that. Boundaries had been set and she'd do her best to respect his decision.

The police station wasn't too far away so she picked up the pace, glancing in shop windows and smiling at people who were out for the afternoon. After signing in, she paced the small reception area until the detective came and greeted her. He looked more dishevelled than he had when she'd seen him earlier. His skin was grey and saggy. It looked like the murder investigation was taking a toll and for a moment, she almost felt sorry for him.

'Thanks for coming, Ms Armstrong. I won't keep you

longer than necessary.' He stepped aside and let her through before moving ahead of her and walking down the hall.

She followed him into an interview room and listened as he explained why he wanted to speak with her so urgently.

'First I wanted to say that I'm sorry for your loss. I know that Mrs Burgess was a friend and finding her must have been a real shock.'

Sloane was suddenly overcome with emotion and choked back the tears – she hated to appear vulnerable in front of the detective. 'Yes. I've known her for a couple of years. She is… was… quite the character. Thank you.' She took a moment to focus. 'Now what's all this about?'

'Everything we discuss in here needs to be off the record. I'd like to get your reassurance on that before I proceed.'

Sloane scrunched her nose. Catching a glimpse of herself in the mirrored window, she realised her thinking face wasn't very appealing but now wasn't the time to be focused on that. 'If you give me a little more detail, it might help form my decision. You've got to understand my position here – there's something going on at that hostel…' Something dawned on her. 'Do you think Helen stumbled across something? She called me *three* times the evening she… died. The public have a right to know if they're at risk…'

The detective raised his hands. 'Hang on. You're jumping ahead, and maybe I should have explained things better. We'd like to work *with* you, give you exclusivity to any breaking news, but nothing gets printed without our approval.'

Sloane leaned back in the chair. An olive branch. *What does he know?* She could probably find out on her own, but would she be burning bridges with her sources if anything she printed shone a bad light on a specific agency, including the police? If she did agree to work with them, they might limit what they shared and that put her at a disadvantage.

She felt torn.

Noah popped into her head then. She'd made a big ask of him earlier and even though he had agreed, there had been hesitation. This offer would allow her to tell him he could back away – and possibly save a friendship that she was keen to keep, now that they'd reconnected.

Sloane steepled her hands and placed her elbows on the table. 'OK, but I just want to be clear on a few things. You've mentioned exclusivity, but I won't be used as a pawn. This' – she waved her hands between them – 'needs to be a two-way street. I have plenty of other sources I can get my information from. I'll share what I've discovered so far and anything relevant that comes up in the future, but I want the same in return.'

The detective leaned forward and opened his mouth but before he could protest, Sloane interrupted.

'I wasn't done. I'm aware that there will be certain bits you can't share with me but in case you haven't noticed, I'm a damned good investigative journalist. Be as vague as you need to be – just steer me in the right direction and don't send me on a wild goose chase, because if you do… this agreement is null and void.' Sloane paused and watched as the detective wrestled mentally with her proposal. His eyes were moving from left to right, as if he was having a conversation with his conscience.

He extended his hand and leaned forward. 'Deal.'

Sloane shook his hand. 'Would you excuse me for a moment? I'd like to make a call.'

'Stay where you are. This feels like a good time for a break. Would you like a coffee?'

Sloane nodded.

'How do you take yours?' He had a foot out the door.

'Skimmed milk and no sugar. If you don't have skimmed, I'll have it black. Thanks.'

Sloane waited until the door had closed before pulling out her phone, but then she had second thoughts about making the call. She looked around the room and spotted the camera in the corner. Although no light was on to indicate they were being filmed, she knew that the room probably had a recording device, so instead she decided to send a text.

Great to see you today. Forget about what I asked you to do earlier. I've made other arrangements. Meant a lot that you said yes though, for what it's worth. Will explain later. Sloane.

She had nearly put an 'x' after her name. She did with all her friends, but she didn't want Noah to think her intentions were anything other than friendship.

If you're sure. Saves me a lot of future grief. Speak Soon.

Sloane smiled as she put her phone back into her bag. The detective reappeared and placed a hot mug of black coffee in front of her.

'Shall we begin then?'

FIFTY-FOUR

Jeanette

W *hat the…?*

'Steph, will you excuse us, please?' Jeanette had never seen Steph move so fast, her eyes on the floor as she squeezed by Anwar in the doorway.

'Why are you here?' Jeanette's heart raced and she felt under her desk for the alarm.

Anwar looked down. 'What are you doing?' He stepped into the office and began to close the door.

'Leave it open, please.'

'Jeanette. I'm not here to hurt you. I haven't hurt anyone… This is all such a mess. I just want to know what happens now.'

She relaxed and then clenched her fists under the desk.

How dare he come here after everything that's happened!

'You of all people know the protocol. You should've received a letter notifying you of your suspension.'

'Of course.' He looked down at the floor. 'Can I ask whether it will be paid?'

Jeanette rolled her eyes; he had some nerve. 'As per the

policy, I believe that until you are convicted, the suspension will be paid. What the hell did you get yourself into?'

Against her better judgement, she gestured for him to sit.

Anwar looked over his shoulder. 'Can I shut the door, please?'

'I'd rather you didn't. Don't worry, unless they've bugged my office, or we start shouting, they aren't going to hear anything that's said all the way downstairs.'

He sat and took a deep breath. 'I know this looks really bad and I'm in way over my head but… the fact is, I needed the money and made some really stupid decisions.'

Jeanette held a hand up. 'Stop right there. This conversation is not confidential so I'm just going to remind you to think about what you tell me.'

He nodded and seemed to change his mind about the confession he had been about to give. 'OK. I don't have any real explanation then. Can I at least collect some of my personal things from my desk?'

'I'll have to accompany you.'

Anwar couldn't look her in the eye. 'That's fine.' He stood. 'For the record, I had nothing to do with Danny Wells's death. I wasn't even here. If you're going to be pointing fingers at staff, Irene and Frank are who you should be looking at more closely. Tweedledum and Tweedledee.'

'What did you call me?' There was a growl in the tone.

Jeanette looked past Anwar and noticed Frank by the staff lockers. *Shit*.

'You heard me. It happened on your watch and it's not the first time you pair have been caught slacking.' The accusation from Anwar hung in the air.

Frank rushed towards the office and Jeanette raced around to stand between the two men. 'That's enough! Frank, go out back. Take the residents for a smoke break, or walk around the grounds. Just get out of here. You both need to calm down.'

Frank mumbled as he turned to leave. 'You'll get what's coming to you…'

'Did you hear that? Did he just threaten me?' Anwar's voice was shaky.

Frank didn't have a violent bone in his body. He was the only staff member who was involved in extra charity work outside of the hostel. Jeanette often wondered how he managed to do everything he did given the hours required. He mustn't sleep. She needed to nip this in the bud though, as she couldn't have the residents witnessing arguments between the staff. 'I imagine he was referring to the trial you'll face. It was on the news what happened…'

Anwar once again looked at the floor, his face reddened. 'Sorry. I just can't believe… Never mind. Can I just collect my things now?'

Jeanette nodded, stepped out of the way, and followed Anwar to his desk. His colleagues stared as he picked up the picture of his family and shoved it in the backpack he had been carrying.

'Don't you all have some work to do?' As disappointed as Jeanette was with Anwar, her team didn't have time to sit around. She watched as he moved things around his desk and when he reached into the drawer and pulled out a plastic bag, she stopped him.

'I'll have to see what's in the bag.' Her hand lay on his arm.

'Huh? I don't know what it is – that's why I pulled it out.'

Anwar opened the bag and inside was a bloodied baseball cap.

'Anwar, please put that down and stay right where you are.

Steph, call the police and let them know we need someone here immediately.'

'What? You don't believe— This had to have been planted here! The whole place was searched. Jeanette, please... don't do this...'

Within minutes the police had arrived and collected Anwar and the potential evidence. Mentally, Jeanette was exhausted. When she had last spoken to the detective, he had confirmed that Anwar had had a rock-solid alibi for the time of the murder. *Had someone planted that evidence or had Anwar been clever enough to elude them all?*

She looked at her team. 'Who else was in here today?'

Amy rattled off the list of keyworkers and residents who had been in the main office and Jeanette wrote them down. DS Brady hadn't attended to pick up Anwar, probably because he was being dealt with by another team – but she had a bone to pick with him anyway. She stomped back to her office and picked up the phone. Dialling his mobile, she waited as it rang. Just as she was about to give up and go down to the station to see him in person, he answered.

'DS Brady speaking.'

'It's Jeanette. Do you mind telling me why no one informed me that Anwar Hussain had been released from police custody?' Her voice shook with rage.

'He was? I thought they were releasing him later today. Someone should have been in touch. Did he show up at the hostel?'

'He did and the police just left with him.'

'Wait, what? Why?'

'When he was collecting some of his things, a bloodied baseball cap was found in his drawer – a secure drawer. I'm not sure how it got there or when, but it had to have been after your officers finished their searches. That was weeks ago. And if that cap has anything to do with Danny Wells's murder and Anwar wasn't involved, you know what that means?'

'It means the killer is playing games...'

'When can I expect you here?'

'I'm leaving now.'

FIFTY-FIVE

Sloane

The detective had ended their meeting early after leaving the room to take a call, but he'd shared some bits of information that Sloane had not been previously aware of about Danny Wells's victim – Emily Nash. If she could catch her contact at social care, they might be able to put her in touch with a social worker from London, which was the birthplace of the victim.

'Long time no speak.' Sam sounded almost happy to hear from her. Usually when Sloane called him he was moaning about his workload or down in the dumps about a horrendous case he had been allocated. All understandable if a little depressing.

'I know. It's been way too long and that's totally my fault. A bit manic workwise. Have you heard about the murder at Ripley House? I might need something…'

'Oh my God, yeah. I wondered if you'd be all over that. You don't live too far away from there, do you.'

'Literally around the corner. Look, I don't want to keep you long but before I ask for a favour, tell me what has you in good spirits. I don't think I've ever heard you sounding so happy.'

'I'm going to be a dad. Me! Can you believe it? I was beginning to wonder if it would ever happen.'

'That's amazing news. Congrats to you both.' Sloane was genuinely happy for Sam and his wife. He had told her before how long they had been trying for a baby and how they had started IVF. When his wife had had two miscarriages, he'd almost resigned himself to the fact that he might never be a father, so this was incredible.

'Thanks. OK, I'm sure you're busy so I'll bore you another time with baby updates. What's this favour you're after?'

'I need a reliable contact in social care – London area, but specifically the south. Do you know of anyone who might be willing to speak with me? To put it into context, Danny Wells was on life licence for a murder. I'd like to include his victim, Emily Nash, in the story I'm writing, but other than old newspapers and a few bits from the police and probation, I don't really have much to go on.'

'That's so weird that you've called, as I actually do know someone. She used to work here and recently transferred to London social care – a hub that deals with specific areas. I'll give her a bell and come back to you. I'm not sure how she'll feel about talking to a journalist though. Don't worry, I'll put in a good word for you.'

'You're a diamond, Sam. Let's not leave it so long next time. We should have lunch soon and you can tell me more about the baby.'

'Agreed! I should know before the end of today so expect a call or text depending on how busy I am.'

Sloane hung up and headed in the direction of the bus stop.

It had started to rain and she could feel the spiky drops hitting her face like little knives. She walked with her head down to avoid any further attacks and when she reached the bus shelter, she sat and pulled out her mobile again.

Scrolling through her emails she read the most recent note from her editor. He was pushing her for an update on the case and Sloane hoped that if Sam came through, she'd have a good piece about the victim and how Danny's murder must have opened some old wounds. Her main article would wait until the killer was caught – it could be her big break.

The bus arrived and Sloane was home in no time. One of the best things about working freelance was that she could work from anywhere, but her favourite place was her home office. That was where she headed after she chucked her soggy trainers on the mat just inside the door.

She started up her computer and, as it whizzed itself to life, she made a flask of coffee. Once she was in her writing and research zone, she hated having to come out of it.

Sloane opened the folder on her computer titled *Ripley_House_Murder_Expose* and searched for the file where she had stored the information on Emily Nash that she'd gathered so far. She wanted to know as much as she could about the victim's background so she could focus her questions if the London social care contact came through.

She re-read her notes where she had highlighted that Emily Nash was raised in a poor environment and been subjected to child protection measures when she herself was a child. She'd moved from various foster care homes and once she hit sixteen she'd left and started living rough on the streets of South London. She had been introduced to the world of sex work at the age of seventeen and soon afterwards her occasional drug use had spiralled into something worse – crack and heroin. She had also been an alcoholic, which seemed to have been a trait in her family as both her parents and her grandfather were known alcoholics. It seemed poor Emily's life had been mapped out from a young age and it made for sad reading. By the time she was twenty-five she had been in numerous abusive relationships and had had a few miscarriages and three children, whose father or fathers she could never clarify.

Sloane had limited information on Emily's first two children, only that they had been adopted out. Apparently, Emily had eventually cleaned up her act and this was why she still had one child in her custody at the time she was murdered. Sloane wondered if she could find out more information on the child that had remained in her care as well as those who had been adopted, but she wasn't holding out any hope as social care records were probably sealed. She noted it down anyway.

When Sloane had contacted Danny Wells's brother, Colin, he'd been short with her and part of her understood that reasoning, but they were still brothers and she had been surprised that he hadn't sounded the least bit upset. They were complete opposites. Neither had had the best upbringing but while one championed prosecuting criminals, the other had become a violent thug who'd ended up getting a life sentence. Colin had told her that Danny and Emily had been in an on-off abusive relationship for many years, so his attack on Emily had not been random but actually part of a sustained history of domestic abuse. Sloane surmised that this was probably the reason her previous children had been removed from her care as Emily wasn't capable of protecting herself, let alone her children from abusive men in her life. Colin had refused to share any more details with her and had told her not to contact him again.

Her mobile buzzed. It was Sam. She crossed her fingers. She needed some good news.

Five minutes later she had the name of a contact and the chance she'd get some of the answers she was searching for.

FIFTY-SIX

Jeanette

Jeanette was still reeling from the fact that no one had forewarned her Anwar had been bailed. Surely one of the conditions of bail should have been that he stayed away from the hostel as he had already been suspended pending the investigation?

It wasn't that she was afraid of him, it was the confrontational tone in his voice when he'd challenged her in front of the team that irked her. She was livid and when the bloody detective got his arse to the hostel, she'd make sure that before he left he understood the meaning of professional courtesy.

Steph popped her head into the office. 'Sorry to bother you but DS Brady is here. Do you want me to bring him through or will you be using a meeting room?'

Jeanette took a moment to compose herself. 'Bring him through. Thanks.'

Steph nodded and turned to leave.

'Just one more thing…' Jeanette called out. 'Don't answer any questions he may have. Leave that to me. I've got a few things I need to get off my chest…' She waved Steph away and stood behind her desk, arms crossed, brows furrowed. He'd know from the start how she was feeling.

DS Brady stopped in the doorway. 'Jeanette, before you unleash on me, can I just apologise for this whole situation. I honestly had no idea Anwar had been released as he's being handled by a different team. I've had a word with my colleagues, and they also send their apologies.'

Jeanette's shoulders loosened and, for a moment, her anger simmered. She hadn't been expecting an apology, but it didn't change the fact that the hostel had been kept in the dark. Anwar's presence could have been received a whole lot differently and the police would have a lot to answer for.

The detective pulled out a chair, ready to sit, but Jeanette stopped him.

'Don't get too comfortable. I suspect you won't be staying long.' Jeanette didn't care if she came across as rude.

One of his big, bushy eyebrows rose and he raised his hands in defeat. 'OK. I get that you're angry, but can we be professional about this?'

Jeanette grabbed the top of her chair, her knuckles turning white as she squeezed, pulling it back so she could sit. She took a few deep breaths; if she answered him now, he'd win, and she wouldn't be able to control the flow of words that left her lips. She sat and waited for him to continue.

The detective looked directly into her eyes as he lowered himself into the chair – he too was waiting for her to speak. They could play this game all day but that wouldn't serve either of them and Jeanette had a shitload of work to do after Steph's revelations.

'I have a few things to say. I won't rehash the incompetence of the police in not informing the relevant people that Anwar had been released' – even though she did just that – 'but a few things were brought to my attention, and I think you need to be aware of them—'

The detective crossed his legs. 'If this is about the bloodied cap, that will be dealt with.'

'Why do you always have to interrupt me?' Jeanette eyed him before reaching across and passing him two pieces of paper. 'Here...'

'What's this?'

She watched as he glanced at the supervision notes. His eyes widened and Jeanette knew he saw the discrepancy.

'Were these records doctored?'

Jeanette nodded. 'Anwar seems to have taken it upon himself to abuse his position of trust... again. Probation will deal with that aspect, but my concern is who he seems to be protecting. Why did he want Ray Southall to remain in the community? Could it be that the two of them were involved in Danny's death? Ray does have form for dealing. He certainly has the connections. What if Danny became privy to this information and was blackmailing them?'

The detective leaned forward. 'That's an interesting theory but do you have any evidence to back that up? We both know Anwar wasn't at the hostel on the night in question, and we've grilled and cleared Ray. Although, considering this new information, we'll have to go through his records and alibi again.' He stood. 'Can I take these?'

'I'm afraid not. I'll have to speak to head office. No doubt you'll get them through the normal channels.'

He shook his head and gave her an icy look. Was he attempting to intimidate her? She worked with offenders who did this daily – did he think she was an amateur? She placed her hands in her lap and stared right back. It was a stand-off.

The silence clearly bothered him more than her. 'Look, Ms Macey… Jeanette. We're on the same side here. Can I at least get a copy and I promise that the correct protocol will be followed re the originals? I'll need the name of every person between Anwar's arrest and earlier today who has had access to this office. It will be easy to eliminate those, like yourself, who have already been cleared in terms of Danny's murder, but planting that cap is another matter. I can wait while you get that together for me.'

Jeanette huffed but the detective made a good point. The killer would love it if the different agencies were fighting each other.

'You already have a list of people who have access to the office – including the remaining residents. We've had no new intakes since Danny was killed and no new referrals. But I'll double-check and send something over to you before the end of play today…'

'I guess we're done here then. Appreciate it.'

Jeanette walked over to the photocopier and produced a copy of the supervision notes for the detective. As she handed them to him, his mouth opened and closed as if he was about to say something but then thought better of it.

'Just spit it out.' Although deep down she thought she knew what he was about to say.

'I hope the probation service has invested in better security since Danny was murdered. Things are escalating…'

FIFTY-SEVEN

Sloane

Sloane crossed her fingers. She needed Sam's contact to come through for her. Social Care were notoriously close-lipped when it came to sharing information, but Sam had assured her that he'd explained the situation to his contact, and they would be expecting her call.

She tapped her finger on the table as the penetrating tone of the ring reverberated off her eardrum.

'South London Social Care. If you know the extension number of the person you wish to speak to, dial that now followed by the hashtag.'

Sloane typed in the four-digit number Sam had given her and waited. The phone rang and she was beginning to think the answerphone was going to kick in. Just as she was about to hang up, a high-pitched voice answered.

'Rose Bagley speaking. How can I help?'

'Hi. My name is Sloane Armstrong. A mutual friend gave me your number. He thought you may be able to help me with an historic case that I believe is on your records.'

'Ah yes. Sam said you'd be calling. I want to make

something clear right from the get-go. I don't want to be recorded or have my name appear in any story that you write. In fact, for the record, this is off the record. Are we clear?'

'I understand and promise that if I do write anything, you'll remain an anonymous source. Do you mind if I take notes though?'

'That's fine and I appreciate you asking. I don't have much time, so let's not beat around the bush. Sam said you were interested in Emily Nash's case. I skimmed through it but I'm not sure what you might find relevant to Danny Wells other than the fact that she was pregnant at the time she was murdered, and it was believed Danny wasn't the father.'

That caught Sloane by surprise. She hadn't known Emily had been pregnant – that titbit had been kept from the media at the time. Was it her infidelity that led to her murder? 'What can you tell me about her children and your agency's involvement? From my understanding, she had two children who'd been adopted out due to her substance misuse, but then she got clean, and in that time had another child who was actually in the home when she was murdered.'

'Yes, that's correct.'

'What happened to the baby? It was a boy, wasn't it?'

'Yes… I'm not sure I'm comfortable with the direction this conversation is going in. What exactly do you want to know?'

'Well, could I maybe get a name? Was he adopted out too?'

The line went silent. Sloane knew she was pushing it, but that information could be key to finding out who murdered Danny.

'Are you implying that Emily's youngest child is responsible for killing Danny? I mean, I can see why you'd think that but surely the police would be looking at that angle? By your logic, he'd have to be on licence himself, given there wasn't a break-in, according to what I've read in the papers. As far as I'm aware, none of the children have been involved in the criminal justice system…'

The social worker was right, but something was niggling at Sloane, and she wasn't prepared to disclose everything she had been thinking. 'I just want the information for background.' She wasn't being truthful, but it wasn't a complete lie.

'I'd have to do some digging, but no promises.'

'That's fair enough. What can you tell me about the other two children? Did they have any contact with their mother before she was killed?'

'Our records show that it was believed that neither of the other two children were Danny Wells's. Seemed to have been a bit of a bugbear with him. They were separated when adopted. I'm not sure how much you know about closed adoptions. At the time of these ones, there was no legal requirement for adoptive families to maintain contact of any kind with their child's birth family after the adoption order had gone through. However, chances are that contact arrangements would've been discussed prior to the adoption and perhaps a voluntary agreement between the two families was arranged. Sometimes the details of the contact arrangements might be included in the court order. But once those kids were taken from her, Emily effectively closed all contact off. I haven't seen any court orders, but that doesn't mean there weren't any.'

Sloane heard papers rustling and waited.

'Hmmm. I can tell you that the adoptive parents were keen to keep Emily involved. They took pictures of the kids which we have on file, but Emily continued to refuse to have anything to do with them… initially. I guess you have to understand she was a heavy drinker and drug-user. Sadly, that was the only thing she cared about at the time. A few weeks before she was murdered though, she did ask her social worker to see the pictures. She'd been clean for a while and had written letters to her kids, explaining why she did what she did in giving them up and suggesting that at some point, she'd be open to seeing them if they wanted. She never got that chance.'

'Why was the adoption closed? I thought that stopped—' Sloane had been digging into adoptions and from what she'd found, that particular aspect had stopped in the late 1970s.

'Yeah, legislation changed in the 70s. Contact is important for kids and as long as it happens alongside therapy it can really help them understand their past and develop a better sense of who they are.' Rose paused. 'Looks like it was actually at the request of Emily. There's some suggestion that she struggled with the decision to sign away her rights and the only way she could cope was to make sure that she cut off all contact.'

'Is there any chance I can have the adoptive parents' names?' Sloane bit her lip.

'No. I really can't do that. But I might be able to tell you who can…'

Sloane's hand ached as she wrote all the information down. She thanked Rose for her help and again reassured her that everything she said would be confidential. She had made sure not to use Rose's name in her notes, on the off-chance that anyone came across them.

Once the call had ended, she skimmed through the pages. Her mind was racing with everything and she was beginning to connect some dots.

If she was right, she needed to know how it fitted with Danny Wells and, more importantly, what was the connection to Ripley House?

FIFTY-EIGHT

Jeanette

J eanette began to question her own managerial abilities as she went through all the changes made by Anwar on Ray Southall's case file records with a fine-toothed comb. So focused on the task was she that she jumped when her desk phone rang, and her stomach muscles tightened. She wasn't up for more bad news. Her hand shook as she picked up the receiver.

'Jeanette. I just got off the phone with a DS Brady, with whom I believe you are familiar? Is there something you need to tell me?' Heavy breathing down the line from the area head of probation made her cringe.

'I was just about to call my line manager, in fact, but wanted to double-check the records to make sure I had all the info correct.'

'The SPO responsible for Mr Hussain's probation investigation will need to speak to you about that. We're going to put an LAO on the file so from now on, his OM in the hostel will need to email over any updates. Make sure no names are used.'

Jeanette wasn't happy but now wasn't the time to argue. 'Did DS Brady mention anything else?'

'Only that they'd be questioning Anwar again shortly. The board is meeting tomorrow to discuss the proposal that we shut down Ripley House until this whole mess is resolved.'

What the hell were they playing at?

'Whole mess? You mean the murder investigation? Bit more than a mess…' Jeanette mumbled to herself. 'Is closing down the hostel the right move though?'

'I'm not sure we'll have any other choice…'

'Hear me out.' An idea formed in Jeanette's mind. 'Closing down the hostel means we'd have to move the residents to other Approved Premises, which are already over capacity and have huge waiting lists. Staff would also have to be moved about and that could cause its own problems. Really, the best thing for everyone is that they stay where they are.'

She paused to let that sink in.

'The media's been all over this, Jeanette. The hostel had significant coverage when it first opened and now a murder? I just can't see how the added attention will balance the need for public protection.'

'The costs incurred by your suggestion would be astronomical.' Surely, he could see that. 'Why not allocate a portion of that towards added security? Maybe a twenty-four-hour trained security guard until everything is resolved, and then it can be looked at again. Additional night staff. A few more cameras that work and which are only accessible to designated individuals. That would ensure public protection but also keep residents and staff safe. I'm afraid that if this carries on for much longer, we will have staff go off sick due to stress and we'll need to hire agency staff just to keep afloat.

'As for the media, there's a local journalist who's been all over the hostel since it opened. In fact, she and Helen Burgess, the volunteer who just died, were bosom buddies. We could invite her to attend head office and explain what measures are being taken and—'

'No. No media.' He cut her dead in her tracks. 'The MoJ are dealing with all that. I'll put your proposal to the board but don't get your hopes up. I need to go now and try to mitigate some of the damage that's already been done. I'll be in touch tomorrow.'

The line went dead.

Jeanette sat back in her chair. Things were spiralling out of control, and she couldn't think straight. Glancing at her watch, she realised that Steph would be going into supervision with Ray shortly.

She headed down to the PO's desk. Steph looked up from her computer and Jeanette could see the concern etched on her face.

'I've updated his home PO on the situation, and they've called an emergency MAPPA meeting.' Steph leaned back and stretched her arms.

'Good. Might make things easier our side if they recall him. Are you ready to start? Let's make it seem like I'm just there to watch how you handle a supervision session.' Jeanette didn't think there was enough evidence to support a return to custody... yet.

The pair walked toward the interview room. Ray stood opposite the door, leaning against the wall with his foot tapping.

'What's going on?' He began to hop from foot to foot, glancing over their shoulders toward the front door as if he was about to bolt.

'Calm down, Ray. Jeanette's here to observe me, not you.

Part of my appraisal. She may ask you some questions, she may not. Now, enough with the antics, let's get started, OK?'

Ray grumbled and reluctantly entered the room, slumping his large frame into the chair. Jeanette had been impressed with how Steph had handled the situation and would be sure to include it in her appraisal when the time came as good evidence of how to deal calmly with conflict situations.

The supervision session revolved around Ray's substance misuse and general offending behaviour.

'Ray, I've been looking over your notes to write my summary for your PO and noticed that Anwar was a lot more involved in some of your sessions than I was aware of. Can you tell me a bit about that?'

Jeanette was pleased that Steph had created a window of opportunity for her to jump in should it be needed.

A blank look crossed over his face. 'Anwar? No idea what you're talking about. I've not had any dealings with him.' He smirked when he realised what he'd said. 'Guess *dealings* wasn't the best word to use…'

They ignored his attempt at humour. Steph pulled out a sheet of paper and began to highlight some dates, reading from the notes. 'Didn't Anwar attend your appointment at RSH with you?'

Ray began to fidget with his sleeve. 'What the hell's going on here? No one's ever attended any appointments with me.' He pushed his chair back and stood. 'I've got my card here – you can see the dates. You sure you got my notes there, Steph?' He pulled out his appointment card and handed it to Steph.

Jeanette glanced over the PO's shoulder and noted that Ray had attended all the appointments, but this wasn't what was reflected in his case notes.

Perhaps that's why Anwar withdrew the missed appointment warning letter?

Steph glanced at Jeanette. 'Uh. OK. Not sure what happened there, Ray. Thanks for clearing that up. I'll take a copy of this to scan into the system and return it to you after the supervision.'

Jeanette didn't hear much of the session after that as she was trying to figure out what was going on. A tap at the door pulled her back into the room.

'Sorry to interrupt. Jeanette, there's a phone call you need to take.' Amy held open the door.

'OK.' Jeanette stood. 'Thanks, Ray. Steph, I'll leave you to carry on your supervision.' Jeanette smiled and returned to the main office. 'Who's on the phone?'

'Your favourite detective. Said it was urgent and when I explained you were busy, he insisted I disturb you. Grumpy sod. I'll put him through to your office.'

'Thanks.' Jeanette jogged back to her office, shutting the door behind her just as her desk phone rang.

'I've been trying to get a hold of you.'

Jeanette stayed silent but turned over her mobile phone to see ten missed calls.

'Hello? Jeanette? You there?'

'Yes. I was just waiting for you to find your manners, but I guess I'll be waiting a while for that…'

'Funny. I'm calling because I spoke to Mr Hussain about Ray Southall's records, and he flat-out denied any tampering with case notes. He was defensive and it felt genuine, so I'm inclined to believe him.'

'I think you're right. I've just been in a supervision session with Ray, and something isn't adding up. I need to confirm a few things with RSH.'

'Ok. Do that and get back to me as soon as possible because if Ray and Anwar are telling the truth…'

The detective didn't need to finish that sentence because Jeanette already knew what he was going to say.

'Someone tampered with the records to cover their tracks and point the finger at Anwar and Ray…'

FIFTY-NINE

Sloane

I n an effort to piece together a timeline, Sloane had strewn all the newspaper articles she had collected on the floor of her living room, but nothing seemed to match up. After speaking to Rose at the South London Social Care hub, she'd managed to track down the child who had been known as 'Baby M' in the papers at the time. He was now living in Leicester, where he'd been moved after his mother was murdered. He had been very open with Sloane and admitted that he had read about Danny Wells's murder but had no interest in the man. He barely knew his birth mother and shared no relationship with any of his half-siblings. He didn't know who his birth father was, but DNA tests showed that it wasn't Danny Wells.

No motive then, was there?

Her mobile phone buzzed underneath the pile of papers, and she patted them down until she located it.

'Hello?'

'Sloane, we just got some info that I think you'll be interested in.' Her editor's words tumbled out in a high pitch.

'Must be pretty juicy. You sound like you just sucked the air out of a helium balloon. Spill!'

'The police are now investigating Helen Burgess's death. Claim they have reason to believe she died under suspicious circumstances and will be appealing for the public's help. I wanted to give you first dibs on the story, given your relationship with her, in case it's—'

The phone dropped from Sloane's hands, and bile rose in her throat.

Suspicions? But it had been deemed an accidental fall… What had changed?

A muffled *'Hello? Hello?'* came from the floor and Sloane returned the handset to her ear.

'Sorry.' She cleared her throat. 'You just caught me off-guard there. Yes, I want the story. Can you tell me everything you know?' Sloane listened as her editor passed on the details. Her hands shook as she noted things down.

'Are you sure you're up for this?'

Sloane smiled at her editor's concern. He wasn't one to share emotion easily but always looked out for his team.

'Absolutely. In fact, I think Helen would have wanted it.' She could almost hear Helen in her ear, pushing her to get involved.

Sloane ended the call and took a moment to let everything sink in. Had Helen stumbled across something linked to the murder at Ripley House, or had it just been a random act of violence? Her editor said a press conference at the police station was planned for an hour's time and she wasn't going to miss it.

She booked a taxi and gathered her things.

———

Twenty minutes later she was standing outside the police station. She dug around in her bag for her ID and went inside to sign in.

The receptionist at the enquiry desk looked her up and down before pointing at the door. 'Pull it gently when you hear the buzz. Someone will be there to show you to the conference room.'

Sloane forced a smile. She knew the drill but didn't recognise the woman so put her condescending tone down to being new in the job. She stood by the door and five minutes later it buzzed and she was led down the hall to the conference room. It was already full but she spied a familiar face from the newspaper and gave him a wave before seating herself beside him.

Sloane leaned over. 'Wasn't expecting to see you here.'

'Just curious. Conrad told me the story was yours, but I'm doing a piece on vulnerable elderly people, and this caught my eye.'

'Has anything happened so far?' Sloane scanned the room and locked eyes with DS Brady. Her heart raced. If he was here, they must feel there was some connection to the Wells investigation. He gave her a nod before joining his colleagues at the front. She was slightly annoyed she'd had to learn about this from her editor after the detective had promised her exclusivity, but now was not the time to bear grudges, despite her fury at being left out.

'Settle down.' The man at the front raised his arms. 'My name is DCI Reese. We'd like the public's help today, which is where you all come in. I'm going to hand you over to my colleague DS Brady who'll go into the specifics. If there's time at the end, I'll open the floor for questions.' Reese stepped aside and Brady took the floor.

'Thank you all for coming. I'll share with you what I can at the moment. We're launching a murder investigation into the suspicious death of a local woman, Helen Burgess. Mrs Burgess, aged sixty-eight years, was found dead in her home by a friend.' DS Brady cast his eyes towards Sloane and for a moment she was grateful he hadn't revealed her name as she didn't want to answer any questions. Ironic really. He continued. 'The police and emergency services responded and initially it was believed to be an accidental death, as Mrs Burgess had form for accidents...'

Sloane was not aware of Helen having been particularly accident-prone, but she assumed the police would have accessed her medical records. The detective carried on for a further fifteen minutes before he opened the floor to the press to see if they had any questions.

Sloane didn't pay any attention to who else wanted to speak. This was her friend and a whole load of questions had built up in her mind. She shot out of her seat and looked at DS Brady. 'Does this murder have anything to do with Ripley House?'

The detective frowned. 'Let's not jump to any conclusions, Ms Armstrong. We don't—'

She interrupted DS Brady before he could give her the usual line. 'Mrs Burgess was very vocal in her concerns about the hostel. In fact, she was convinced someone in that hostel was spying on her. What did the police do to investigate her concerns? Could this death have been prevented?' Sloane's jaw tightened. She thought she saw the detective flinch.

'I'm not at liberty to discuss anything in any more detail.' Brady looked around the room. 'Anyone else have any questions?' He didn't wait for a response before stepping away from the microphone.

DCI Reese stepped forward, ending the conversation and any further questions by asking for members of the public to come forward with any information. The crowd of press personnel started to disperse, and Sloane heard someone calling her name.

It was the detective.

'I think we need to talk.'

SIXTY

Killer

There's a buzz around the hostel when a voice booms over the radio airwaves telling its listeners about some new information that's come to light regarding the death of Helen Burgess.

Shit!

I'm confident that nothing will place me at the scene, but it doesn't mean I'm not concerned. Helen hadn't factored into my plans; it really was just an unfortunate accident. A tinge of guilt courses through my veins.

'Bloody bullshit.' A resident comes storming into the communal living area and throws himself into the oversized beanbag chair. He's not trusted by many in the hostel as he's known for trying to stitch people up if it means he gets something he wants in return. Sympathy would not be his friend today though.

I lean in and listen as the man rants about accusations, and staff trying to screw him over.

'Why the hell would they do that?'

The man punches the side of the chair.

What a muppet.

'Trying to get you recalled would be my guess?' another resident pipes up. 'These fuckers are always on our cases, like they're just waiting for us to fucking fail so they can send us back.' The man turns and looks at me, waiting for my take on what's happening, but there's no way I'm going to get involved. Instead, I shrug my shoulders and walk out of the room. 'I'll leave you to your conspiracies.'

I don't have time to listen to all the moaning because I need to find out more about why the police believe Helen's death wasn't accidental. Maybe they think it was random – there had been a few burglaries in the area. Let's hope so, otherwise I could be screwed.

I pat my pockets in search of my fags. The nicotine's calling and without even bothering to check with anyone, I walk out of the back door.

Screw the rules, I'll just have a quick one.

My eyes can't help but drift over to look across the fence at Helen's property and a shiver goes down my spine.

Damn!

I see my first mistake – hopefully my only one. Beads of sweat form on my head. I wipe them away quickly.

I jog two by two down the steps and head to the end of the garden. Large bushes have been planted on each side of the area and along the back of the fence. They're overgrown, which will work in my favour.

A quick look over my shoulders to make sure no one's around and I won't be disturbed…

I lean between the bushes on the side of the fence that joins the hostel to Helen's house, poking my arm through and feeling about until my hand tips the hard object. The wooden crate is still there.

Bloody hell.

I can't believe how reckless I've been. After what happened with Helen, I didn't have time to come back and remove the box. Then, with all the police presence, I couldn't risk being seen nosing around the end of the garden. It had completely slipped my mind – and that's how people get caught.

Stupid move.

With the police reopening the case, it's now or never. I push my hand through the bushes once more, trying to grab hold of the box, but the branches scupper my attempts.

'Oi! You're not supposed to be out here on your own. Jeanette will skin you alive if she sees you!' It's Steph. I'd recognise her voice anywhere. She has a distinct accent, giving away her Staffordshire background.

'Yeah, snuck out for a quick fag but thought I saw something down here…'

'Oh, really?' She begins to descend the stairs.

'It's nothing.' I pull my hand out and head back towards the stairs to stop the nosy cow from coming down and spotting the crate. 'Just a cat. I shooed the bugger away.'

Steph stops midway. 'Yeah, they're always coming in and doing their business in the bushes. Cute but such pests.' She laughs. 'Get inside before Jeanette sees you. I won't mention anything this time…' Her head tilts.

'Appreciate it. Thanks.' I squeeze by her and return inside. 'Catch you later.' I duck past the communal room and head upstairs to the second-floor bathroom. Once inside I lock the door and lean against the sink to catch my breath.

That was close.

I open the window, look out into the garden, and my heart skips a beat. Steph is still outside and now another member of staff has joined her.

Bang! Bang! Bang! Bang!

The door shakes and I nearly wet myself.

'Hey, you gonna be long in there? I'm busting for a piss and the other bathroom's being used,' a husky voice shouts.

'Two minutes, mate.'

Shit!

I rub my head. Suddenly it feels like everything's falling apart and with only weeks until my transfer out, now is not the time to panic.

I glance out of the window again, but Steph and the other person are nowhere to be seen.

Did she find the crate? I need to know.

I flush the toilet and turn on the sink faucet, splashing water on my face. I look at my reflection in the mirror.

More banging on the door. 'Come on! I'm going to piss myself here.'

I yank open the door and can't help the tight smile on my face. 'It's all yours.'

I return downstairs and see Steph chatting to the kitchen staff in the hallway by the back door. I wonder whether to approach her and ask her more about what she was doing in the garden but figure that might seem suspicious.

Steph catches my eye and waves me over. The volunteers move away as I approach. I don't realise I'm rubbing my hands together until Steph looks down at them. That's when I feel how clammy they are.

'I think I will have to have a word with Jeanette.'

My voice croaks. 'Ah, really? Why?'

How will I explain how I knew where the crate is if the police get hold of it?

'There's a bigger problem out there.' She points down the garden.

Here it comes. I want to cover her mouth and make her go away. I wait for her to carry on, as my shoulders tense.

'Yeah... rabbits or moles. Digging into the veggie garden. We'll have to get it sorted.'

My shoulders loosen. 'Oh! Good spot.'

Steph walks away.

She will never know how close she came to being my next victim.

SIXTY-ONE

Sloane

S loane hung back as the crowd of press and media left the room. DS Brady also waited, his face blank, giving nothing away. Once the room was cleared, Sloane blurted out, '*Is* this connected to the hostel? Was Helen murdered because of something she knew?'

The detective's face remained unchanged. 'Ms Armstrong, you're no stranger to this game so c'mon, you know I can't confirm anything for you right now. The reason I asked you to stay is because I thought this might happen and, given our conversation about transparency previously, I thought I owed you an apology. More so than most because of your personal connections to Mrs Burgess. This was all sprung on me last-minute. I'm sure we both have the same goal – the truth, and to get justice for the victims and their families. Right? Let's not ruin that by running before we can walk.'

'Please, detective. Name a time I have ever spread or written information that wasn't factual. Can you just get to the point?' Sloane placed her hands on her hips, her patience wearing thin. She appreciated the apology, but it would have meant more if he'd at least given her a quick heads-up in a text.

'I was trying to...' the detective grumbled. 'I'm here to make an offer of sorts. You'll have to report this in the story, but as you and Helen were close, I'd like to go through a few things with you if you have time. We could do that now?' He paused and cleared his throat. 'But if you're too busy, I'd ask that you steer clear of Ripley House while we continue our investigation, and we can catch up when you are free?'

Sloane's cheeks burned. 'You've some nerve, Brady. I've time now to chat, so let's get it over with so that I can go do *my* job.' She turned on her heels and stomped out of the room with the detective in tow. Sloane waited outside the door and followed him into one of the interview rooms. She had no idea what she could offer to the investigation, but if clever, she might learn more than she would have otherwise.

'Can I see your mobile phone?' The detective held out a hand.

Sloane pulled her phone out of her bag and showed him the screen. She couldn't help but be a bit smug, knowing he was checking to see if she was recording and even though the thought had crossed her mind, she figured his mistrust of the press, of her, would have led to him wanting to check it.

'Satisfied?' She made a move to take her phone back, but the detective placed his hand over hers.

'Thanks. Can you leave it on the table please?'

Sloane laughed. 'Of course. You do know that I can retain conversations in my mind, right?' She tapped her head.

'I do. But at least it would be your word against mine without any recording to back it up.' His lip curled. 'Shall we just get on with things? Can you confirm how you knew Mrs Burgess?' DS Brady's eyes were locked on hers. He would be looking for any sign of deception from Sloane, but she had nothing to hide.

'Really? You know all this but—' She sighed. 'OK, I met her about two years ago when Ripley House was first opening. She'd formed a group – a neighbourhood watch scheme to complain about the hostel opening in the area. I was doing a story and we started chatting. A friendship soon followed.' Sloane looked at the floor.

'I found it curious that after all her protestations and complaints about the hostel, she ended up working there as a volunteer. In the kitchen, right? Do you know why she did that?'

'Helen was pragmatic. The hostel was opened and not going anywhere. I guess she wanted to make sure she kept an eye on things, so when she saw they were advertising for volunteers, she applied.' Sloane shrugged. 'If you can't beat 'em, join 'em, right?'

'In the time she was there, were there any incidents?'

'In what sense? I mean, there was a murder. I'd say that was a pretty big incident...' Was this guy for real? Sloane's sarcasm had not gone unnoticed. The detective was asking questions she was sure he already knew the answers to – from Helen herself, no doubt. Was he testing their friendship? Or pointing a finger?

'No need to get smart, Ms Armstrong, but if you need things spelled out, did anyone from the hostel openly threaten Mrs Burgess? Did she ever tell you she was concerned for her safety, other than what we already know?'

Sloane thought for a moment. 'Hmmm. She'd been afraid once when she thought someone had been inside her home. She'd heard noises – or she thought she had – but it turned out to be nothing. Wait... Not long before she died, she had gone around to the hostel. She was furious because she believed someone from there had been in her garden.' Her lips quivered as she held back the tears. Sloane was surprised at how overcome with emotion she was. The realisation that her elderly friend had been murdered blindsided her. 'Excuse me for a moment.' She took a tissue from her pocket and blew her nose. Thoughts of her sister popped into her head, specifically the time when the police had come to tell her family she'd been murdered. The hairs on the back of her neck stood on end.

'I'm not a monster, Ms Armstrong, and I understand that this may be difficult for you, but I do appreciate it. When you're ready, could you tell me if Mrs Burgess named anyone or had any idea who might have been in her garden?'

'All I know is that she felt strongly that it was one of the hostel residents. Maybe she came across something or overheard something when she was at work. Have you spoken to the staff? Jeanette Macey probably knows a lot more than she lets on.'

'Hmmm. OK. Thanks for your time. You've been really helpful. On a final note, I just want to reiterate how important it is for you to let us do our job.' He looked her in the eye. 'Please don't go to the hostel and start stirring things. We don't want to tip anyone off.'

'I heard you the first time, detective.' Sloane stood, gathered her belongings, and waited to be escorted from the building. Once outside, she pulled out her phone. The detective said not to *go* to the hostel. He never mentioned anything about calling.

SIXTY-TWO

Jeanette

News of the investigation into Helen Burgess's death concerned Jeanette. The last thing the hostel needed was more bad press and with Helen having been a volunteer, it was inevitable that a connection, whether right or wrong, would be made. Helen had been very vocal about her dislike of Ripley House, and with her outburst and accusation about someone being in her garden... Jeanette's head thumped. Once this hit the press – or, worse, Sloane Armstrong got her claws into it – heads would roll.

Her chest tightened as the office walls appeared to be closing in on her. She had an overwhelming urge to run out of the door and never come back. It was only a fleeting thought as she'd never leave someone else to clean up this mess.

What she should be more concerned with was how her team were coping. She walked downstairs and stood just outside the door into the main office area, where she saw her team huddled around Steph's desk. Every now and then someone would look her way and despite the icy glare she gave them, they carried on as if she wasn't even there.

She was losing respect, losing control. The old Jeanette, the one who just wanted a peaceful life with no conflict, would probably have accepted that, but not now. A fire burned inside her. Enough was enough.

She smacked her hand against the doorframe and cleared her throat, waiting for her staff members to acknowledge her presence. When they didn't, she unleashed the anger that had been pent up for the last few weeks.

'I'm sorry, has everyone suddenly gone deaf? I'm assuming that your case records and assessments are all done and up to date?'

Blanks stares met her, and this only fuelled the flames.

'You all seem to have so much free time to stand around and chatter. I hope you're docking that off your timesheets. Do I need to be contacting the courts and field teams to let them know you have the time to take on extra reports?'

The room was silent.

Steph opened her mouth to speak but Jeanette held up her hand. 'Save it. I don't want to hear your excuses. What I do want to see is you all back at your desks *working*. Whatever it was you were gossiping about no longer gets mentioned during work hours or I *will* deduct every single minute of wasted time off your time sheets. Everybody understand?'

For just a moment, a small part of her felt bad; she hated having to micro-manage but they were leaving her little choice. She waited as they returned to their desks and a few incoherent mumbles and grumbles followed. Jeanette dismissed them from her train of thought.

She took her time going back up to her office, but it seemed the team had got the message as they focused on their computers rather than chitchatting with each other.

Once back in her office, she gulped in some air, needing to

calm down, and waited for her body to stop shaking. She'd never had to speak to her staff like that, but she'd never been in this situation before either. She'd surprised herself, but she wouldn't let her team undermine her authority. There was too much to lose right now.

Jeanette reached across her desk and went to pick up the phone handset with the intention of ringing her line manager but before she could, her work mobile rang. She instantly regretted answering the call as soon as she realised who it was.

'I can guess why you're calling.' She tapped her finger on the arm of her chair.

'I'm sure you can. I wanted to reach out to see if you have something to say before I print my story?'

'All in the name of professional courtesy, is that what you're going to tell me next? That's not like you, Ms Armstrong. What I don't understand is why you keep asking even though you know I can't speak to you. Any statements will have to come from the comms department at head office.'

'Really, Jeanette?'

Jeanette was surprised at the tone in Sloane's voice. She sounded deflated. Where had her fight gone?

'I know Helen could be an annoyance but in the grand scheme of things, she was a member of your team, and a good friend to me. I get that things were not always smooth sailing and, believe me, I know she could be a bit... fiery, but surely you'd want to know if her murder had anything to do with the hostel?'

'What?' That had thrown Jeanette. 'Who said her death was linked to Ripley House?' As shocked as she was to hear this latest development, she'd be lying if she said she hadn't had the same thought herself. She wouldn't say that to the journalist though. She could just imagine what sensationalist story would be whipped up from one passing comment.

'It has to be connected. Two murders within such close proximity? That can't be a coincidence. Helen's death was made to look like an accident. We both know she had some strong views. Did she find out something about one of your residents?'

Jeanette tapped her phone. 'Hello? Can you hear me?' *Tap. Tap. Tap.*

'What the heck? Of course I can. Why'd you do that?'

A little smirk crossed the manager's lips. 'I thought there might be a connection problem as you keep asking me things that I won't... that I *can't* answer. I know you and Helen were close and I really do sympathise – no one deserves to die that way, especially alone. But I can assure you – and this will be the only bit of information you'll get from me – that Helen did not come to me or anyone on my team, as far as I know, to raise any specific concerns about any of the residents.'

'Hang on. We both know that's not true.'

Jeanette paused and thought for a moment. 'Are you referring to her complaint that someone was smoking in her garden?'

'Yes. She was upset and afraid. Shortly after, she was dead. Like I said, I don't believe in coincidences.'

Jeanette stood. 'You're jumping to the wrong conclusion. The residents were all spoken to. Measures were put in place. There's no way any one of them could have been involved. Have you forgotten about all the recent break-ins? Perhaps Helen confronted a burglar. Between us, Helen was old, possibly forgetful. I even told her if she was really concerned, she should call the police. I mean, someone could have been watching her house for days, but she declined any assistance from me.'

'So that's it? You're just going to pretend none of this is happening?'

'I'm sorry you feel that way, Ms Armstrong. I've said all I'm going to say on the matter. Please don't call me again.' Jeanette ended the call and fell back into her chair. Spinning around, she stared out into the hostel's back garden, her eyes drawn to the fence that separated it from Helen's yard. Her gaze halted at the large bushes near the back.

Something there had caught her attention.

It couldn't be…

SIXTY-THREE

Sloane

The bloody nerve!

Sloane looked at her phone, checking that she hadn't accidentally hung up on the probation manager.

She hadn't.

Grumbling to herself, she headed to the bus stop. Right now, all she wanted to do was get home and go through everything she and Helen had worked on – their conversations, texts, notes – maybe there was a clue amongst all the scribbled notes as to who could have done this. She knew it was a long shot, but it was all she had to go on.

The bus journey took longer than expected thanks to road works and this added to her frustration. The road crew were standing around a cordoned-off manhole, smoking, texting, chatting. She should have been home ages ago.

The bus finally came to a stop a few feet from her home. Sloane raced up the path to her front door and immediately headed to her office. There had to be something. She pulled up her notes on her laptop, skim-reading the bullet points and shorthand. When that was a lost cause, she rifled through the various notes in her legal pad.

There was nothing.

She slid down the wall in defeat. Helen had told her that she feared someone was watching her, but she didn't have any clue as to who it was or any insight into who it could be.

A thought struck her. She rummaged through the basket of stationery bits – paperclips, staples, and the like – until she found what she was looking for.

Helen's spare key. Sloane had been given the key one time after her friend had a strange fainting spell, but she'd never had the need for it since.

Sloane knew that forensics had gone over the property already but her experience working on stories related to crime cases told her that a fresh pair of eyes could spot things that others missed.

She changed into more comfortable clothing and got her exercise in by jogging at a comfortable pace the two blocks to Helen's home. She stopped outside the hostel briefly and was tempted to ring the buzzer, but the DS's voice boomed in her head, reminding her that it could lead to serious repercussions if she did. Normally she'd ignore those pesky voices and do what she pleased but finding out the truth about Helen's murder was more important than defying the police's advice.

She knew which battles to fight. This wasn't one of them. Not yet, anyway.

Sloane walked up the stairs to Helen's front door. Her hands shook as she placed the key in the lock and turned. She had to nudge the door with her shoulders once she heard the lock click. She smiled to herself then as a memory popped into her head. Helen was always complaining about the door jamming and Sloane had suggested a bit of WD40 would do the trick if she sprayed it every now and again, but Helen had said that had always been Malcolm's job and it seemed she had never followed through.

Once through the front door, Sloane stared at the darkened bloodstain on the floor. No one had been back to clean, and it just reminded her of how alone Helen really had been. A pang of guilt at all the times she had fobbed the woman off stuck in her throat. She began to wonder if coming here was a good idea. The house no longer felt like a home, and she realised how much she'd miss the old busybody. Sloane's eyes glistened.

No time for sadness, though

If Helen had had concerns, would she have written them down?

Helen had always carried a pocket-sized notebook on her person and Brady had never mentioned it, so there was a chance it hadn't been found.

Sloane knew her friend hadn't been tech savvy, so the police wouldn't find anything on her phone or iPad. Helen had been old school and the address book on the side table by her landline just reinforced that. Who had address books these days?

She stepped over the bloodstain and made her way upstairs. All the doors were closed, so she opened them one by one in search of Helen's bedroom. The first door she happened across was the main bathroom. It was so different from the small one downstairs, and it made her realise that in all her time visiting her friend, she had never once ventured upstairs. It was pristine.

The second door was a sewing-room-cum-spare-bedroom. Her eyes were drawn to a rocking chair with a home sweet home pillow, which faced the window and overlooked Helen's back garden. Helen had loved knitting and sewing – she had given Sloane a hat and gloves set for Christmas last year and Sloane had made a mental note to find them and wear them more often.

She closed the door and went to the final room, the one she had been looking for – the bedroom. When she opened the door, her nostrils were assaulted with the smell of Chanel No. 5 – Helen's signature scent. The room was dark with the curtains pulled across the windows. Sloane touched the wall in search of a light switch and flicked it on.

The bed was still made. Helen hadn't even had the chance to go to sleep before her attacker took hold. The police had obviously been in this room though as the closet door was open, boxes had been pulled out, and the contents of her jewellery box had been spilled out over her dresser; items had been knocked over, drawers haphazardly left opened. Instinct made her start putting the figurines back in their place until she remembered why she was here.

Sloane took a deep breath before she walked over to the first night table on the left side. She sat on the bed and pulled the drawer completely out. She reached under the top and felt around. Nothing there. She rummaged through the items, but nothing stood out to her, so she replaced the drawer as she found it before moving to the other side of the bed and did the same. Nothing.

Sloane glanced over her shoulder at the closet and headed over. Moving the boxes with her feet, she began to go through all the items of clothing with pockets. She was beginning to feel disheartened, feeling that she had wasted her time, when her hand touched something. She pulled out a small notebook from the pocket of a cardigan.

What do we have here?

Her fingers were positioned to start leafing through the little black book when a noise startled her.

Someone was in the house.

SIXTY-FOUR

Jeanette

Jeanette hesitated for a moment, edging closer to the window to get a better view. Was she just seeing things? Was her mind playing tricks on her? Her tired eyes trying to fool her?

Sometimes this house felt like a prison. Even though she had a key to come and go as she pleased, the energy inside sapped her soul, took over her thoughts, and created illusions that would scare the most die-hard horror fans. But she had chosen this job, so she needed to pull up her big-girl pants and stop faffing about.

She pushed her chair out and headed down the creaky stairs to the garden. A few of the residents were standing by the back door. Steph was there, clipboard in hand, jotting down their details and letting them out one by one.

'Just taking these guys out for a fag. You might want to speak to Pete at some point.'

Jeanette stared past the men and into the garden. She'd only been half listening to Steph. 'Why?'

'Think we have rabbits or something. Found a few holes

and a lot of the veggie garden has been decimated. If Helen were here, she'd be disappointed. She loved making a big pot of stew...' Steph sighed and walked away, mumbling something about a group that was due to start in an hour.

Jeanette remained at the door. Maybe it was a rabbit she'd seen in the bushes. After all, it hadn't moved – might have been scared. She removed her glasses and gave them a wipe on her sleeve before replacing them. From this angle nothing could be seen. She was halfway out the door when her work mobile buzzed in her pocket.

'Hello?'

'Ms Macey. I'm calling from Recovery Starts Here. I've got a very agitated Ray Southall here with me. He's informed me that his probation records have been doctored? Is that correct?'

Jeanette's jaw tightened. She didn't appreciate the confrontational tone of the keyworker's voice, nor the fact that this supposed professional felt it was appropriate to have this kind of discussion in front of a client. 'Can you hang on a moment?'

She returned to her office and shut the door.

'Hello? Are you still there?'

'Yes, I'm here. I needed to go somewhere private as I wasn't in my office when you called. I'm glad Ray felt he could discuss the situation with you, but I'm a little concerned you feel it's appropriate to have this conversation with him listening in.'

'Ray's fully disclosed his concerns about recall and the allegations that he has missed appointments and that he's tested positive. I wanted to make it clear to him that I and this agency played no part in this, but also to confirm with you that he has attended all of the keywork sessions and continues to test negative for any substances.' There was smugness in his tone, and although Jeanette could appreciate his point of view, she couldn't help the anger rising.

'I've noted that down and I'll be sure to pass the information to his home probation officer. I'm not prepared to discuss anything further with you at this time. In fact, could you put your line manager on the phone?'

'I… uh… yes. Yes, I can. I'll put you through now.' The tone in his voice had changed and Jeanette couldn't help feeling slightly satisfied at putting him in his place.

Jeanette sat down at her desk and started spinning a pen between her fingers while she waited for the call to be transferred.

'I understand you wished to speak with me? How can I help?' Jeanette could almost feel the frosty attitude through the handset.

'Hi, this is Jeanette Macey. I'm the SPO at Ripley House and I've just had quite a concerning conversation with one of your staff members.'

'What seems to be the issue?'

'I don't appreciate having a keyworker call me to discuss a situation with the client present and listening in. Had your member of staff waited until the client left, I would have felt comfortable giving a more detailed explanation. When it comes to multi-agency working, I try to avoid the us-versus-them mentality because it isn't productive.' Jeanette took a deep breath before continuing. 'You may have seen on the news that one of the residents was murdered here recently. You also may have seen that one of my staff members has been arrested for supplying drugs.' Jeanette wanted to be as open with the RSH manager as she could be, because she knew they would also be under pressure with the same investigations and allegations. 'Although these are separate investigations, and your agency is named, to then call me and ask questions in front of one of my residents was wholly inappropriate.'

'Ms Macey. The keyworker you spoke with is new to the agency and perhaps trying to prove his sincerity to his client. We operate in an open and transparent fashion here, and often have three-way discussions but, saying that, I agree that the call was not appropriate and I'll speak to him.'

Jeanette had been preparing for an argument so the manager's response caught her off guard. 'Ah, thank you. I'm glad we're on the same page. I think a meeting is probably in order at this stage, so I'll talk to the relevant people and get the ball rolling on that. Will you be attending the next priority crime group?'

'Yes, I'll be there. Thanks for bringing this to my attention. I'll update you at the PCG.'

Jeanette ended the call and logged the conversation onto Ray's case record as a manager oversight, detailing as much information as she could. As she finished and was closing the case records, a faint but piercing scream caught her attention.

What the hell was that?

She rushed to the window outside her office but couldn't see anything so ran down to the main office.

'Did you hear that? Where did it come from?' Steph burst into the main office and looked around.

'I think…' Jeanette walked over to the big bay window at the front of the house and looked to the left. 'It can't be…'

When a second scream was heard, Jeanette reached for the phone. 'It's from next door. Helen Burgess's house.'

SIXTY-FIVE

Sloane

When the bedroom door creaked open, Sloane grabbed the lamp from the nightstand and waited, her body pressed tightly against the wall. She was ready for a fight.

The moment she saw the large boot at the bottom of the door, she came out screaming, lamp raised high over her head and poised to crash down on the intruder's skull.

'You'd better stop right there. I'm trained in martial arts and if you take one more step, I'm going to kick your ass!' Her voice shook, dispelling any confidence she was trying to get across and potentially exposing the lie about martial arts.

The man came forward into the light, his eyes wide, like a deer caught in headlights. Sloane screamed again.

'Stop!' The man raised his arms in submission. 'I'm not here to hurt you. I just want to know who you are and why you're in my aunt's house. I've rung the police.'

'Your aunt? The police?' Sloane lowered the lamp to her side. 'Shit…'

'Yeah, shit. Can you put the lamp down on the floor? I'd feel safer if I knew you weren't going to use it against me.'

'How do I know you are who you say you are?' Sloane took a step back and gripped the lamp tighter. For all she knew, this guy could be a burglar – or possibly Helen's killer, coming back to collect his prize now that the police presence was gone.

The man pulled out his wallet and rifled through it until he found what looked to be a photo. He held it out for Sloane to examine. 'This is me, my mum, and her sister, Auntie Helen.' He pointed out a younger-looking Helen Burgess.

Sloane's body relaxed. 'I'm sorry. I didn't realise Helen had relatives in the area.'

The man blushed. 'The family fell out. Stupid really, but sadly nothing can be done about it now. I still don't know who you are though...'

'Oh sorry.' She held out her hand. 'I'm Sloane. Your aunt and I were friends. She was a wonderful woman. I'm sorry you never got to know that.'

'Doesn't explain why you're here.'

Sloane didn't want to give the man anything more to regret. 'I missed her. She gave me a key to her house before she... passed. Wait, how did you know I was here?'

The man gestured for Sloane to follow him. When they got downstairs, he pointed to a small camera above the front door. 'That notifies me if anyone breaks in. With the house being vacant and my mother not ready to go through my aunt's things just yet, I installed this for a bit of extra security earlier this morning. It streams to my phone. I was heading back home after grabbing a late breakfast when I was notified.'

The pair jumped simultaneously when a loud *bang, bang, bang* on the door interrupted the nephew's explanation.

'That must be the police.' Helen's nephew opened the door and Sloane stood back out of view. She hoped she wouldn't have to speak to the police as they might not be so forgiving

313

this time; they might even follow through on their previous threats of arrest.

'It's OK, officer. Turned out to be a false alarm. A friend of my aunt's dropped by to check on the house.'

'OK. Could I just come in and check please?' The officer mumbled something into the radio on his shoulder and Helen's nephew stepped aside, letting him into the front hall.

A knowing smile crept across the officer's face. 'Hello, Ms Armstrong. Why am I not surprised?'

Helen's nephew looked between the pair. 'You know each other?'

Before Sloane could explain, the officer jumped in. 'She's a local and very vocal journalist for the *North Warwickshire Herald* and we've spoken before, haven't we, Ms Armstrong? Has she been bothering you? We could arrest her for trespassing.'

'Hang on a minute. I wasn't trespassing. I have a key and was just explaining everything before you arrived.' Her eyes pleaded with Helen's nephew not to push this further.

The nephew gestured for the officer to stop. 'There's no need for anyone to be arrested, but maybe you should leave now, Ms Armstrong. My family and I are grieving and my mother is having a hard enough time as it is. I don't even know why the press would be interested in any of this.'

The police officer went to put his hands on her arm to lead her out, but Sloane moved away. 'I can walk myself out, officer.' She reached into her bag and pulled out a card and handed it to Helen's nephew. 'If you or your family want to know anything about Helen, please call. She was a real character and a good friend. I won't rest until her killer is caught. You have my word on that.' She went to step outside.

'Her killer? She fell down the stairs.' He paused, taken aback. 'What are you talking about?'

'Sir, I'll explain everything once Ms Armstrong leaves the property.' The officer glared at Sloane.

She was curious as to why Helen's nephew hadn't been informed that the police were treating Helen's death as suspicious.

As if reading her mind, the officer continued, 'Your parents were told last night, but it seems they haven't passed on the message. There was a press conference this morning. I'm sorry. Had I known you hadn't been told...' The officer pointed at Sloane. 'I think you should go now before I arrest you.'

'I... uh... only got back today and haven't spoken to my parents yet. I...'

Sloane felt guilty at being the cause of further grief to the family. It hadn't been her intention.

The officer closed the door on Sloane, leaving her standing outside on the doorstep. She heard loud sobs through the door and a pang of guilt hit her.

She'd leave the poor man in peace.

Sloane made her way off the property, eyeing the second officer standing by the police car.

'You lot are making a shambles of this whole situation.' The words were out of her mouth before she could stop herself. The policewoman remained tight-lipped and stone-faced at the insult.

'I've been asked to make sure you leave the area or arrest you for obstruction.' The officer took a step towards her.

Sloane snapped then. 'Obstruction? My friend has been murdered, probably by someone who lives in that hostel.' She pointed at Ripley House and spotted Jeanette Macey staring at her from the front window. Some of her team were watching too from the opposite window. Her blood boiled though when she noted a few of the residents were watching and laughing.

The fucking nerve of them…

Sloane stomped over and stood outside the hostel on the public pavement – she couldn't be accused of trespassing then.

'That's right, you heard me. One of you is responsible for this. You think I won't find out? You don't know me then. Rehabilitation my arse! Mark my words, I will do *everything* in my power to make sure *you*, whoever *you* are, are caught, convicted, and put away for life this time!'

The officer started walking towards her.

'Don't bother, I'm leaving.'

Sloane turned sharply on her heels and headed back towards her own home. She meant what she'd said. Anger was bubbling beneath the surface and she felt like she was on the verge of exploding.

No matter what it took, she'd make sure the killer of Helen Burgess and Danny Wells was unmasked.

SIXTY-SIX

Killer

That fucking journalist!

Why doesn't she just drop it? She should be glad I got rid of Danny – she's pro prison. I guess I can understand why she's upset about Helen but in the grand scheme of things, she was only using her to get what she could information she could about the hostel. Why else would someone her age be friends with Helen?

I scratch my head. There's no way I can be tied to Helen's murder. I removed anything I touched. I panicked when I realised what had happened. Maybe positioning her to look like she fell actually drew more attention…

I'm second-guessing myself. Why would *she* be snooping around?

Damn.

My chest tightens as my breathing shallows. This is not how things were supposed to turn out. Bloody Danny Wells. It's all his fault – if he'd just chosen someone else as his victim all those years ago, none of this would be happening now. He's ruined my fucking life.

The voices in my head emerge. Sometimes it feels like they're coming from the walls of this shitty hostel. Telling me that it isn't right. As if they're my fucking conscience. I smack my leg to pull me out of the invading thoughts but it doesn't work. My justifications are ridiculous – even I know that – and I don't want them in my head anymore. It's my integrity I'm getting sick of – butting in without an invitation. Jeanette would be pleased to see all that group shit does work. Even when I don't want it to.

Fuck right off!

'I'm not like him… I'm not like Danny,' I whisper.

Realising I've voiced my thoughts out loud, I look around, worried that someone might have heard me. Heard me sounding like him. Victim-blaming. Haven't I learned anything? I cringe when I think about Danny's court case and the quote in one of the national newspapers: 'If that dumb bitch had just kept her mouth and legs closed, I wouldn't be facing a life sentence now.'

My skin itches. Danny's seeping into my thoughts, and I'd rather die before I turn into someone like him.

But if you don't do something…

You'll never get away with any of it.

Come on, you're so close.

She needs to go.

SHUT UP!

The room seems to shrink and the walls are closing in on me. I need some fresh air, so I grab my hoodie and leave the hostel for a walk to clear my head. I look at my watch. I'll be back in time for the drug testing, or else they'll become suspicious.

I'm not paying attention to where I'm walking until I look up and realise I'm outside Sloane Armstrong's house. I overheard her giving her home address to that detective and made a mental note. At the time I hadn't realised why but it all makes sense now. I was being pulled by some inexplicable force – that must be it. The universe is telling me to tie up all the loose ends before I go. I'm not sure how long I stand outside, staring at her house, before a young woman with a pram nudges me and clears her throat.

'Scuse me. I need to get by.'

Shit! What's the time?

I step out of her way. If I don't return to the hostel soon, questions I'm not prepared to answer will be asked.

The crisp air fills my lungs and I feel more in control. I pick up the pace and reach the hostel with moments to spare. Once inside the foyer, I lean against the wall to catch my breath.

'Hey, can you give me a hand?' It's the RSH keyworker; she points to some boxes by the side of the door.

'Sure.' I bend over and pick them up with a grunt. 'Where do you want them?'

'If you could put them in the drug-testing room, that'd be great.' She has a nice smile, almost comforting – like she knows I need that just now.

'Of course.' I place the boxes in the testing room and then make my way to the communal living area.

Three men are on the couch, playing cards. The TV is showing the news, and I manage to catch snippets of the conversation.

'That's some fucked-up shit,' one of the men observes and the others nod in agreement. 'Bet one of us gets the blame too. They're always more than happy to point the finger our way. Don't even need any evidence to kick our arses back inside.'

Another resident speaks up. 'Nah. You're wrong there, mate. After my last recall, I appealed and got out. My last PO tried to get me back inside because they said I was associating with known "criminals".' The last word said with his fingers in quotations. 'But they had no evidence, and the parole board reviewed my case, agreed with me, and let me out. It was bullshit. You need to educate yourself on this stuff, lads, or you *will* end up back inside.' He taps the side of his head.

The keyworker pops her head through the door. 'Hey, fellas, testing is going to start in ten minutes so wrap things up and make sure you attend at your specified time.'

The cards are collected, and the TV turned off but the chatter continues.

I check my watch. I need to be in the drug-testing room bang on four-thirty. I'll have time to think about what happens next once the testing is finished.

Though I already know the answer.

SIXTY-SEVEN

Jeanette

Seeing Sloane Armstrong being escorted away from Helen's home no longer surprised the probation manager. Trouble followed the journalist like a bad smell. But when Sloane turned sharply and glared at Jeanette, she got goosebumps. The journalist's icy stare was uncalled for, and Jeanette was relieved to see her turn away and head in the opposite direction. The last thing she needed was a scene outside the hostel.

What had made Sloane scream? Jeanette pressed her face against the glass, standing on her tiptoes and peering in the direction of Helen's house. A young, animated man stood speaking to a police officer. Her curiosity got the better of her.

'Just popping out front for a few minutes,' she called out and headed over to the neighbour's property.

'Hello, I'm Jeanette Macey. From next door…' She pointed at the hostel. 'Helen used to volunteer for us. I heard a scream and just wondered if everything was OK?'

The young man looked her up and down. His eyes were

slits, his jaw tight. 'You're from the hostel? Was it one of your lot who murdered my aunt?' He took a step towards her, but the police officers stepped between the two.

'Everything's under control here. Nothing for you to be concerned about. Why don't you go back now?' The officer's eyes were serious but apologetic.

'Yeah, go back and do your job properly before someone else is murdered. You should be ashamed of yourself!' The nephew spat.

'I'm sorry for your loss. Helen was a kind woman and did a lot for us at the hostel.' Jeanette wanted to come across as sincere. 'I'll leave you to it…'

Helen's nephew was still shouting as she closed the front door at Ripley House.

'Pissing folk off again, eh?' One of the residents smirked as he headed towards the drug-testing room.

Jeanette wanted to respond but bit her tongue. Getting into something with one of the offenders wouldn't be setting the right example so she ignored the remark and returned to the main office.

'What the hell was that about?' Steph turned her chair in Jeanette's direction.

'Helen Burgess's nephew. I just went round to see if I could find out why Sloane was there but I didn't get the chance. He thinks someone from here murdered Helen.'

Steph coughed and turned back to her computer. An awkward atmosphere filled the room.

Jeanette walked over to the PO's desk. 'Do you have something to say?' She was already on edge and didn't need her team hiding things from her. They needed to be working together at this time and it wouldn't do anyone any good if they started turning on each other.

'Come on, Jeanette.' Steph tilted her head. 'Helen came in here ranting that she was going to get everyone recalled. They're already anxious enough as it is with that threat because of Danny's murder. They'll all be walking on eggshells. Can't be a coincidence that she was pushed down the stairs and suffocated, can it?'

'Wait... what? Where did you hear that she was pushed and suffocated?' Something clicked at that very moment. The cause of death sounded vaguely familiar.

'Police released it to the press while you were out. It was just on the radio.'

Jeanette sprinted to her office and logged in to the computer. She was finger-tapping on the desk while she waited for the Delius entries to load.

'Fuck's sake. Why does this always happen when I need it?' she grumbled to herself.

When the case records had finally loaded, Jeanette scrolled through the names of the residents until she came across what she was looking for.

Ray Southall
OFFENCE(S): Murder. Aggravated Burglary.
LICENCE: Yes

She opened the induction appointment records and a lump formed in her throat when she saw that the victim of his murder was an elderly woman. Ray had form for drugging and sexually assaulting elderly women but on this occasion he claimed he had been in the house to burgle. When he was upstairs, rummaging through a room, she caught him and threatened to phone the police. The old lady turned to run downstairs, presumably to go to the phone and ring the police.

When he realised this, he pushed her down the stairs. Confirmed in the autopsy by the bruise on her back. When he got to the bottom of the stairs and saw she was still breathing, he plugged her nose and covered her mouth, watching her die.

Jeanette reached for the phone and dialled the detective.

SIXTY-EIGHT

Sloane

Sloane was torn. She didn't know what she should do with the notebook that she had taken from Helen's house. It could be nothing, and if she called the police and gave them the info and time was wasted chasing shadows, she'd get the blame. But it could be evidence...

Her head was buzzing. She could go through it and write an article for the newspaper, hinting she might have info that would not only reveal Helen's killer, but also the person who murdered Danny Wells. Sloane bit her lip so hard she drew blood. If she was wrong though, her integrity would be called into question and that was not something she would take lightly.

She kicked the cushion that was at her feet across the room and looked at the names Helen had written down – four in total. Two of the names were no surprise and Sloane couldn't recall from her own research whether they had any previous offences or recent concerning behaviour that would warrant them risking their liberty. Or maybe that was it – they were trying to *protect* their liberty.

The other two names did shock her, and Sloane wondered why Helen had included them as neither had ever really been mentioned in the conversations they'd had about the murder.

She reached across and pulled her bag towards her. Shoving her hand inside, she felt around for her mobile phone and called Noah. He might be able to add some context to the names – that is, if he was willing to help her.

'Hey, I meant to call you and check in. How did your call with social care go?'

'It went well – really well. But that's not why I'm calling. I have a favour to ask…' Her voice dipped.

'Why don't I like the sound of that? Let me guess, you're looking for info only the police can access?'

'Well, not exactly true. Others do have access, but they don't like me enough to help.'

Noah laughed down the line. 'What is it?'

'Oh, thank you. You're a star! I really appreciate it, so—'

'Hang fire on the praise. I'll hear what you have to say and then make a decision. We're friends, but you know that there are some things I won't do. We clear?'

'Crystal. OK, so you may have heard on the grapevine that Helen Burgess's case is now being investigated as a murder.'

'Mmmm. Yes…'

'Well, I found a list of names in a notebook in one of Helen's cardigan pockets. They could be nothing but… what if one of them was involved in Danny Wells's murder and Helen was silenced because of what she knew?' Saying it out loud made it seem more real, and Sloane shivered.

'That's a big leap, isn't it? Do you have anything other than names that links them to the crimes?'

Sloane had figured he might ask her this and something

suddenly dawned on her. 'When Helen was complaining to me about someone being on her property, she mentioned something about cigarette butts being scattered on the ground. I think she told the police… or maybe the probation team at the hostel…'

'So, one of those names could be linked to any DNA found on the cigarettes. Is that what you're thinking?'

'Exactly. So, if I give you the names, do you think you could help?'

'No.'

That took her by surprise. 'You're not going to help me?'

'No. That could land me in a shitload of trouble. It's not my investigation and if you're right then you need to be speaking to the lead detective on the case.'

'But that's why I need you to check. This is only a guess, and I don't want to waste anyone's time. I don't even know if the police took her complaint seriously or collected the cigarette butts as evidence. If you could at least find that out, I promise I'll speak to the detective in charge.'

'No can do. I've told you what you need to do, and I think it's best I go now before one of us says something that we can't come back from.'

'Fine!' she huffed. 'Thanks for your help anyway.' She knew he was right, but she was still annoyed.

'Look, don't get stroppy. I hope you get the answers you're looking for but be careful. If you're right, there's a murderer out there who's killing people that can identify them. I don't want to be attending your funeral next.'

'OK. Speak soon.'

Noah was spot on. Her life could be in danger if the wrong person found out about the list. Her stubborn nature got the best of her though, and even though she might regret it, she called the one person who wanted these murders to be solved as much as she did.

'I could have you charged with harassment, you know.'

'Hear me out first. I think what I've got to say will change your mind, Jeanette.'

SIXTY-NINE

Jeanette
___

Jeanette leaned back in her chair, waiting for whatever bullshit the journalist was going to throw her way. Did she really have time for this? Everything around her was crumbling, so she had nothing to lose by entertaining whatever it was that Sloane was so keen to share. 'So, what do you have to say? I don't have all day.'

'I take it you've heard about Helen – how her death has been deemed suspicious? What you might not be aware of is that Helen made a list. I think she may have discovered something about Wells's death and was killed to make sure it didn't go any further.'

Jeanette gasped. She wasn't prepared to admit to Sloane that she had been wondering if that was the case herself. 'What the—? I mean, how... who... That still doesn't explain why you're calling me. Shouldn't you be calling the police?'

'What have the police done so far? I'll involve them when I have enough to give them but all I have at the moment is a list of names and nothing more than that. They'll probably sit on it for a few months. Who knows what could happen between now and then. I need you to do me a favour…'

Jeanette chewed on her lip. She wanted to know the information Sloane had, but it could place her in an awkward situation, especially if it led to someone being recalled. 'I'm not making any promises, but I'll hear you out.'

'OK. That's all I ask.'

Jeanette could hear the excitement in Sloane's voice.

'First though, can you check if Helen's nephew has left her property? He parked a silver car in the drive. Let me know if it's gone.'

'You'll have to hang on then. This phone isn't handsfree.'

'I can wait.'

Jeanette laid the handset on her desk and jogged through to the main office. At the front window, she saw the car was gone.

Irene called out to her, but she waved her away. 'I'm just on a call…'

'Car's gone.' Jeanette grabbed her side, a sharp pain taking hold. She balanced the phone between her ear and shoulder as she massaged the area with her free hand.

'OK, that's good. Do you know if the police investigated Helen's allegation about a resident from Ripley House trespassing on her property?'

'I don't think she called the police. She burst in here, really upset and shouting about getting everyone sent back to prison, but there was no police involvement, as far as I'm aware. I dealt with the matter internally and didn't hear anything about it afterwards.'

'That would be because she was murdered…'

The comment stung as the journalist no doubt wanted it to.

'Here's what I think: someone in your hostel was worried about what Helen knew – whether real or imagined, someone felt threatened. I need to check a few things first, but I'd like to drop by when I'm done…'

'I really think you need to call the police with whatever information you have. Who's on the list?' A part of Jeanette didn't want to know because if something more did happen, she wouldn't be able to live with herself for taking no action. But she wasn't the police – and Sloane shouldn't be poking the fire. She was going to end up burned… or worse.

'Are you sure you want to know? You're not going to like what I tell you, so I'm giving you every opportunity to turn a blind eye.'

'Stop playing games.' Jeanette paused before she said something she'd regret. 'I asked for the names – why wouldn't I want to know? I work with these people. I'm not fragile – I know exactly what type of people they are. It's hard to shock me at this stage. Will you just spit it out before I lose it?' Her leg shook.

'OK, but two of the people aren't residents…'

Relief washed over her. 'That's good news then, isn't it? Who are they? Some of the drug users that hang around the area?'

Sloane was silent for a moment. 'No. They're members of your staff…'

Everything stopped.

Sloane was talking but all Jeanette could hear was muffled words, something along the lines of '*You should've listened to me from the start.*' The handset dropped from her fingers, bounced off the desk, and hit the floor.

SEVENTY

Sloane

D own the line, Sloane could hear the deep breaths Jeanette was taking and she waited for the Senior Probation Officer to absorb the information just delivered to her. If she were in Jeanette's position she'd be feeling pretty concerned and probably a little foolish right now too.

'I know it's a stupid question and not something I'd normally ask you, but are you OK?'

'I'm silent because I didn't want to be right. You've just confirmed something I'd been wondering myself, only I wasn't prepared to visit that avenue just yet.' Jeanette sighed and her honesty piqued the journalist's interest.

'Why? Has something else happened?' She'd need to tread carefully or Jeanette would shut down the whole conversation. 'I mean, why would *you* think a colleague was involved? If it makes you feel any better, our conversation can be off the record for the time being. I just want to find out who's responsible for the murders and you want Ripley House's reputation to remain intact. We don't have to work against each other.' Sloane was surprised at how sincere she sounded. Would Jeanette believe her?

The silence was becoming uncomfortable. She wanted Jeanette to open up and see that by putting their heads together, it would be in both their interests, but she was concerned the SPO would only be looking at the hostel's reputation rather than the bigger picture. Her suspicions were confirmed when Jeanette next spoke.

'No. I can't discuss this any further. I think we need to call DS Brady. If we both share our concerns, he's going to have to act and take it seriously.'

It was Sloane's turn to sigh. She didn't agree. The police were chasing their tails and with no forensic evidence linking anyone specific to both crimes, it was unlikely they would take this circumstantial evidence as anything but hearsay and fake news. 'I can see we're not going to find any common ground here, but I do understand where you're coming from. I tell you what, I'll speak to the police, and we'll see what they have to say.'

'I can't believe I am actually saying this but... thank you. It has to be this way. I can call DS Brady too if you think it will help substantiate what you tell them?'

'No!' Sloane pinched her lips together, immediately regretting shouting. She hadn't wanted to sound so panicked. 'I mean, I need to speak with them anyway about the cigarette butts, but I can always let them know that you have your own concerns – the ball is then in their court whether they want to speak to you further. It's better this way, don't you think?'

There was some mumbling in the background. 'Uh, yeah. OK. Look, I need to go now but keep me posted.'

'Sure.'

The call ended.

Sloane stood and stretched her legs. She had no intention of calling the police. Instead, she pulled out her own notebook and started cross-referencing all the information she had on the people Helen had listed in the little notebook.

If it took her all night, she was going to whittle down the list and identify who was responsible before they had the chance to kill again.

SEVENTY-ONE

Killer

'**B**loody hell.'

My phone wakes me out of the deep sleep I've finally managed to fall into. Why didn't I put the damn thing on silent? The ringtone tells me it's my mother. It's too early for me to be up so it must be an emergency. I sit up in bed, pick up my phone, and try to sound cheery.

'Hey, Mum. What's up? Bit early to be calling, don't you think?' I throw the blankets off and scratch my legs.

'Oh, I'm so glad I caught you. Someone's been asking about you. A journalist. She was very persistent. Wanted to know all about your background.'

Now I'm awake!

That stupid little bitch!

To be fair, I'm not all that surprised that Sloane Armstrong had finally started to piece everything together, but I need to know exactly what my mother told her. It's too soon.

'Calm down, Mum. There's nothing to be worried about. She's just doing her job. With everything that's been happening, I probably should have warned you that someone might be in touch.'

'But why? What's going on?'

I shake my head in disbelief. My parents live in a world of blissful ignorance – they always have – and in some way, I'm envious. They don't follow the news. So I shouldn't really be surprised, but given the circumstances I'd have thought they might have heard… something.

'Mum, I thought you knew. Danny Wells was murdered.'

I hear a gasp down the line. 'Oh my God. When did this happen?'

'A few weeks ago. It made the national papers. Has no one been in touch with you before now?' I should have prepared them. My bad.

'Why would they be? It's got nothing to do with you.' She repeats her earlier thoughts, as if by saying it over and over again it will make it true. I can hear her annoyance now.

'Of course it doesn't. But you know what the press are like. They'll poke and prod until they find something they think they can twist to make their story more interesting. It's all just a load of shit – I don't want you or Dad to worry about anything, OK? If the journalist calls back, just hang up on her.'

'Are you sure that's the right thing to do? What if she makes up lies and prints something anyway? Maybe I should just—'

'Nothing, Mum. Don't say a word. Trust me on this. Everything will sort itself out. I promise.' My fists clench. I need to get my mum onto a new subject, or she'll just harp on for hours, convincing herself to do the opposite of what I've asked. 'My transfer should come through soon. I can move back down to be closer to you and Dad. That's good news, isn't it?'

'Oh, that's wonderful news! How long have you been keeping that from us?'

'I didn't want to say anything until I knew for sure. You know what probation can be like – lots of paperwork. You can't just up and leave a hostel. It just made more sense to wait until I had more definite news.'

'Can I tell your father? He's going to be so happy, and we've so many little projects you can help us with. We try to keep ourselves as active as possible, so our old bones don't seize up.'

'Why don't we keep this between ourselves for the time being – at least until I have a confirmed date. I was thinking once this gets sorted, I could take you both away for a bit. A holiday would be great, wouldn't it?'

'How wonderful! You're too good to us. Your father is going to be so surprised. OK, I'll keep a lid on things for now but promise me you'll let me know as soon as you do, so I can tell him. He'll be suspicious of me going around with a big smile on my face.'

We both laugh at that. My mother is one of the kindest souls I've ever come across in my life, but you'd never be able to tell it from her face. It always looks to be in a constant scowl.

'I swear, I'll let you know as soon as I can. Look, I need to go and take care of a few things. Remember, not another word to anyone, not even your friends, OK? I'll deal with the press situation.'

I end the call and haul myself out of bed. It's going to be a long day, but I can always catch a nap later if need be. I pull on my jeans and grab a clean hoodie from my dresser.

The rest of the house is silent as I make my way downstairs and out of the door. I head into town and stop at a café, where

I grab a large coffee and a bacon roll. I eat outside, people-watching.

I need to do something about Sloane Armstrong before she uses that annoying brain of hers and jeopardises all my plans. I'm sure Jeanette's already putting the pieces together. I'll have to avoid her as much as possible; at least she's focused enough on her own shit to stay out of mine. If the two of them put their thoughts together, I'm done for. I'm confident enough though that it'll be difficult to trace anything back to me, but it's a risk I'm not willing to take this close to freedom.

Maybe I should just take off now? Screw waiting for the transfer. I could deal with the repercussions after the fact – it would all be easy to explain. Sick parents? Job offer? It's not like I'm a risk to the community…

My hands hurt and when I look down and I realise I've been squeezing them so tight that there are nail marks on my palms.

If people just minded their own damn business, Danny Wells would have been the only person dead, and they all could have gone about their business as the case grew cold. But the bastards *had* to go and stick their noses in. So now they need to pay.

I stand, stretching my arms, and begin walking.

This ends now.

SEVENTY-TWO

Jeanette

'I t's all kicking off again – you might want to go out there.' Steph stood in the doorway. 'They're pointing the finger at each other, saying we're doctoring their records to get them recalled.'

'Oh, for fuck's sake...' Jeanette welcomed the interruption from Steph but wasn't pleased with the reason why. 'What's got them so riled up?'

'They're watching the news. It's not looking good for us. Apparently, poor practice here calls into question whether the public is really safe from them all. And don't even get me started on what they're saying about the sex offenders...'

Jeanette ran her fingers through her hair. 'Tell me. I need to know what I'm going to have to defend.'

'Well, according to the latest news stories, we don't monitor their movements, we allow them to roam the streets, to hang around outside of schools, and even invite children into the hostel.'

'You can't be serious. That's preposterous. Surely no one in their right mind would believe that. Where the hell do they come up with this shit?' Jeanette expected a call from her line manager any second but first she'd have to deal with the residents. 'I'm coming down.'

Steph nodded and left Jeanette. Had Sloane stabbed her in the back? She took a deep breath and headed out to what would no doubt be a war zone. The extra security that the MoJ had agreed to would certainly come in handy now.

When she arrived in the communal living area, the men were shouting and pointing at each other and the security guard was standing in between them. She walked over and picked up the remote, switching off the TV.

'OK, enough now! If this doesn't stop, you'll be right about one thing – warnings will be issued and for some of you, that could lead to recall. I'm confiscating the remote and telly until you can all behave like calm, rational adults.' She motioned to the security guard. 'Take this and put it in my office, please.'

'You can't do that! It's against our human rights,' one of the residents shouted.

'I'm afraid you'll find that I *can* do it. TV is a privilege, not a right.' She looked around the room at all the angry faces. 'Where are Ray and Jack?'

'Out. At work, I guess.' Steph didn't sound too convincing. She should know this information, not be *guessing*. It played right into what the news was reporting. What the hell was going on? This was a hostel they were running, not a fricking circus.

Jeanette needed to know where the residents had got off to so early, otherwise the press would be half-right. Although residents were not locked in twenty-four-seven, with everything going on, she needed her staff to be more vigilant in monitoring their movements.

'There's a keywork session in' – she looked at her watch –

'forty minutes. I suggest you all calm down before then or I'm serious, next I'll have staff go through all your rooms and remove the TVs from there too. If you don't want that to happen, focus on what you need to do to avoid that. I'm not playing around – consequences will follow.'

The men glared at her but quietened down soon enough. She returned to the main office.

'Taking the telly away was a bold move,' Steph commented.

'I had no choice. The more they watch, the more worked up they get. I meant what I said; the ones in their rooms will be next if this carries on.'

Steph shook her head. 'Jesus. We'll have a riot on our hands if you do that.'

'Well, let's hope it doesn't come to that. Where's the sign-out sheet?'

Steph pointed behind Jeanette to the clipboard by the reception window. Jeanette glanced at the names and tapped the board. 'When Ray and Jack return, can you let me know? And please make sure that anyone else who leaves signs out. We really need to make sure that every process is followed – as our policy and practice here have already come into question.'

Steph huffed. 'I can't speak for anyone else, but my records are all up to date, so let them try to catch me out.'

'No need to get defensive. My comment wasn't aimed at you specifically, Steph. Just in general. We're a team so we need to have each other's backs but if you do know of someone who isn't following the proper procedures, I need to know.' She paused and looked around the room. 'That goes for all of you...'

The other officers gave her a brief glance before returning to their work.

Back in her office, Jeanette recalled her conversation with Sloane. She was beginning to question whether the journalist had any intention of calling the police. After what she had just said to her team, she knew what she needed to do.

She picked up the handset and dialled DS Brady's number.

SEVENTY-THREE

Killer

I'm watching her leave her house.

She's dressed in leggings and a sweat top, and I see her adjust her earphones – she must be going for a run. That'll give me enough time to see what she's found out so far and ultimately decide her fate. I'd planned on waiting until the evening but after speaking to my mother, I decided it couldn't wait. It would also be easier to avoid any curious onlookers during daytime hours when errands or jobs would leave the neighbouring homes empty.

My head is a mess. What should I do with Sloane? It must be necessary. I can't keep doing this. If all she has is guesses, nothing concrete, I could easily prepare some answers to the inevitable questions and my original plan would not be lost.

But if she has anything else…

I look around. The street's quiet. I try to look as casual as I can as I cross the road and stroll towards the back of the property. Her garden is enclosed so it's less likely that any of the surrounding houses will see me and raise the alarm.

The back door's locked, so I try the windows. Each one is

secure. I guess I shouldn't be surprised. To the left of me is a pile of loose bricks, and I pick up a broken one and use it to smash the glass. It'll look like a burglary when she comes back.

I reach through the glass with precision, my hoodie pulled over and around my fist – there's no way I'm going to cut myself and leave DNA. I unlock the door and step inside. Catching my breath, I go through the plan in my head before I take any further action. A mistake now would be unforgiveable.

Within a few steps I'm in her living room. Papers are strewn about a small table, the floor, and even on her couch. I walk around and look at the notes, removing from my pocket the gloves I nicked from the drug testing room and putting them on. My eyes are drawn to a piece of paper that has four names in bright red at the top and what looks like 'reasons' written below. My name is there with a star and question mark beside it.

Fuck.

But what does it mean? Does she have any evidence or is it just a guess? I comb through everything, looking for my name on other pieces of paper. My contacts are highlighted; I can see that she's been thorough in her checks, making connections with the right people. Will I need to take care of them too? Has she spoken with them already and shared her theories?

A pain shoots through my head.

If she has, my disappearance after all this will raise some red flags if these people come forward.

My neck burns; my hands shake.

Pressure. Lots of pressure. I put my hands up and push hard against my temples.

No relief.

A sound at the front door pulls me out of my thoughts.

Keys jangling.

I look around the room and find what I'm after.

I pull open the door to a small closet stuffed with coats and other things that she clearly wanted out of the way. I squeeze myself in and wait.

SEVENTY-FOUR

Sloane
_____

S loane placed the earphones in her ears and fiddled with the music app on her phone. Finding 'Mr Brightside', she cranked up the volume to stop her brain from going over every bit of information she had researched. She needed to separate herself from it now; needed to return with a fresh pair of eyes and a clear mind-set.

As she headed to the park, she smiled or said hello to the people who came across her path. A few smiled back; most looked away. She found it curious how some people were made uncomfortable by the simple gesture of a smile. A smile can't kill you – yet these same people who avoid kindness get manipulated because they become too trusting and they're the ones that end up... dead.

Where the hell did that come from?

Sloane paced herself, her breathing comfortable, and with each stride she started to slot information together, narrowing the list from Helen's notes from four people down to two, and when she thought about who those two were, goosebumps rose on her arms.

One person was in a position of trust and could use it to get all the information they'd need. But could they really be a killer? It seemed unlikely, but Helen had clearly thought otherwise.

The other though… they had form. Previous convictions for robbery, burglary, and murder, all to get money for their next fix; currently on licence for murdering an elderly woman – an MO quite similar to Helen's murder, in fact.

What Sloane hadn't figured out was how Danny Wells fitted in to the situation. Why would Wells be targeted? Was it drug-related?

Did the killer value their freedom so much that they would kill again? All actions so far said they would.

Her concentration on her thought process cost her, though, as her foot caught on something and her body was propelled forward. She placed her hands out in front of her to cushion the landing and narrowly avoid ending up face down on the gravel path. That was her first mistake. The second mistake came shortly after as she tried to stand, and a pain shot up her leg, making her lose her footing again and landing her on her arse.

Dammit.

A stranger rushed over to her. 'Ouch. I saw that fall. Are you OK?' He held out a hand and pulled her up.

Her wrist ached and she held it out in front of her, swivelling it from left to right.

'If you can do that, it can't be broken. You'll want to get some ice on it though. Probably a sprain.'

Sloane gave the man a crooked smile, an attempt at masking her discomfort. 'Yep, you're probably right.' She tried to walk but the ache in her foot made that difficult.

'You'll want to get that checked out too. Saying that, even if any of your toes are broken, they'll only tell you to rest… You should probably sit down for a moment. I can call an ambulance if you need me to?' He held up his mobile.

The stranger was only trying to help her but he was beginning to get on her nerves. 'It's fine. Just a dull ache now. I'll just take a moment…' She headed towards the park bench. 'Thanks though…' She didn't want him to think she was completely ungrateful. The man shrugged and watched as she hobbled to the park bench.

'You sure you don't want me to call anyone for you?' He approached again.

'No thanks. I don't live too far away. I'll just wait here a moment and then head back.' She hoped he would take the hint. Sloane rubbed her ankle as she waited, the action relieving some of the ache; a few more minutes and she'd be able to walk on it without wincing at each step. Her wrist was starting to swell slightly. She used her good hand to push herself off the bench and lowered her foot to the ground, testing it by slowly bearing some of her weight on it. There was a dull pulsating sensation, but nothing too bad. She'd live. So much for a long run this morning.

Sloane hobbled back to her house and leaned against the wall, digging around in her bum bag in search of her keys. Once inside she headed straight for the kitchen; an icepack or two should do the trick.

She spotted the broken glass from the back door immediately.

'What the fuck?'

Her gaze quickly shot around the room. She pulled her mobile from her pocket, unlocking it so she could dial 999. It was then that she heard a noise behind her. Sloane turned around and was face to face with a masked intruder.

'I'm giving you the chance to go. All I have to do is hit one button and I'll be connected to the police.'

The intruder stepped forward and before she had the chance to connect the call, he punched her in the face.

SEVENTY-FIVE

Killer

I'm standing over her limp body. The punch was instinct, to stop her from screaming out and calling for help.

Now what the hell am I going to do?

I look around the kitchen for something to tie her hands with and find some frayed rope in one of those 'throw everything in here' drawers.

That'll do.

I cup my hands under her arms and lean her up against the cupboard door. I ignore her moans as I wrap the cord around her wrists. She's coming around.

I watch as she tries to move her hands before realising they've been tied. She winces and, even though I probably shouldn't, I do find the attempt comical. She's determined, that's for sure.

'Just sit there while I think of what I'm going to do.' Disguising my voice as much as I can, I pace the floor. This wasn't how things were supposed to be.

At the moment, the journalist believes I'm a random

burglar. I scratch my head. The knitted balaclava is itchy, but I'm glad I brought it with me.

I could get away with this. She doesn't know anything. Who would believe her anyway?

'M-my wallet is in my bag over there.' She raises her clasped hands and points in the direction of the front door. 'Take whatever you want…'

'Shut up! I need to think.' I look down at her. The minute my back's turned, she'll try to escape and call the police. *Just like Helen.*

No. No. No. I need to make sure that doesn't happen.

I notice her eyes widen and I follow her gaze, looking down at my leg. A card is sticking out of the top of my jeans pocket.

'Shit.' I stuff it back in. 'We have a problem now…'

'I won't say a word. I promise.'

I want to believe her, but I know that would be a mistake.

'I'm afraid I can't take your word for it. I know from experience that you're a liar.'

'Did you kill Danny because of what he did to—?'

'Shut up. Shut up. SHUT UP!' I pace around the room.

'Was it you who killed Helen? She was harmless.'

'That's what you think. Why didn't you tell her to leave things alone? Her death is on *you*. You hear me? She didn't need to die…' I growl.

Out of the corner of my eye, I catch her moving. The rope around her wrist hangs loosely and suddenly she's up on her feet. I stretch my arm out and try to grab her, but she dodges to the left and I tumble forward.

Fuck!

She's heading towards the back door.

'Where do you think you're going? We're not done here.'

I run towards her and pull her back by her sweat top – had

her hair been long enough, I would have grabbed that. A scream escapes her lips, leaving me no choice but to cover her mouth with my gloved hand. I can feel her trying to bite me. Why is she making this harder? She's leaving me no choice.

I drag her towards the living room. Her legs are kicking out in a feeble attempt to try and make me loosen my grip.

'Would you fucking stop and listen? You're making this worse than it needs to be!'

She continues to thrash in my arms, and I drop her on the floor. As I'm about to straddle her, she kicks out – narrowly missing my groin. It's clear she isn't interested in the truth.

I snap.

'You stupid bitch! You should've just left it alone. I didn't want to have to do this.'

I bang her head against the floor, and, placing my hands around her neck, I begin to squeeze.

SEVENTY-SIX

Jeanette

'DS Brady. I'm so glad I reached you. Look, there's something Sloane knows and I'm not sure she's going to share it with you so...'

'Is she with you now?'

'No, why?'

'Look, Jeanette. We've had some of the DNA results back. Did Sloane tell you where she was when she spoke to you?'

'DNA?' Finally, this could all be over, Jeanette thinks. 'I think she was at home. What's this all about?'

'And where's Frank Brown?'

'Frank? He isn't due in until later. He popped in earlier as he had a short-notice meeting and needed to check some case notes. What's going on, detective?'

'I've tried Sloane's mobile but it's just ringing out and going to voicemail. Do you know where Frank was going?'

'He had a three-way meeting at Recovery Starts Here. Stay on the line – I'll call them.' Jeanette picked up the desk phone handset and dialled.

'Hi, it's Jeanette Macey here, SPO at Ripley House. Can I speak to Frank Brown? He's there for a meeting.'

Jeanette could feel the blood draining from her face as the receptionist told her that Frank had rung earlier to say he wouldn't be able to attend as the three-way clashed with an urgent appointment he couldn't cancel. She ended the call and relayed the information to the detective.

'Shit. I'm going to have to go. If Frank returns, don't do anything to tip him off. I'm sending someone to the hostel now.'

Jeanette's heart raced.

Frank was the killer?

No, Jeanette refused to believe that.

Why? It made no sense.

What did he have to gain from murdering Danny Wells?

SEVENTY-SEVEN

Sloane

Sloane grappled with the hands around her neck but the more she fought the tighter he squeezed. Her legs thrashed and his body bounced on top of her, knocking the air out of her lungs, but she wasn't going to give in.

She turned her head and saw her sister – the picture on her mantelpiece – staring at her; urging her not to give up now. Was this how her sister had felt? Bolts of energy surging through her veins and willing her to fight, then weakness... and a feeling that it was too late.

'Please...' She choked, trying to get the words out. 'Haven't... you... done... enough?'

The hands around her neck loosened and Sloane realised it was now or never.

She reached up and pulled the mask off. She wanted to see the face of the man who would end her life; wanted to look him in the eyes so he would never forget her.

Frank Brown.

Helen had been right.

She could hear her mobile ringing and patted the floor in the direction of the sound, but it was too far out of her reach.

'Why? Why couldn't you just leave it alone? If you and that nosy bitch had just dropped it, none of this would've happened.' He moved his knees forward and pinned her arms down.

She tried to speak but his fingers gripped her throat tight. She wanted to tell him that she'd help him if he'd only let her go.

Everything made sense now. He was the other boy – Emily Nash's neglected son.

Sloane wasn't ready to give up. She thought she heard her sister's voice whispering in her ear.

It's not your time yet.

She kicked her legs out in defiance and the hands around her neck loosened.

There was a loud bang. Muffled voices. A bright light.

He smashed her head against the floor once more and the darkness took over.

SEVENTY-EIGHT

Sloane

ONE YEAR LATER

S loane looked at the headline again, pulling her shoulders
back. A strange feeling came over her. Her emotions were
all over the place. A call from her editor earlier to remind her
about a podcast interview had brought a smile to her face.
He'd sung her praises, but her eyes welled up when the reality
hit her that she nearly died for this article. She picked up the
newspaper and looked over her work to prepare for the Zoom
call she was waiting for.

A killer who slit the throat of the man responsible for his estranged
birth mother's murder over twenty years before has himself been
convicted of murder.

Frank Brown, a probation service officer at Ripley House
Approved Premises, targeted DANIEL (Danny) WELLS in the
hostel after luring him into the communal living room under the
false premise that he had some drugs to sell.

According to the police, it is believed Brown snuck up behind the
unsuspecting Wells and slit his throat from ear to ear, quickly
disposed of some of his clothing, and then calmly returned to his post

where he carried on as normal with a colleague. Almost an hour later, Brown offered to do the rounds and check that the residents were in the hostel. At the time, he told police that during these rounds he stumbled upon Wells's body and raised the alarm. The body was discovered at 12:30am on the twentieth anniversary of the day his birth mother was found dead in her flat.

A source informed me that in the weeks leading up to the murder, Brown had become increasingly preoccupied with making sure he was on the work rota that particular day. Just a day before, police later learned, he had purchased a small quantity of drugs so that he could set his plan in motion. In hindsight, colleagues at Ripley House said they should have sensed something was wrong as Brown's behaviour had changed.

Sloane scoffed at this. For all of Jeanette's sermons on the probation service's ability to assess risk and put in place the appropriate measures to monitor offenders, the manager and her whole team had been completely blind to a killer operating in their midst. The Google alert popped up on her screen and she logged in. She had to steady her hands as she clicked the mouse, and a face filled the monitor.

'Hi, Sloane. It's great to finally meet you. Are you ready to start?'

Kieran Sherlock smiled. He was an ex-lawyer turned podcaster and his show, *Crime UK*, was followed by over twenty-five million subscribers.

'Yeah, just give me one sec.' Sloane took a large swig of water and after swallowing, signalled to Kieran that she was good to go.

'OK. I'm going to start by summarising the crime, and then I thought it would be great if we could just talk through some of your views and then wrap it up with perhaps something you've come away with after this experience. I'll start recording now.' Kieran's voice changed as the red recording light flashed in the corner. He welcomed his subscribers, read out the bio that Sloane had provided, and then jumped straight in to telling his listeners what they were about to hear.

'For those of you unfamiliar with the case, let me pull you out from under that rock you've been hiding under and share the highlights. Danny Wells was released on life licence after being granted parole for murdering Frank Brown's birth mother, Emily Nash. Frank and another sibling had already been removed from their mother's care due to concerns raised by social services about Miss Nash's ability to protect her children from her partner, her alcohol misuse, and general neglect. However, it looked like she had been trying to turn her life around and meet her children – until Danny Wells put a stop to that by holding her against her will, savagely beating and raping her, and leaving her to die while her youngest child slept in another room. Did I get that right, Sloane?'

'Yes. I learned that Brown had been tracking his victim after getting a job as a probation service officer in various locations over the years. After the internal probation investigation, it came out that he'd been accessing case records for Danny Wells, and when Brown had discovered the date of release and where the convicted murderer would be housed, he set his macabre plan in place – putting in for a transfer to work at the newly opened hostel.'

'Well, that's creepy as fuck. How in the hell did he go undetected for so long?' Kieran adjusted his mic.

Sloane shrugged. 'I wondered the same. The professionals say he snapped but I don't believe that one bit. In order to cover his tracks, Frank Brown murdered Helen Burgess, a volunteer at the hostel, when she guessed his identity following a confrontation in her home. He was obviously concerned she'd call the police. A second member of staff at the hostel, deputy manager Anwar Hussain, was a person of interest in the case, however it transpired he was involved in the supply of drugs in unrelated offences...'

'Wait, what? Another probation officer was committing crimes?' Kieran's eyes widened and Sloane nodded.

'That's right. The police had a separate investigation going which initially saw Anwar arrested for Wells's death, but a solid alibi had him released on bail and suspended from his probation duties until the matter had been resolved – ironically, he's now on probation for those drug offences. Let's not forget the gardener, Pete Price, who was also cleared of any charges despite having the finger pointed at him. A source told me he was dismissed from his duties at the hostel when probation learned he was stealing tools and selling them on. They also found a barrel in the cellar full of hooch – he was supplying the prison-style alcohol to the residents.' Sloane shook her head. 'Pete was charged with theft and is currently undertaking community payback. It seemed the hostel was hiding more than one demon under its roof.'

'What a shitstorm. Fact *is* stranger than fiction and that couldn't be truer than in this case. I'm going to pull you back for a moment. The police investigation eventually led to Brown's arrest after delayed forensic evidence came to light and a warrant was issued to search his property, where police recovered a hoodie with Wells's blood on the sleeve cuff as well as the missing murder weapon – a knife from the hostel kitchen. Seems like it was a solid case. What can you tell us about that?'

'My source in the CPS said... hang on, let me just grab my notes.' Sloane reached across and grabbed the piece of paper she'd written the quote on. My source said, "This was a premeditated, targeted, and brazen execution of a man in a secure environment that was supposed to protect the public from further harm and keep their residents safe. Frank Brown knew his victim well. He'd spent years monitoring his whereabouts, his rehabilitation in prison, and his eventual release on life licence into the community. He'd even worked in the victim support unit of probation for a short period and contacted Colin Wells, who works for the CPS in the London Borough of Southwark, to advise him of his brother's upcoming parole at the time. Brown believed that Mr Wells was responsible for taking away his opportunity to form a relationship with his birth mother over twenty years before. That's why on the anniversary of the day his mother's body was discovered, twenty years later, he took it upon himself to carry out what he believed was a revenge killing. In his own words, he was ready to 'kill to avenge the death of (his) mother'."' Sloane put her note down, letting those words sink in.

'Unbelievable.' It was Kieran's turn to shake his head. 'During the trial Brown initially claimed that he had witnessed Anwar Hussain killing Wells. Why do you think he did this?'

'Brown said he had not disclosed that at the time because Hussain had threatened him. A lie, of course. The police found evidence to the contrary in Brown's flat – computer searches, a notebook with details only the killer would know, and later, probation records showing that Brown and not Hussain had been accessing Wells's information online. That, along with Hussain's airtight alibi, assisted the prosecution to be able to prove that this was a lie.' Sloane shuddered at how easy all the lies had come to Brown.

'Brown was convicted of murdering Mr Wells, Mrs Burgess,

and the attempted murder of you, Sloane Armstrong, following a trial at Coventry Crown Court. What listeners may not know is that you've had your own personal experiences of the justice system… or failures of, is probably a better way to phrase it. Has this changed your views on parole or, how can I put this, did you find that at any point you could understand, maybe empathise with, Brown?'

Sloane sat back. She'd been wondering when someone would bring this up. 'My sister's killer has sent me letters for years.' She looked over at the coffee table where are the letters currently lay. 'I never read them… until the trial was over. I wanted a better understanding of why this man decided one day that my sister was his target. Why he had to take her life and ruin mine… my parents'… everyone who knew her.'

'Did you find the answers?'

'In a way, yes. He had suffered his own trauma as a child. He had turned to drugs and spent much of his life in and out of prison. A mistake saw him released from prison early and he wanted drugs to celebrate. I spent my early years hating this man for choosing her, and it turns out he didn't specifically target my sister – it was opportunistic. He broke into her home, hadn't known anyone was there… and when she confronted him—' A lump formed in Sloane's throat. She took a sip of water. 'When she confronted him, he killed her. Can we take a moment?'

'Of course. Let's move on. Why don't you tell us what's next for you?'

Sloane was grateful to the podcast host. 'I'm taking a bit of a sabbatical of sorts actually. Someone close to me' – she brushed over the tattoo on her thigh – 'once suggested I think about writing a novel, so I'm going to share my sister's story and how it impacted those who loved her. I'll be interviewing her killer to get a better understanding of things… I learned a lot from the experience with Frank Brown, and perhaps I had been holding in my anger, much to my detriment.'

'That sounds like it will be a fascinating book. You'll have to come back to discuss it. Well, Sloane, it's been an insightful and interesting conversation. Thanks for joining me on *Crime UK* and best of luck on that book.'

'Thanks for having me. I look forward to chatting again in the hopefully not-so-distant future.'

After ending the Zoom call, Sloane headed to the couch and stared at the letters. She'd already discussed her idea for a non-fiction novel with her editor and he'd put her in touch with a few agents.

She'd channel her frustration at the criminal justice system into this book and make sure her sister's killer was never released.

Sloane smiled. He wouldn't see it coming.

SEVENTY-NINE

Jeanette

Jeanette still couldn't make any sense of things. She'd been reading all the newspaper articles and interviews with Frank on the TV but found it hard to digest. How long had Frank been fantasising about killing Danny Wells? At the trial, it was said that he'd been tracking the Danny Wells's whereabouts for some years. How many others within the service had joined in order to exact some sort of revenge and deal with their own personal traumas? It was a disturbing thought and went against everything she believed her job encompassed. She shivered.

Had Frank not been caught, how many more would have died at his hands? Frank had only told the media and the court what he wanted them to know; her own training and discussions with other professionals since the trial had confirmed that there were many theories that tried to explain why some people 'snap' and become violent. She couldn't shake the question and picked up the card from the criminal psychologist she had bumped into at the trial. She'd offered to answer anything Jeanette wanted to know, so she picked up the phone and made the call.

'Hello?'

'Hi. It's Jeanette Macey, from Ripley House. I hope you don't mind me ringing but I need to get things straight in my head and decided to take you up on your offer.'

'Ah, no problem. I'd be happy to help. What did you want to know?'

'I guess I'm struggling to understand what you testified to at the trial… about Frank snapping. I mean, it seemed to come out of the blue twenty years later…'

'I can see why you're sceptical. Although a person's snap into violence may come as a total surprise, in most cases there is a psychological build-up to that point.' The psychologist paused. 'There's what we call a pathway to violence which starts with thinking and then fantasising about a plan – and there may be a more explicit planning phase that other people don't particularly notice.'

Jeanette took a moment to absorb what had been said. The doctor was right. No one had noticed this in Frank, not even his adoptive parents – his mother was inconsolable at the trial while Frank stared blankly at her from the docks.

'In Mr Brown's case, once he disposed of Mr Wells, he had to cover his tracks and that's when the fantasy of killing others turned into intention, leading him to murder Mrs Burgess and to attack Sloane Armstrong.'

Jeanette shook her head. 'He was a probation service officer. Surely he knew there were other ways?'

'He knew…' The doctor's voice dipped to almost a whisper. 'Sadly, it seems his overwhelming belief that Wells took away the opportunity for him to get to know his birth mother overrode any logic. The other killings were a necessity, until he could move on to the job he had lined up for himself.'

'What you're saying is that he made the decision to end Danny's life before he even joined the service?'

'Yes, I believe he did. A person like Frank who has already decided to kill someone may develop what they call an "eerie composure", firmly believing that the moment to turn back has passed.'

Jeanette's stomach turned.

'Despite the planning during the build-up, many experts have found that a perpetrator often cannot recall particulars about the moment of the attack. You'd think they'd give it a lot of thought, but they go into some kind of dissociated state where their feelings are split off from what they're doing. Like they're on autopilot...'

'And that's how they carry on with work as if nothing had happened...' Jeanette shivered at the thought that she had signed for his transfer into another area – he could have got away with it and she would have helped him. 'But why had no one else picked up on his desire to kill? Why did he feel it was the only way?' Jeanette needed to understand as she was struggling to sleep and focus on her own work, thinking about what had been happening right under her nose. Criticism from the press, from colleagues, from the residents... it was becoming too much to bear.

'I personally feel that Mr Brown was suffering from a condition called delusional disorder – in particular the "persecutory type". This causes people to believe that someone is plotting against them.' The doctor excused herself and Jeanette heard a cough. 'Sorry about that. Scratchy throat. Right, where was I? Oh yeah, Frank has said over and over again the notion that Danny took his mother away. Now, *we* know Danny's index offence was not premeditated. Danny had an on-off relationship with Emily Nash and then snapped while heavily under the influence of alcohol and drugs in a binge that had lasted for days. Once he realised what he'd done, he had to avoid getting caught. But Frank saw it all as a purposeful act to prevent him from meeting his mother.'

'I suppose you're right; his own life experiences contributed to Frank just... snapping.' Jeanette hadn't known about Frank's background before the trial but sadly it was one she was all too familiar with, having worked with violent offenders for most of her life.

'Exactly. Before he'd been removed from his mother's care, he may have experienced or witnessed violence or abuse early in life. Why some people snap and others don't is still a mystery.' The doctor mumbled to someone else in the room. 'I'm really sorry, Jeanette, but I'm needed. If you have any more questions, let me know and perhaps we can meet up in person. I know it's easy for me to say, but none of this is your fault. You couldn't have known or predicted what Frank might do and right now, he's where he needs to be.'

Jeanette thanked the psychologist and ended the call. She knew the woman was right but couldn't help feeling that she had ignored the signs because she had become numbed to it – not something she expected to have to deal with from her colleagues.

Jeanette paced up and down the corridor outside of her office. She had a decision of her own to make. She walked over to the window and looked directly at the FOR SALE sign that had been stuck on Helen's front lawn for months now. It suddenly dawned on her as she thought about the whole situation that no matter where you lived, the daily papers and news media were filled with similar instances where 'normal' law-abiding individuals with no history of violence suddenly 'snap' and attack violently.

Jeanette ran her fingers through her hair. As inexcusable and perplexing as the thought was, it was not incomprehensible. She returned to her office and sat down, resting her chin in her hands.

She clicked on the email from her line manager informing her that Frank had been sentenced to life without the possibility of parole for twenty-five years, due to the mitigating circumstances presented by his defence. A tear rolled down her cheek and she brushed it away.

Jeanette picked up the letter from Frank asking her to visit him, but she was in two minds whether she could do it or not. Ripley House was being closed down, she was being moved to a different role in the probation service, and the rest of her team – those that weren't too traumatised by what had happened – were being dispersed to various locations that were short-staffed.

Jeanette clicked through to the email she had drafted that morning – her resignation – and her hand hovered over the send button. She hit send, then leaned back in her chair and her shoulders relaxed.

She was done with probation.

EIGHTY

Frank

I sit on the hard bed and stare out of the tiny window of my cell, wondering how one man could have ruined my life so completely. The trial made me see things from a different perspective, as did talking to all the psychologists who highlighted my obsession. It turned me into what I had hated most about Danny Wells – a killer with no conscience.

Well, that's not completely true.

I do have remorse for what I did to Anwar – setting him up to look like he was the killer. And to that old lady from next door, Mrs Burgess. They didn't deserve that, I know this now. The guilt I feel about the journalist though is somewhat diluted. Her stories piss me off. She has her own agenda and it has nothing to do with justice. She needs to watch herself or one day she could end up like me. I didn't understand any of this at the time – my mind was in overdrive – and I now I'm ready to move on. If only they hadn't been a threat to exposing me.

No! There I go again blaming others…

I pace the floor of the small cell. My new home.

In hindsight, I'd never have gotten away with any of it and I should've just confessed after I killed Danny. I could've made it look like he was attacking me, like it was self-defence. At least then no one else would have died and if I'd had to serve any time, it would have been for manslaughter.

I walk up to the window and touch the bars, staring out at the freedom I will never see again.

Whilst on remand, I contemplated ending my life – taking what I perceived to be the easy way out – but I knew deep down that I needed to suffer for what I'd done. I will never be free. An ex-PSO in prison doesn't make many friends.

My solicitor said the CPS would be going for life without parole. They called me a cold, vindictive killer who would do anything to stay out of prison. I understand why they feel that way – if I had been assessing myself, I would have said the same.

Keys jingle outside my door and the loud clunk as it is unlocked tells me my visitors have arrived. I turn and follow the guard to the visitor's area.

My adoptive parents came to visit me once before the trial. The look of devastation on their faces nearly broke me. Today will be their last visit; I can't bear to put them through any more pain. Pre-trial they had been in complete denial, begging me to tell them that the police, the papers, everyone had got it wrong.

I was close to trying to fight my case, to deny my involvement and explain that Sloane was threatening to tell the world it was me just for a big break in the story. But I knew it was too far-fetched and there was too much evidence against me. I was tired of lying, tired of running from the truth.

My neck burns, and when I touch it, the heat on my hand is

a reminder that the anger is still within me. I suppose it will dissipate and maybe I will find peace.

And maybe not.

I see my mother first as I walk into the visitation centre. Her eyes are sunken, her skin looks saggy – like she's aged twenty years – and my heart feels heavy. My father stands up next to her and waves me over. His hair has turned completely white and his hand trembles.

'I'm sorry, Mum, Dad. I wish I could say it wasn't me… but it was. You both need to accept that and forget about me. I don't want to cause you any more hurt…' A pain shoots through my stomach as I watch my mother collapse to the floor.

I rush over to her side, only to be pulled away when the guards come over.

'Step aside, Wells.' The guard points to his left, and then mumbles something about needing assistance. 'You'll have to go back to your cell now.'

'What? Can't I wait until the ambulance arrives?' I look around and the guards' faces tell me they have no sympathy.

'No. Now go.'

'Wait!' My father holds out a while envelope. 'This came for you. You need to see it.'

I break free from the guard's grasp and take the letter before my arm is jerked back and I'm pulled out of the visitor's area. The last thing I see is my father crying.

Back at my cell door, I wait as the guard unlocks it and steps aside.

'I'll keep you posted about your mother. You're not going to harm yourself, are you?'

'No.' I throw myself on my bed and lie down.

All I've ever wanted is a family – people who love me – and

I had it all along. My parents, my friends, even my probation colleagues. I was so fixated on a woman who gave me away because drugs and alcohol were all she lived for. Did she even love me?

I remove the tape that my father had used to reseal the envelope. What had been so important that he'd felt he had to deliver it in person? I unfold the letter and read.

Talk about a kick in the teeth.

I reread the words before crunching the paper into a ball and throwing it against the wall.

99.9% accuracy. DNA evidence proving that Danny Wells was my father.

I guess the apple doesn't fall far from the tree after all.

Acknowledgments

Since 2019, things have been really difficult for me and I found myself struggling to write until the idea for *6 Ripley House* popped into my head and my editor gave me the thumbs up. I'm hoping readers will enjoy this standalone novel as much as they enjoyed the DC Maggie Jamieson series.

As always, I'd like to thank everyone who has cheered me on and supported me so far on my writing journey. I'm so grateful to be able to share my stories and I can't do that without any of you.

I'd like to thank my family and friends both near and far, for the tremendous support they have given me – I love how you champion my books!

I need to thank my amazing editor Bethan Morgan for her patience, understanding, guidance and belief in me as a writer and to the whole One More Chapter team – you strengthen my words, challenge me and make me want to be a better writer!

Special thanks to my beta readers, the Crime & Publishment gang, all the authors, crime writing/reading community and festival peeps who have been so incredibly supportive, inspirational and kind. You have no idea how much it means to me – you know who you are and a thousand #thankyous would never be enough. Too many to name, but I love each one of you!

To the reading/blogging community and my blogger friends, I want to name you all, but I can't – so if you are reading this and thinking "is she talking about me?" the answer, as always is – *Hell yeah, I am*! Love you all. Special mention to Anne Cater for organising the blog tour via Random Things Tours. She is an absolute legend!

A massive thanks to the Bookouture team (both the authors and my colleagues) for all the amazing advice and cheers! It blows me away every-single-time!

I will always mention Coventry & Tamworth Probation/ Tamworth IOM; Stafford IOM; and all my remarkable ex-colleagues within the Police and Probation Service. Your dedication and professionalism continue to astound me – you will never be forgotten, especially in my books!

Finally, a massive thanks to all the readers. There are just no words to convey how much your support and reviews have meant to me. You make me believe I can keep on doing this and give me a reason to write.

A Note from Noelle

This novel is based in a fictional town in North Warwickshire. I've used some literary licence for certain things in order to keep the reader turning the pages – but don't assume something couldn't possibly be the case, as fact is often stranger than fiction!

Having been a Senior/Probation Officer for 18 years I have a lot of experience in procedures and processes. Any errors to police procedure / probation or any other agency mentioned within the story are purely my own or intentional to move the story forward.

YOUR NUMBER ONE STOP

ONE MORE CHAPTER

FOR PAGETURNING BOOKS

One More Chapter is an
award-winning global
division of HarperCollins.

Sign up to our newsletter to get our
latest eBook deals and stay up to date
with our weekly Book Club!
<u>Subscribe here.</u>

Meet the team at
<u>www.onemorechapter.com</u>

Follow us!

𝕏 <u>@OneMoreChapter_</u>
f <u>@OneMoreChapter</u>
◉ <u>@onemorechapterhc</u>

Do you write unputdownable fiction?
We love to hear from new voices.
Find out how to submit your novel at
<u>www.onemorechapter.com/submissions</u>